Apart from the hunt staff there were only about ten of us up. Amongst them was the Prince and I noticed that he rode shorter than most, almost a steeplechasing seat, and that he had his horse in a snaffle, something practically unheard of in those days when you were considered almost undressed to come out in anything other than a double bridle. I noticed, too, that there were one or two glances cast in my direction, wondering no doubt where I had come from in my old black coat and bowler hat on the little mare. The Prince, I was grateful to see, was concentrating his glance on hounds and on what they were doing. And he was right, for hardly had they checked than they had it again and were driving forward.

'Don't go there,' I called out instinctively. 'You'll break your neck.'

'It's my bloody neck, isn't it?' was the reply, and as he launched himself at the fence I saw that the rider I had so addressed was none other than the Prince of Wales. His horse was foam-flecked and I guessed pretty well beat like the rest of us for he'd come far and fast but, driven into it, he rose at it gallantly enough. The next moment there was an almighty crash and then, before my horrified eyes, I saw a riderless horse galloping away. Of the heir to the throne there was no sign.

John Welcome is a distinguished novelist and biographer. His racing novels *Grand National* and *Bellary Bay* were widely reviewed; *Grand National* was a bestseller. His biographies include *The Life of Fred Archer*, *The Sporting Empress*, *Elizabeth of Austria* and *The Life of Bob Sievier*. He has contributed to newspapers and magazines, including *Country Life*, the *Field*, *Horse and Hound*, the *Spectator* and the *London Magazine*.

ROYAL STAKES

John Welcome

Mandarin

A Mandarin Paperback
ROYAL STAKES

First published in Great Britain 1993
by Sinclair-Stevenson Ltd
This edition published 1994
by Mandarin Paperbacks
an imprint of Reed Consumer Books Ltd
Michelin House, 81 Fulham Road, London SW3 6RB
and Auckland, Melbourne, Singapore and Toronto

Copyright © 1993 by John Welcome

A CIP catalogue record for this title
is available from the British Library
ISBN 0 7493 1613 6

Printed and bound in Great Britain
by Cox & Wyman Ltd, Reading, Berkshire

Dedicated in affectionate
memory of the late
Brigadier J. J. ('Plunk') Plunkett CBE
friend, companion and sometime mentor
in many happy racing days

HUMPHREY CULLENDER'S
Statement

About a year or so back we were having trouble with one of our authors or, rather, he was having trouble with his writing and desperately looking to us for help. I'd better explain before I go any further that I am a literary agent, a partner in the firm of Cullender and Colton, and the author in question, Max Melville, who wrote stirring tales of World War Two on sea and land, had done very well for both himself and us – until now. He had dried up, he said, and was suffering from writer's block and, indeed, practically everything else save housemaid's knee. His contract provided for his delivering his new novel in two months' time and he had scarcely started it. In fact he had run out of ideas after about ten thousand words and had already torn up two drafts of that. He ended his last letter with a sort of *cri de coeur* – what on earth was he to do?

My partner and I discussed it and it was decided that I should go over and see him. He lived in the west of Ireland in a sort of expatriate enclave and to tell the truth I was not looking forward to the trip as I thought there was very little help I could give, but he was a valuable client to us and he'd been paid a whopping advance on the promise of those three books so it was up to us to help him if we could.

When I arrived he told me that his mind was clogged up, he could not sleep at night and inspiration would not come. I made all the right reassuring noises and suggested that he make his mind a blank for a bit and that somehow, somewhere the flow would return. He was so depressed I doubt if he paid much heed, but in fact it all worked out in the end and the third of his books was one of his best; but that, really, has had little to do with what came out of my visit.

Towards its end we were sitting on his terrace looking down to the cliffs and to the waters of the bay on whose shores he lived, when he suddenly said: 'Good of you to take the trouble to come over, Humphrey. Wish I could do something in return. Tell you what, why don't you go and see Dermot de Lacey down the bay. His father died recently and he's winding up his affairs. The old boy must have been nearing ninety but he had all his faculties. I knew him quite well. Once or twice he mentioned he was writing a book. It had something to do with some sort of racing sensation in the family. You were in racing yourself, weren't you?'

'I rode a bit until the money ran out and I had to earn a living,' I said.

Because of my connection with the Turf, slight though it was, we had handled one or two racing books and done well enough with them. I was therefore vaguely interested though no more. The old saying that everyone has a book in him is a fallacy which has been proved many times over, and goodness knows how often have those dreaded words: 'I've written a book, care to have a look at it?' been dropped into an agent's ear. It was more than likely, I thought, that this would be a dreary sludge of ill-digested reminiscence fit only for a publisher's slush pile. On the other hand there is always the off chance of striking pay dirt, I had a day to spare and I thought it just possible that my visit and the fact that he had had someone to talk over his problems with had set Melville's mind travelling again and I didn't want to be in his way.

I have an idea that the very same thing had occurred to him and that he wouldn't be sorry to see the back of me for a while. In any event he went on pretty quickly: 'Dermot has found the typescript. There's something about the Duke of Windsor when he was Prince of Wales in it, I believe. They went hunting and racing together back in the twenties. No harm looking, is there? I told him you were coming over. I'll go and phone him now.'

Without giving me time to refuse he shot off inside to the telephone. In a few minutes he was back. 'You're bidden to lunch tomorrow,' he said. 'One o'clock. It's a couple of miles down the road. I'll direct you.'

I'm bound to say that it was in no very sanguine mood that I pulled up before the De Lacey bungalow next day to be greeted by a man whom I took to be Dermot de Lacey of whom I had been told. He was tall and angular, greying a little at the temples and aged, I thought, in the late forties. The first thing I saw when he brought me into a spacious living room was a pair of framed photographs. One depicted two men in steeplechasing jerseys with whips in their hands smiling at the camera in a parade ring, the other of the same two hacking home from hunting. One of them was unmistakably the young Duke of Windsor looking boyish and happy, the other I presumed to be De Lacey's father, the author of the book. Both were signed across the corner EDWARD P.

'Yes,' De Lacey said, following my glance as he mixed me a king-sized gin and tonic. 'That's my father with the Prince or HRH as he always called him. I'd better explain that I don't know the first thing about racing or field sports of any sort for that matter. I'm into computers and they're my life. I was a dreadful disappointment to my father who wanted me to follow in his footsteps – or horsesteps might be a better word.'

'It often happens,' I said non-committally.

'He'd ridden over two hundred winners,' he went on. 'And was proud of it, that and his friendship with the Prince, and he would never allow a word against him to be spoken in his presence despite all the things that happened later on. I remember once his exploding to me not long before he died. "I heard some young pup calling him all wet," he said. "I'd like to know how long he and those like him would have lived with him in a fast forty minutes from Ranksboro Gorse." What on earth does that mean?'

'It's a famous covert in the Shires and hounds ran like hell from it,' I said.

'I see, or rather I don't,' he said. 'We didn't have much to do with each other after I left school and went to a technical college, although we never really fell out and met and talked on and off.'

'What about the book?' I said.

'It's there.' He pointed to two blue-bound folders lying on a side table. 'I found it in a drawer after he died. We knew he was writing it, of course. My wife has written a bit herself. He didn't get on with her either, called her a blue-stocking, that dates him, doesn't it? She tried to find out about it.'

'And did she?'

'Only a little. My grandfather ran into trouble, racing, back in the twenties. It was never really referred to in the family when I was growing up, you know the way it is in families. If it was mentioned at all, which it very rarely was, it was just called "the trouble" but it did rather hang over my grandmother and to a certain extent him, I think. He said he wanted to write a bit of unwritten history that ought to be told.'

'Did that concern the Duke of Windsor?' I asked, remembering what Max Melville had mentioned to me and the photographs on the desk.

'It did. You'll find it all there. He knew him well as a

4

young man and he never lost his admiration for him or his loyalty to him.'

'He took his time about telling it,' I said.

'Yes, well, he'd lived a full life and it was only late on that he came to live here and to put it all down.'

'Emotion recollected in tranquillity.'

'What's that? Oh, yes, and the effort of recalling and writing was quite something, too, at his age. Then he said he had to wait until people in it were all dead. But he insisted that it was worth doing. He wanted justice done even in a small way to a man he idolised in his youth. Come to lunch.'

We went into a kitchen with a dining area where an elderly woman whom I was introduced to as the old man's daily-cum-house-keeper, was busy at an Aga. 'I'm a bit at sixes and sevens here,' he explained. I wonder what you'll think of the manuscript. It's redolent of the twenties. My goodness it was a different world then, wasn't it?'

'I'll tell you the truth when I've read it,' I said. 'That's my job. I hope you won't be offended if I don't think it's quite up to scratch.'

'Of course not,' he said as we returned to the living room. 'I don't know whether you'd care to take these away,' he went on indicating the folders. 'Or start on them here. I can leave you alone. I've lots to do going through things and generally clearing up and I expect you'll be able to reach a verdict pretty quickly.'

As I've said I had the idea that Max Melville's writing cylinders were beginning to fire again and he would be happy to have me away for the afternoon. 'Thanks,' I said. 'I'll do that if I may.'

Settling myself in an armchair and with no very great expectation I picked up the first of the folders and opened it. Then I began to read. Here it is.

1

I was in my last year at school when my father was warned off the Turf. The warning-off was the result of one of those doping cases which took place years before the stewards relaxed the rule placing absolute responsibility on the trainer if one of his charges was tested positive for dope. He had a winner at Ascot who was tested, traces of a prohibited substance were found and that was that. The penalty then was mandatory and he had to go.

There was, however, more to it. My father trained at Newmarket. He had forty horses in his care (they didn't have strings of two hundred or so in those days, he used to say fifty was enough for one man to manage and perhaps even that was too high); he trained for and mixed with several members of the Jockey Club and other swells, and he had a devoted staff, all of whom had been with him for years. Just before Ascot some sort of gastric infection had scourged the human element in the stable and he had been forced to take on temporary substitutes, three of them stable lads.

He had been hit hard by the decision as you may imagine. It didn't break him for he was not the sort of man to be broken by misfortune. I suppose you could say that what it did was to anger him, to make him determined to find the real culprit and why it had been done. To that end he hired the best firm of private detectives he could get and they quickly came to the conclusion that it was an inside job. The older permanent staff were cleared and suspicion focused on the three temporaries. They had gone, of course, but the enquiry agents found two of them in different stables and satisfied themselves of their innocence. The third was a different matter. He had disappeared. Somehow, however, they managed to trace him to Liverpool where he took a boat to America and there they lost him – irrevocably. The two other temporaries testified that he was a bit of a loner – that they knew nothing about him or his background and that he had left before they did, once Ascot was over and the permanent staff began to return. There was, too, the enquiry agents said, at least a suspicion that the name he gave when he was taken on was not the one he had been christened with. All the evidence, such as it was, pointed to the fact that he had been paid to do the job by someone with a grudge against my father or for some other deeper reason but in any event the trail had run cold.

Then my father had had his stroke. He had received a message, my mother told me, to meet someone who could give him information about the doping. He did not tell her the actual venue for the simple reason that he did not know it. All he was told was that he was to go to the Royal Albion Hotel at Brighton on the eve of Brighton races and there he was to be telephoned to arrange the meeting. He had left home optimistic that something at last might be going to happen to help him, he was in good spirits my mother said, but the next thing she heard was that he had been found in his car near Beachy Head, unconscious and incapable, having been struck down by a stroke. He had, although I was unaware of it at the time, suffered for years from high blood pressure. My mother had endured humiliation from the shame and indignity of the warning off, and now this second tragedy, just when there had seemed to be some hope of finding the truth, was a terrible blow to her.

Here I think I had better say something of my parents. My mother was a cold, hard, determined woman. She was one of the best of her sex across Leicestershire when my father married her and that was not a crown she was prepared to surrender lightly by giving birth to and rearing what she herself described as a brood of snivelling brats. She had one child, myself, and after that, I believe, firmly refused to have another. I don't think, looking back, that sex interested her, indeed for all I know she may have hated it. Certainly when I was growing up whenever they were together they occupied separate rooms and to a large extent went their own ways though, as often happened in such cases, more frequent then than now when easy divorce is the norm, there remained some bond of mutual interest and shared affection between them. So when the crash came she took it as a personal humiliation and withdrew into herself, going to the house in Ireland we had then, hunting with the local pack which she found 'drearily provincial' and drinking, if not to excess, then more than she should. By this time I had moved on to my first term at Oxford where I, too, found myself slightly the object of curious glances amongst those with whom I mixed, and snide remarks being made about 'the chap whose father was warned off for doping, y' know'.

My father was tall and lean. He reminded me always of those lines of W. H. Ogilvie's, 'One was a lancer long of limb, it took a good one to stay with him – ' He trained at Madagascar House (I never knew why it was called that), Newmarket where he lived during the flat season. In the winter he hunted from Melton and in Ireland – flat race trainers didn't spend the winter months in Barbados in those days. Sometime before I was born an aunt had left him a place in Westmeath and he loved it.

Kilbarry House was really our base and that was where, by and large, I was brought up. My father spent the early part of the hunting season there. Later, after Christmas, 'when hounds really begin to run' he would go to Melton where he mixed on even terms with the swells and cut most of them down, too, over their own country. It was that ability to ride in front and stay there which brought him into close acquaintance and something approaching friendship with the Prince of Wales, who was also hunting from Melton then and liked to do just the same.

When he was at Kilbarry he took immense pains with my introduction to and education in hunting and racing. We were both lucky in that, unlike some children of horse mad parents who turn against it all, I loved it from the start. He mounted me on the best, by which I don't mean putting me up on some flashy brute that cost a bomb and was too hot for me, but chose carefully something that could jump safely and would carry me over anything, or precious nearly. When we went out together I can see him now, he who loved to get on and be up with hounds, waiting for me, looking back to see if I was all right, choosing the places and gradually teaching me by his example and following him to have an eye for country, to know what hounds were doing and to take my own line. And afterwards at tea before a roaring log fire I can see him, too, his long legs stretched towards the flames, talking to me as if I was his equal, discussing the hunt, the fences we jumped and the way we and the fox had gone. Then, in the evenings, he would read me the sporting poets he loved, Whyte-Melville, Bromley Davenport, Ogilvie and Lindsay Gordon, whose rhythms have remained with me all my long life. And it was the same when I started to ride in point-to-points. He bought me an old patent safety to educate me and gradually brought me on so that I didn't have to begin on some useless tearaway cast-off as others have done. Whatever success I later achieved as a gentleman rider (we called ourselves that in those days) and amateur huntsman, I owe it to him. No wonder that I, along with many others, refused to believe that he had been involved in a doping scandal, and was desolated by his stroke and the thought that he would remain a hulk, unspeaking, unable to move, cared for by nurses night and day in an upstairs room at Kilbarry for as long as breath was left in him, which the doctors said might be years.

So, in a way, it came as no surprise when my mother summoned me home from Oxford and I was told she wanted me in the library at Kilbarry. I can see her now, too. She had just come in from hunting and was standing in front of the fire, still in her habit, a whisky and soda in her hand, tall, angular and handsome. She looked wonderful on a horse, they used to say. She was one of those women a habit sets off and, oddly enough, I think it was then for the first time that I saw in her what must have captivated my father all those years ago. 'I'm taking you away from Oxford,' she said abruptly. 'Sit down. I want to talk to you.'

It was then that she told me the full details of my father's warning-off, his struggles to nail the culprit and the suspicious circumstances surrounding his stroke which I have mentioned earlier and none of which I had known before. 'I went to him,' she said. 'When the warning off notice appeared in the Calendar. To stand by him. I felt I owed him that. We had dinner together in London and he told me he was certain he had been framed. When I asked for his reasons for this he wouldn't elaborate, he said it was a delicate matter and it was as well I didn't know too much, that that might have been his trouble, that he knew too much and there were those in high places who wanted to ruin him. He was bitter about it and remorseful, too, saying how much he felt the shame he had brought on us both but he was damned if he was going to lie down under it.'

'Is that why he employed the detective agency?' I said.

'Of course, and when they found out about that third lad

disappearing he was more than ever convinced. "Shipped out," he said. "I wonder who paid for his passage."'

My mother took a cigarette from a silver box on the mantelpiece, lighted it, inhaled deeply and stared for a moment into the fire. 'He came back here, you know, during that awful time,' she said. 'He thought of sueing the Jockey Club for their wording of the warning-off notice, and bringing everything into the open, but he decided in the end not to. "It would mean involving some I owe both loyalty and friendship to," he said. "And much else besides for that matter. I will not do it."'

'I suppose by that he meant his friendship with the Prince,' I said.

'He must have done though always in this affair he spoke in riddles. He did murmur something about a plot against the Prince, but even then, I could tell, knowing him, that he was holding something back. He said all along, too, that he didn't want his troubles to involve you and me. But talk of a possible libel action was freely bandied about in hunting and racing circles. There were even paragraphs about it in the gossip columns. That dreadful man who writes *These Names Are News* had a spicy bit in his column. I don't know if it is a coincidence but shortly after that your father got the message to go to the meeting in Brighton to meet someone who could tell him more about the whole affair. You know what happened then, or, rather, you don't because nobody does.'

'Are you telling me the stroke wasn't a pure accident?'

'I'm sure of it. Why was he telephoned, why was his car found somewhere near Beachy Head? There were marks on his body which were never explained. Something terrible happened. Someone wanted him out of the way and didn't care how. And he can't tell us and never will, the doctors say.'

'But, Mother, who?'

'That stable lad who disappeared, he must know some-

11

thing. Whoever set up the whole thing must have had resources and power and covered their tracks well. For all I know there were those who had sufficient influence to stifle enquiries.'

A silence fell between my mother and myself then. She lighted another cigarette and stared again into the fire. 'It was at Melton,' she said, 'that it all began. He said as much. The truth lies there, or some of it anyway. I want you to go to Melton and see what you can find.'

Melton! My heart leapt at the very words – Melton Mowbray in High Leicestershire, the Mecca of all hunting people. But Melton without horses offered no prospect at all. My father's string had all been sold and dispersed. 'But how – ' I wondered aloud and then a thought struck me. 'Perhaps if he was friendly with him the Prince would help – '

'Don't be a fool, boy,' she snapped at me. 'One doesn't ask Royalty for favours.' Her next words told me that she had thought it all out, as indeed I might have guessed, for that was her way. 'What I want you to do from the first,' she said, 'is to keep your eyes and your ears open. There's bound to be talk. Someone there knows more than he, or she for that matter, is letting on. There's a friend of your father's, a Captain Terrier, he was veterinary officer in your father's regiment and he's now the veterinary officer looking after the Remounts at Melton. He's always on the look out for civilian rough-riders. I've written to him. He'll give you a trial. If you pass he'll take you. I've no doubt you will.' She left me in no doubt, either, that she did not expect me to let her down. 'I've told him,' she went on, 'that I want you to get experience in both riding and veterinary before you make up your mind what you'll do with horses. He knows nothing of your real purpose. You'll be unpaid because if you ride for hire you won't ever be able to ride races or point-to-points as an amateur again. I'll make you a sufficient allowance to cover all that.'

It was a marvellous opportunity for at that time of my life

there was nothing else I wanted to do save spend my time with horses. I'd be right on the inside, as it were, and perhaps there would be the chance of a hunt with one of those splendiferous Shire packs of which I had so often heard my father speak. There was also the spice of adventure in the search for clues to my father's humiliation and disgrace. Oxford would have to be abandoned, but I had not been up long enough to make firm friendships and, as well, I had not been unconscious of that aura of being somehow different which seemed to attach itself to me. I was eager to be off, and to look for wider horizons. 'When do I start?' I asked.

'As soon as you can get on to the mail boat,' my mother said.

And that is how and why I, Danny de Lacey, first came to Melton Mowbray.

2

The Remount depot at Melton was situated outside the town in a three hundred acre farm where the offices and tie-up lines were. There was, too, a large paddock with a jumping lane down one side and a set of schooling fences. Standing by the gate into this when I arrived a few days later was a man whom I recognised from my mother's description as Captain Terrier. Below medium height, he had a knowing eye behind thick glasses, a humorous quirk to his mouth, and a general air of briskness and efficiency. After greeting me he looked me up and down, nodded and said, 'Come to ride, have you. All right, let's see you do it.' With that he called up another rank, who was standing by, holding a horse that was already saddled and bridled. I had a feeling I was being set up for something as there was a slight smile, I noticed, on Captain Terrier's lips. The horse, a common looking devil of a type I was later to classify as a trooper, was brought up and I approached him warily.

'Walk him round, out the gate, bring him back, canter, and then take him down the jumping lane,' he instructed me.

The big trooper was a rotten mover, that I knew immediately, and as we approached the gate I felt him tighten himself under me. I guessed then what was coming: he was going to nap. Three strides from the gate, before he had time to do anything, I let him have one, hard, down the shoulder. He gave a snort of surprise, shook his big ugly head and walked out as quietly as a kitten. From trotting a little way down the path I turned, brought him back and put him into a canter round the paddock. As I expected, he had a rough, ungainly action and he sent up a few signals before entering the jumping lane, but by that time I had him where I wanted him and he lumbered along down it and over the obstacles effectively if not prettily.

'That's enough,' Captain Terrier said when I pulled up beside him. 'Get down now and come along and meet my chief.'

Colonel 'Pirate' Probert had been badly wounded in the war, losing a leg, and had been given the job of commanding the Remounts at Melton. He had acquired his nickname because he had a piratical air about him which was accentuated by the rolling gait caused by his artificial leg. He was, as I was to find out, no respecter of persons nor was he inclined to suffer fools gladly. He ran the Remounts as if they were a feudal feoff of his own and woe betide anyone from the War Office or elsewhere who tried to interfere with him. But there was kindness and sympathy behind the outward piratical, keel-hauling appearance, and if you did your job for him or even tried to do it, he would go to lengths to help and encourage you.

'New recruit, Colonel,' Captain Terrier said, saluting, as he brought me into his office.

The Colonel gave me a piercing stare from a pair of unblinking grey eyes. 'You're Dick de Lacey's boy, aren't you?' he said.

'Yes, sir,' I said, wondering if I should be standing at attention.

'Well, if you're half as good as your father, you'll do,' he said, and continued to stare at me in intimidating silence while I thought to myself that my father had left memories behind him and, that being so, I would not be entirely unknown, which must be a help in my quest. It wasn't much but at least it was a start. 'You can't be on the strength, you know,' he said breaking the silence. 'We shan't pay you anything. If we did you'd lose the right to ride as a GR if you want to, as I imagine you do.'

'My mother has explained that to me, sir,' I said.

'How is she? Living in Ireland all the time now, they tell me. Hunting away, I hope.'

'Yes, sir. But I think she misses the Shires.'

'Once here, never forgotten,' he said. Then his lips gave a twitch and a humorous glint came into his eyes. 'You'll be acting, unpaid supernumerary rough-rider,' he said. 'Be on parade at 8.30 tomorrow. Good luck.'

So I started with the Remounts and loved every minute of it. My goodness it was an education for anyone who wanted to work with horses. There would be seventy or eighty of them in at any one time, divided into troopers, and those likely to make officers' chargers. It was the task of the civilian rough-riders, of which I became one, to take these out in designated batches of five or six a day and get them going. I was a bit apprehensive at first that the other riders would resent my presence, but in the event they didn't. They made me welcome, showed me the ropes and were generally helpful. From them I learnt that the Pirate, as they always called him, and Captain Terrier, or Captain Pat as he was universally known, were expected to hunt the officers' chargers, on the good old theory then still strongly held in the upper army echelons that hunting was the best possible training for horse and man in any future war. They made good use of that theory and the opportunities for sport which it offered, culling the best of the drafts for themselves and, as I was told with many a nod and wink, that it was a very considerable time, usually well after the hunting season finished, that these were passed on to the regiments. Some of the real stars, I learnt, remained at Melton for several seasons and even ran in point-to-points.

At the time I joined, Captain Pat had found something quite special. She was a small mare called Dainty. I've clean forgotten her breeding now but she must have been damn nearly in the book. Captain Pat was, like myself, a handy weight. He could ride all right, too, and on her he had shown the Meltonians the way on more than one occasion, so much so that he had made quite a name for himself and her. It was, in fact, through her that something happened about ten days after my arrival which was to change my whole way of life and further my quest.

It was a dark, misty morning, I remember, and there was a sort of stir and bustle in the yard when I arrived.

'HRH is coming,' Captain Pat greeted me. 'Says he wants to look over our lines. I know what he wants,' he said, turning to Pirate who had just joined us. 'He's after my mare. I've been told he has his eye on her. If he gets her he'll break her up like he does the rest of his horses.'

'It'll be treason or something like it if you try to refuse,' Pirate said. 'After all, everything here is the property of KGV.'

Captain Pat looked at his watch. 'We'll see,' he said. 'We've about half an hour.' They moved away and I saw them engaged in earnest conversation before walking towards the line of brick built stables where Dainty was housed.

I wasn't down to go out with the first lot and I hung around to get a glimpse of the man who had been my father's friend. It was just about half an hour later that he came into the yard. He was wearing a very well-cut tweed overcoat and one of those wide-brimmed caps affected in those days which a later generation were to refer to as 'gor-blimeys'. He walked with the brisk, springy step which was characteristic of him and, as I later learnt, of his way of life, for he was a restless man, always wanting to move from one experience to the next. At his shoulder was his *fidus achates*, Major 'Flinty' Westcough, his ADC, best friend and Master of Horse. It was my first sighting of Flinty, too, though even in the short time I had been there, I had heard much about him, how he was regarded – as he said himself, or so I was told – as a dose of salts to the proprieties, how he was frowned on by the Establishment (though that term had not been coined then) and how the Prince relied on him for good company, good cheer and good advice on their horse-coping expeditions.

'Good morning, Captain,' the Prince said, extending his hand as Captain Pat saluted him. 'Bloody awful weather, isn't it?' Then he lost no time in coming to the point and that was another of his ways as I was to discover. 'We've come to have a look at that little mare you've been cutting us all down with, Captain,' he said. 'I'm a spot short of horses at the moment and from what I hear she might suit me down to the ground – eh, Flinty?'

'That's so, David,' Flinty said, and I noticed his easy use of the first name. I saw, too, how his glance darted about, sizing everything up. It even lingered on me for a moment before passing on, no doubt dismissing me as being of no account. As I was soon to find out the Prince, too, had taken in everything in the yard at a glance and registered it all in that photographic memory of his.

'Very well, sir,' Captain Pat said. 'By all means. But I'm afraid – ' He led the way towards Dainty's box.

I was intrigued by that last sentence and I followed at what I hoped was a respectful distance. The door of the box was opened and the two of them filed in, followed by Flinty. They were out again in a moment or two, a look of disappointment on the Prince's face. 'Well, Terrier, can't be helped, I suppose,' I heard him say to Captain Pat.

'Yes, sir, I'm very sorry but she must have got a bang on the tendon that day from Barkby Holt,' Captain Pat replied.

Then the Prince and Flinty moved off, got into their car and were driven away.

As soon as they had gone I made a bee line to Dainty's box. Inside the mare was standing, looking contentedly at nothing in particular. On her near fore was a large yellow blister – or what looked like one. Going nearer I was bending down to examine it when I heard a voice behind me. 'It's odd, you know,' the voice, which was Captain Pat's, said. 'These injuries, they often show themselves when you are least expecting them.'

I straightened up and turned to look at him. If his tongue wasn't in his cheek it was as near in it as makes no matter. 'A slight mixture of paste and paint often effects the cure,' he said then. Our eyes met; there was more than a suspicion of a twinkle in his, and I think it was from that moment that my real friendship with Captain Pat began.

3

The friendship grew steadily as the days progressed. Captain Pat was a bachelor who lived alone. Although he and Pirate were firm friends and got on splendidly in their work together, Pirate had his wife and family nearby, and as well lived and mixed on easy terms with the swells and the Braden Lodge set at the country club which was their home from home. Captain Pat told me that he did not aspire to that lifestyle nor could he afford to since he lived on his pay or, as he said, tried to. Though he loved his work I think he was lonely and longed for someone to talk to. From him I learned that his grandfather had been Irish and that the name originally came from a Huguenot family who had settled there called Terrière and over the years they had dropped the accent and the final e. He had, I discovered, stayed with my parents at Kilbarry on one or two of the buying expeditions to Ireland with Pirate to find the troopers and officers' chargers they put through their hands. These visits must have happened during the school terms since, as he said, he did not know of my existence until my mother had written to him. 'Your father,' he said, 'was a fine trainer and a fine man and a hell of a fellow to ride to hounds.' He looked at me under his eyes in a manner I later learnt to know and which I christened his 'wise old owl' expression. It was as if he was expecting me to say something, giving me the opportunity to broach a subject he was unsure of opening up himself. Here was at least a chance of learning something more if Captain Pat knew it, and I took it.

'My mother,' I said, 'thinks that there was more behind the warning-off than ever came out at the hearing.'

He hesitated a moment before commenting on that and I wondered if he would simply dismiss such suspicions as the fantasies of a wounded wife and widow. But he didn't. 'She's not the only one,' he said slowly. 'Things are going on in high places. Pirate knows more than I do, for he mixes there and I don't, and he's let a word or two drop here and there. This place, you know, is full of gossip and intrigue. Some say HRH doesn't want to be King. Others have it that it would be as well if he isn't. I don't know, I'm only a vet and bit of an outsider. But your father was very close to him – '

'They think they found the lad who administered the drug,' I said. 'He was shipped off pretty quick to America and there he disappeared. Did you know that?'

'No, I didn't know,' he said. 'I've said enough, probably too much. Come on, let's get these horses out.'

Two days later he went down with flu and a day after that I was summoned to his bedside. He was sitting up wrapped in a flannel dressing gown, very red in the face and racked with a cough. 'I've been thinking,' he said between bouts of coughing and cursing. 'That little mare of mine, she isn't doing herself any good shut up and eating her head off. She needs a hunt and you'd better take her out tomorrow.'

'But,' I said. 'That blister – and what about the Prince, what will he say?'

'We both know about the blister, and as for HRH, he's away in South Wales or somewhere opening something.'

My heart leapt – a day in the Shires on a known

performer, what an offer! 'Gosh,' I said. 'I'd love to, but are you sure?'

'If I wasn't I wouldn't be giving her to you, would I? But now listen to me a minute. I said to you once that I was a bit of an outsider here, well, that's true, too, when we're hunting. We're semi-professionals, somewhere between the rough-riders and second horsemen and the nobs, so you need to take care. You'll want to have a cut if I know anything about you, and she'll carry you anywhere and you can put her at anything, that little mare. But above all don't push on or barge at gaps or gates. It's all too easy to do in that big crowd when you're aching to get a start. But don't do it. They're very jealous. If you do you'll be damned out of your boots and remembered for it.'

'I'll try,' I said.

'You'd better, because if you don't they'll come to me and say don't send that boy out again on that mare of yours or anything else. There may be the best part of three hundred people out, and that's where the pressure at the start comes from. But you'll find that out of that lot only about thirty or forty have a real go. The mare can gallop as well as jump, take one or two of the first fences in your own place and you're there. Don't jump on anyone. Enjoy yourself. I wish I was coming with you. Curse this cough. Good luck.'

I went out walking on air.

Captain Pat's words had not really prepared me for the size and swagger of a Shire field, so I almost gave a gasp of astonishment when I arrived at the meet the next day. It was a clear and brilliant morning with a touch of frost in the air, just such a day as to heighten the anticipation, stir the nerves and set the adrenalin flowing. I don't usually suffer from nerves but the fact that I knew no one, that I was an outsider in all this galaxy, did set me back a bit as I looked around me and wondered how I was to hold my own and get through them once hounds really ran.

Everywhere there were red coats, many of them swallowtails with aprons worn beneath them to preserve the pristine perfection of their white breeches, top hats shining and ironed to the nth degree, ladies in faultless habits and toppers being put up by grooms as smartly turned out as themselves. All of them hailed each other with cries of familiarity which made me feel more of a stranger than ever. And there were the horses, my word the horses! Big blood horses, ninety per cent of them were, all full of quality and costing the best part of five hundred guineas – work out that in present terms – and each one ready to adorn a Munnings picture.

Coming from rural Ireland it almost struck the sight from my eyes as I lurked inconspicuously at the back, drinking it all in. And then something happened which drove all other thoughts from my mind.

A car drove up and there was a little buzz of anticipation as a door opened and an unmistakable figure stepped out. It was HRH. The Prince of Wales had either changed his appointments or returned from South Wales sooner than expected.

There was very little I could do about it save make myself even more unobtrusive if that were possible. The Prince was immediately surrounded by a press of admirers and those anxious to be seen talking to him and to enjoy even for a brief few minutes the glitter and glamour Royalty reflects. It was unlikely, I thought, that I would come to his notice, and above all, whatever happened, I told myself that I wasn't going to sacrifice my first chance, and probably my last, of a day in the Shires.

Almost immediately after the Prince's arrival we moved off. I was later to learn that he detested hanging about at the meet, 'coffee-housing' with sycophants, and that the Master and hunt staff knew this. He was impatient to get on and get down to the serious business of riding the legs off his contemporaries in the first flight and, unfortunately, like many of the hard-riding lot, off his horses too, which explained Captain Pat's reluctance to let him have the little mare. He was a competitive man and this was, I think, one of the reasons, apart from the thrill of it, that riding fast over fences and pitting his wits against hounds and his fellows so much appealed to him. But there is no doubt he truly loved his hunting and, as Captain Pat was later to say, he had the blood and guts of the thing in him.

Mindful of the warnings I had received from the sickbed, and indeed of the presence of the Prince, I took good care to keep to the back of the field as we crammed down a laneway. The first draw was a spinney set on the slope of a hill. The whole three hundred of us were penned up below it and behind the field master standing at a gate at the head of the lane. Then, as the draw progressed, we were allowed to file out and spread across a hundred acre field still under the field master's watchful eye and command.

I was just about the last out of that gate, praying all the time that they would not find before I got clear or I would be lost in the press and hopelessly left. The moment we reached the turf the little mare's ears went forward. She knew where she was and I could feel her excitement mounting under me. Through those ears I had my first view of that unending sea of galloping grass fenced by big, black uncompromising raspers, the very sight of which made my pulses quicken. Then they did find.

There was a screech from the whipper-in at a far corner, his hat held high. In a second, or so it seemed, hounds were out driving forward in a dappled cloud, their music a clarion cry in the clear, frosty air.

'Hold hard! Hold hard, damn you! Give them room!' came from the field master behind his uplifted hand as he admonished two swallow-tailed thrusters. Out on the right I felt my way forward, keeping a wary eye on that uplifted hand. As hounds topped the first of the fences below and in front of us he dropped it. 'Now you can go, those that want to,' he called out, at the same time catching hold of his own blood hunter's head.

The line surged forward and I let the little mare go. I had already picked a place in that first fence. The mare jumped into her stride and we were off. At first the sheer pace of the thing, compared with the sedate way we hunted over banks in Ireland, took my breath away. We were at the fence almost, it seemed, as soon as we had started. A regiment could have jumped it abreast. I steadied her. She shortened her stride and then – flip! – a binder flashed beneath us. We were over without a pause and galloping on towards the next. It was a hairy stake and bound and it went beneath us in the same effortless fashion.

I can still recall the thrill of that first hunt in Leicestershire. It was the most exciting thing I had ever done. In front was the clamour of hounds running straight and hard, under me was the mare who knew her business better than I did. She never touched a twig as she flicked those big, black fences behind her.

For a full twenty minutes we were at it as hard as we could lay legs to the ground. Then, mercifully enough for me at any rate, they checked. Looking around me I saw the truth of what Captain Pat had said. Apart from the hunt staff there were only about ten of us up. Amongst them was the Prince and I noticed that he rode shorter than most, almost a steeplechasing seat, and that he had his horse in a snaffle, something practically unheard of in those days when you were considered almost undressed to come out in anything other than a double bridle. I noticed, too, that there were one or two glances cast in my direction, wondering no doubt where I had come from in my old black coat and bowler hat on the little mare. The Prince, I was grateful to see, was concentrating his glance on hounds and what they were doing. And he was right, for hardly had they checked than they had it again and were driving forward.

They hunted a trifle more slowly now and not quite so

straight. Even so the pace was strong enough. The mare hadn't been out for the best part of a week and the check had barely given her breathing space. That burst had taken something out of her, and when I saw hounds swinging left-handed, I thought I could cut a corner. Turning, I jumped a fence almost at right-angles. Hounds were breasting a slight rise a field in front of me. Separating us was a stout post and rails with a boggy take-off and a fearsome drop and ditch beyond it. The mare was tiring and she wasn't mine. I couldn't risk breaking her up and besides I remembered one of my father's admonitions that one should have sense as well as courage. As these thoughts went through my mind, I saw that another rider had jumped the fence behind me and was cantering towards the timber.

'Don't go there,' I called out instinctively. 'You'll break your neck.'

'It's my bloody neck, isn't it?' was the reply, and as he launched himself at the fence I saw that the rider I had so addressed was none other than the Prince of Wales. His horse was foam-flecked and I guessed pretty well beat like the rest of us for he'd come far and fast but, driven into it, he rose at it gallantly enough. The next moment there was an almighty crash and then, before my horrified eyes, I saw a riderless horse galloping away. Of the heir to the throne there was no sign.

It is difficult to describe my thoughts at that moment. No one else had followed us; hounds had disappeared and so, for all I could see, had the rest of the field. Shire fields anyway were not prone to stop and count casualties. I was alone with the Prince, apparently knocked out, at the bottom of a deep dark ditch, from which a fearsome fence separated us.

Fortunately a fence to the left presented no such problems. I jumped this and found that a convenient gate would let me out into the field where I thought I would find the Prince – preferably not dead! He was half-sitting, half-lying on the side of the ditch, a hand to his shoulder and his face a grimace of pain. 'Are you all right, sir?' I asked as I jumped down from the mare.

'It's my blasted collar bone,' he said. 'It's gone again.' Then he looked at me and his look lingered for a moment. 'I've seen you before,' he said with that instant recognition and recall which seems a prerogative of royalty. His eyes left me and dwelt on the mare. 'I've seen that mare, too,' he said, while thoughts of the Tower of London raced through my mind. Then, suddenly, he began to laugh. 'Convey my compliments to Captain Terrier,' he said. 'And tell him I hope his camouflage is as successful in war as in peace.'

Just then, mercifully for me, there was the sound of horses approaching. I looked up to see a rider leading a horse and coming towards us. It was the faithful Flinty who had seen and caught the Prince's loose horse and come back to look for him. He jumped down and, throwing the reins to me, walked towards where the Prince was. 'What happened, David?' he asked.

'Collarbone gone,' was the reply. 'Taking on something I shouldn't on a tired horse. The youngster here warned me.' He gave a rueful grin, as he nodded in my direction.

For the first time Flinty recognised my existence. Turning to me he snapped, 'Don't stand there gawping, boy. Take off your stock and I'll make a sling for His Royal Highness.' He did, too, very neatly and effectively when I ripped it off thinking at the same time how well he had seized the opportunity of avoiding having to disturb his own beautifully tied neckcloth.

The Prince insisted on being put up on his own horse again, and they moved off towards the gate by which I had entered the field, but not before Flinty had hissed at me: 'Keep your mouth shut about this or it will be in all the papers tomorrow.'

I followed at a respectful distance and found that a cluster of farm buildings let us out on to the road where our ways parted. There was no hope now, I realised, of getting back to hounds with the pace they ran and in a strange country. Consoling myself with the thought that it would be time for second horses anyway and I hadn't got one, I made my way slowly back to Melton.

Next morning I was with Pirate discussing arrangements for the day, telling him something of my adventures and wondering aloud if the Prince's recognition of the mare would have any repercussions on him and Captain Pat.

'I shouldn't worry on that score,' Pirate said. 'He laughed, didn't he? We'll hear no more. Say what you like about him, too, and some do, he's a sportsman.'

Scarcely had he said this when a car drew up and Flinty strode into the yard. 'Where's that brat who picked up HRH yesterday?' he demanded in his usual arrogant way.

'He's here beside me,' Pirate said shortly. He had assumed what was known in the yard as his 'hanging from the yardarm' expression. It was apparent to me that there was no love lost between him and Flinty, and I wondered if an explosion was imminent. However none came, possibly because Flinty didn't give him time.

'He wants to see you,' Flinty barked at me. 'Braden Lodge. Six o'clock. Make sure you're on time.' He nodded to Pirate, turned on his heel, and strode out of the yard.

'Bloody man,' Pirate said under his breath as his eyes followed the retreating form.

Here I think I should say a word about Flinty because from there on I had much to do with him and came to like him where many didn't. I know what they said of him but he was a royal favourite and royal favourites down the ages have never been greatly loved. Bounder and cad were two of the adjectives they used about him, but these were two of the adjectives they used about the Prince later on when he fell from grace. It is true that Flinty's antecedents weren't of the bluest of blood (I never did discover just what they were) as decreed and desired by the starchier members of the Court, and it's true, too, that he could be arrogant and off-putting, especially with those below and beneath him, but I believe that much of that arrogance came from an inner insecurity and his knowledge that those entrusted by the Court to 'look after' the Prince and to control some of what they regarded as his wilder escapades looked on him as an upstart and a bad influence. Once, however, he accepted you, which he did me, reluctantly at first and then I think and believe, quite genuinely, he was fun to be with, which was, of course, what originally attracted him to the Prince who was fed up to the teeth with the stuffier courtiers always preaching to him. And, my goodness, Flinty knew horses, and how he could ride them! He could cut them all down across Leicestershire when he had the cattle under him, and sometimes when he hadn't. And that didn't endear him to the courtiers either, who were mostly fishing and shooting people who couldn't see the way he went if they came out at all.

'A horse-coping Indian cavalryman, the worst of all types,' I once heard one of them describe him, and there was something in the horse-coping bit at least, for he bought most of the Prince's horses or they were bought on his advice but ninety-nine times out of a hundred he would try them first – he smashed himself up once quite badly doing this – and I've no doubt he took his cut on those deals. If he did, he deserved it, for he kept at bay those other predators anxious to stick one into the Prince for big money, and I never heard he got him a wrong 'un.

Anyway, as instructed by him, I presented myself at Braden Lodge at six o'clock that evening. It is not every day that a naïve youth from the depths of the Irish countryside is introduced to Royalty, and I won't conceal the fact that I was nervous. Pirate had given me something of a briefing and rehearsed me. 'Above all,' he said, 'when you're introduced, don't bow from the waist like an alderman, he hates that. The way to do it is from the neck, it's a sort of half bow, half nod. Here, I'll show you – ' And he did and then told me to go and practise it in front of a mirror. When I had done this and thought I had it right, I put on my one and only dark suit and hoped I would pass muster.

A special suite of rooms had been built on to Braden Lodge for the Prince and there was a separate entrance which allowed him to come and go as he pleased. A manservant opened the door and let me in.

The Prince's suite was on the first floor. Flinty met me at the head of the stairs, introduced me and I made my nod. HRH was sitting in a chair between the fire and the door dressed, I remember, in casual clothes – whip-cord slacks, an open-necked shirt with a polka dot silk square loosely knotted about the neck, a Fairisle sweater and a hacking jacket one sleeve of which was empty. With his free arm he waved me to a chair opposite.

My first impression of him was of a pair of blindingly blue eyes, my second was of the impress of a personality which hit you the moment you entered the room. This, allied to his quick smile and the instinctive ease of manner which went with it, made me think in that instant, and I have had no reason to alter the opinion since, that here was the most vital and attractive human creature I had ever met or was likely to.

'De Lacey, eh,' he said to me. 'Any relation to Dick de Lacey?'

'He was my father, sir,' I said.

'The dickens he was. Well, I'm damned. No wonder you can ride. The only thing I ever saw of him in a hunt was his back and you look to be following in his footsteps. Several people were asking who you were. Did you give Captain Terrier my message?'

'I did, sir.'

'I hope he's duly ashamed of himself.' He laughed again, and then added, 'I'll have that mare off him yet.' Scarcely pausing, he said, 'Give the boy a drink, Flinty.'

Flinty crossed to a side table where, as far as I could see, every imaginable form of bottle and drink was laid out. There was a huge silver cocktail shaker with which he busied himself. 'Cocktail,' he said to me lifting an eyebrow. 'White lady all right?'

It was the cocktail era; mixed drinks were the fashion then. I had little experience of them, or of drinking at all for that matter, but I could scarcely refuse. A brimming glass was placed before me. It tasted delicious whatever it was, though I warned myself to be careful of its effect. HRH, I noticed, had a straight whisky and soda.

'Your father,' he said, sipping his drink, 'was very harshly treated. The Jockey Club should think again about that rule but I sometimes wonder if they ever think.' It was, I thought at the time, to say the least of it, an indiscreet remark to make to the victim's son on first acquaintance, but as I was later to realise he was never discreet nor, in his position, had he any reason to be if he didn't want to, but it did not increase his popularity in certain Court circles. He had a peculiar, rather rasping voice, utterly unlike the usual upperclass English accent with its clarion notes and tones. It had, I thought, the hint of the Teuton in it somewhere, and I later heard one of those who disliked and disapproved of him describe it as 'damn cockney'. Anyway I listened entranced as, finishing his drink and demanding another, he went on chatting to me as an equal. That was one of the greatest things about him, he never patronised, never talked down whoever you were, except, of course, when he took one of his few furious dislikes to the pompous and the would-be grand when he could be perfectly bloody. 'Ireland,' he said. 'Tell me about hunting there. I've always wanted to have a go over the banks, you know. I've heard so much about it and the sport of it all. It sounds the greatest fun. Your father was to arrange it for me. There was talk of a house in Tipperary. Then the stiff-necks stepped in and

31

stopped it. Said it was too dangerous. Someone would take a pot shot at me. All damn rubbish.'

'It's sport,' I said. 'Real fox-catching. And there aren't big fields to get in the way. I don't think, though, from what I saw yesterday, that it's as exciting as it is here.'

He laughed again. 'Excitement,' he said. 'Is that what you're looking for? And I made you lose that hunt. We must do something for you then. I'll be out of action for a bit. I know what I'll do to make it up to you. You must hunt one of my horses for me. Pepperpot. He can hunt Pepperpot tomorrow, Flinty. See to it, will you?'

At that moment the telephone rang. 'Get it, Flinty,' the Prince said, gesturing with his good arm.

Flinty went to the instrument which stood on the table beside the drinks and picked up the receiver. He listened attentively for a minute or two and then, covering the mouthpiece with his hand, turned to the Prince. 'It's Marston,' he said. 'Do you want to speak to him?'

The reply was a vehement shake of the head. 'No. Not under any circumstances. I suppose the old fool has heard of my break and is trying to make what he can of it.'

'You've got it, that's just what he's up to,' Flinty said and, turning again to the phone, spoke into it: 'I'm sorry, Lord Marston, he's not available at the moment. No, it's not a bad break, I assure you. He's quite fit and well and able to get about. No, no, nothing at all, nothing like that, it was just one of those things that happen. Yes, I'll tell him.' He put the phone down and turned to us with a smile.

'Wants me to stop riding to hounds I'll be bound,' the Prince said.

'That's about it,' Flinty answered.

'Damned old fool,' the Prince said. 'He's one of the interfering gang at the Court. They don't want me to live. What they want is a tailor's dummy while they pull the strings.'

'He said he supposed you were riding recklessly,' Flinty

said with a grin. 'I told him nothing of the sort. It was a pure accident.'

The Prince got up with a wince of pain from his injured arm and began restlessly to pace the room. 'If they'd only leave me alone,' he said. 'And allow me to lead my own life. They don't want me, that's the truth of the matter.' Then, suddenly catching sight of me, he went on. 'Your father wasn't like that. That's why they had no use for him.'

After another minute or two there was a nod from Flinty and I knew I was dismissed. I walked home slowly, thinking things over, or trying to, for when one is twenty the prospect of hunting a blood horse belonging to Royalty in the Shires next day is apt to concentrate all one's thoughts.

4

Next morning Flinty called for me in the open, boat-bodied two-seater Rolls which was HRH's personal conveyance and which only he besides its owner was permitted to drive. He smiled at me in a friendly fashion when I climbed in beside him and we drove off at a high speed along the traffic-free roads. 'You've no idea of the hit you've made,' were his first words to me. He had evidently decided to be amicable, and I wondered at it, remembering his arrogant bearing when he came into the yard the day before. I knew his reputation for having his eye firmly fixed on the main chance and I had half expected a surly acceptance. When he next spoke, however, it did much to explain his attitude. 'You're in luck,' he said. 'He likes you. Play your cards right and there's no knowing what he'll do for you. He likes chaps with fire in their bellies, not those mealy-mouthed buggers at Court. You heard him last evening about Marston.'

'Who is Marston?' I asked.

'He's the Grand vizier, the leader of the crowd who don't like him or don't want him for that matter. They're trying to mould him to their image and he won't have it.'

My thoughts were fairly far away just then from the

Prince and his problems. They were centred on the coming day and what it would bring forth. 'This horse Pepperpot,' I said. 'What's he like? Is there anything I should know about him?'

'You're in luck again. He's a bit of an old sheep unlike a lot of HRH's which take a pretty good hold. HRH started the wrong way round, you know. Put himself under the care of Jack Anthony and Harry Brown with a view to riding races. They taught him to pull up his leathers and sit up against them. He hasn't, let's face it, the best of hands, and that's why they're in snaffles and nearly all pull. But Pepperpot, he wants a bit of kicking along to get him going. Once he wakes up he'll gallop till kingdom come.'

By this time we were meeting signs of a hunting morning. Grooms leading horses were on the grass verges and smart cars were beginning to fill up the roads – horse boxes and trailers were, of course, virtually unheard of then. I'm ashamed to say that after this lapse of time I can't remember just where the meet was, and my hunting diaries were all lost in the war. What I do remember was that the car was instantly recognised and that people pulled aside to make way for us and allow us to pass.

Flinty drew up beside where the Prince's grooms were holding the horses. Once out of the car he busied himself taking off his fur-lined overcoat and donning his swallowtails. I'm bound to say he looked magnificent in them for he had the figure to carry them and the hawk-like face to set the whole thing off under the gleaming topper. I noticed, though, that there were very few greetings to him and only one or two curt nods of recognition, while many curious glances were directed at me. Shire fields in those days did not take to strangers, or talk to them either, and Flinty without his patron and protector was left alone.

I walked over to where the grooms were holding the horses. When I asked for Pepperpot they eyed me superciliously in the way royal servants can do, as if they could scarcely believe that this nondescript creature was going to ride one of the horses in their care. One of them nodded to another who brought the horse forward. Looking at him I almost gasped in delight. He was a big, rangy, blood hunter, a dark bay, the best of all colours. He was about as unlike Captain Pat's Dainty as two horses could be and despite what Flinty had said I wondered would I hold him in a snaffle amongst all that thundering crowd once they got going.

As I was settling myself in the saddle I saw that one of the field had detached himself from a group and had come to a halt a few yards away from me. He was looking me up and down with a fair amount of insolence in his glance which was, as I was later to learn, the sort of greeting a stranger could expect from members of a Shire field. He was a handsome sort of chap with a clipped moustache and something of a presence about him. 'Saw you out a day or so back,' he said. 'You're young De Lacey, aren't you?'

'That's right,' I said, wondering what was coming next. His stare continued but it had mellowed considerably. 'Come from Ireland, have you?' he said. 'I believe you're with the Remounts.'

'Yes, as a learner,' I said.

'Hm. I hope we have a fox for you. He'll carry you well,' he said, transferring his stare to Pepperpot. 'One of HRH's, isn't it? I see you're with Westcough,' he added as he moved away.

Slightly mystified by the approach I watched him go, resolving as I did so to ask Flinty about him, but almost immediately we were moving off.

I've heard it said or read somewhere that one hunt is enough for any book, and I don't intend to go into detail of that day, which in any event has little to do with my story, save to say how I got on with Pepperpot, which did lead to a development later on. It wasn't, as it happened, a very brilliant day's hunting. During the morning we hung around without finding, and all about me I could hear murmurs from that fashionable field complaining of slowness in the huntsman and lack of foxes, and more than one of them cursing fractious and overfed horses playing up, all of which made me glad of Pepperpot living up to Flinty's recommendation of his gentlemanly behaviour. I noticed, too, with a certain amount of amusement, that those who recognised Pepperpot were inclined to make way for me at gates and gaps.

Round lunchtime the field began to thin, people drifted away as boredom took hold and the rich and ritzy members conserved their energies for another, better day. I myself began to wonder if we were in for a blank day and a disappointment for me on this big blood horse which I felt instinctively would not be such a sheep once hounds were running.

It was beginning to rain when hounds were put into a thick wood. Of those of us who were left by then some were going this way and some that and I was at a loss which lot to join when Flinty came up to me. 'Follow me,' he said. 'I know this place. With any luck we'll be there when he breaks.'

He led the way round a corner of the wood. We jumped a small set of rails and hardly had we done so when hounds opened. I saw Flinty cock an ear, listening. The clamour rose and came nearer. There were only about six of us there, one of whom I saw was the man who had spoken to me at the meet. Suddenly, silently, a big dog fox slipped across the fence bordering the wood and sloped away across the grass. The next second hounds were out and, after them, the huntsman. I don't know where the field master was and I don't suppose any of us cared. We had it to ourselves and, by Golly, we were off!

Flinty never lost an instant when hounds ran. He was into his stride and away. So were the rest. They hadn't come to hang about. Immediately I saw what Flinty meant when he said Pepperpot took a while to warm up. They were over the first fence, all six of them, line abreast, before he had caught hold of his bit. 'This won't do. Come on, you old devil,' I said to him and gave him a couple of backhanders. The result was immediate. He stood back and jumped that first stiff cut-and-laid so big he nearly had me off. Then he started to gallop, and what a gallop it was! Those long strides of his seemed to devour the ground. This, I realised, was the real thing, a true Leicestershire horse all blood and quality, the sort you dream about and the dream comes true. I had them caught or very nearly by the time we reached the second of those big black fences. I saw that though they had come back to me a bit, Flinty hadn't. Do what I could, I could never get to him during that hunt, and all I saw of him was his back and his flying coat-tails, and none of the others could either.

I seem to have contradicted myself by describing more of the hunt than I meant to but I've nearly finished. I suppose we ran for the best part of twenty to twenty-five minutes when hounds cast up in sheep stain and we lost our fox. It doesn't seem very much I know to those outside the Shires, but in those far off days of all grass, much of it ridge and furrow deepened by recent rain, it was enough to get to the bottom of nearly every horse who shared that burst. Actually, only four of us finished it, the others had come to grief somewhere. All I knew was that I had been carried by one of the living best and I longed for the chance to do it again. Dainty, Captain Pat's mare, had been brilliant, but it was for her a matter of skill, cleverness and timing. Here was something different – a surge of supreme power behind the saddle that gave one almost the feeling of flight as one met one right and took off into space.

One of those who had finished was the man from the meet and as I looked I saw him go up to Flinty and speak to him. Then they both glanced at me as people do when they are discussing someone. I didn't think much of it at the time, I was too busy reliving those marvellous minutes across the grass and thinking of the fences I'd jumped. I was my father's son, after all, and riding one of the Prince's horses, so it was natural enough, I supposed, for notice to be taken of me.

But back in the car I remembered it. 'Who was that chap who was talking to you when we finished?' I asked. 'He had a good look at me at the meet.'

'Roger Gretton,' Flinty said. 'He's a member of the old guard, one of the few of them who hunt, incidentally. He wanted to know how you got hold of HRH's horse and what the devil you were doing here. What the devil *are* you doing here, anyway?' he said.

I was tempted then to confide in him. I felt that he had no animosity towards me, unusual perhaps in a Court favourite, but I was so young no doubt he didn't see me as a threat. It seemed to me, too, like Captain Pat had said, we were both to some extent outsiders, which formed a bond between us. But I didn't. Some innate caution restrained me; I had been sent to look, listen and confirm, not to confide, and to say the least of it I was still feeling my way in a very strange land. 'I'm here to learn about handling horses and something on the veterinary side,' I said. 'Captain Pat was the vet in my father's regiment.'

He gave me another sharp look as the Rolls purred contentedly along in front of us. 'Hm,' he said. 'Your father and Roger weren't exactly soul mates.' Then he changed the subject. 'You're bidden back to tea now. Tea and poached eggs. I expect you could do with them. And HRH will want to know how the horse went and pretty well every fence you jumped, I shouldn't wonder.'

He was in the same chair in which he had been sitting the night before but this time there was someone else with him. I'll never forget the first time I saw them together. She was standing beside him, her hand on his shoulder, a tall girl with a mass of russet hair, an oval, open face and a friendly smile. She was dressed in a tartan skirt (women didn't wear trousers in those days) and a two-piece, a rope of pearls at her neck. She moved with the easy grace of, I thought, a tigress. I really don't know why I thought of that comparison because there was nothing feline about her, but there was something vibrant just the same, something which matched HRH's own electric personality. Between them they seemed to bring an extra dimension of light and brightness to the room. Such was Lady Valerie Spenlove, always known as Lady Val, and this was my first meeting with her. She smiled at me and from that moment I was entranced.

I had heard something about her from my mother. A lot of nonsense has been written before and since about the Prince of Wales' sexual prowess or lack of it, some alleging that he was all but a neuter, others that he rivalled his grandfather as a sexual athlete. The truth, as usual, I believe, lay somewhere in between, but that he liked women there was no doubt, and Lady Val was the then chosen one. The liaison was known and talked about in that set of course but the press as we called it in those days, the word 'media' not yet having been applied, were then more discreet where the couplings of Royalty were concerned, as was to be amply evidenced a few years later in the Simpson affair.

It was, I think, Lady Val's dash and go out hunting which first attracted her to him.

She had plenty of money, my mother had told me and, superlatively mounted, was considered to be one of the best women to go in the Shires, rather as my mother had been a generation before her, and I think my mother was secretly jealous of her though she tried not to show it. The money and the title came from her father, an ironmaster, one of 'the hard-faced men who had done well out of the war' and, according to my mother, 'a rough old divil' who had conveniently died a year or so back leaving Lady Val, his only child, to inherit his fortune and the landed estate, Huntercombe, he had bought with it. He had also bought a title, an earldom, if you please, from Lloyd George, with the munificent donation he had made to that shifty gentleman. It was one of the few earldoms Lloyd George had sold, in fact it may have been the only one for all I know. Certainly he had been known as Lloyd George's earl and was laughed at and looked down on in the highest sporting circles, despite his success which his steeplechasers – two Grand Nationals and an early Gold Cup – had brought him. His beloved daughter, Lady Val, had been brought up with horses and had proved she could out-ride most if not all of those who laughed at her and her father. She took some awful falls in the process of proving just that, and it was rumoured that the Prince had first made her acquaintance when pulling her from under her horse after one of them. At Huntercombe, which numbered amongst its other attractions a swimming pool, rare in those days, and a private golf course, she entertained him and his friends discreetly if lavishly, my mother saying with a faint curl of her lip that those week-end parties were mostly male orientated. Whenever and however the friendship with the Prince began, it was in full flight when I first came into their circle.

'Well, who won the hunt?' were HRH's first words as soon as we entered the room.

'He did, sir,' I said, nodding towards Flinty.

'That's Mastermind,' the Prince said. 'We haven't had him long. He's all right, is he, Flinty?'

'Suit you down to the ground, David,' Flinty said. 'Takes a hold and gallops and jumps.'

'I'll have a go on him as soon as this damned arm of mine mends. What about Pepperpot? How'd he go?' He looked at me.

'Like a dream,' I said. 'I've never ridden one like him.'

'He's one of your favourites, isn't he, David?' Lady Val said.

'Came from Ireland originally,' the Prince said. 'Your father got him for me.'

'Only four of us in at the finish,' Flinty said. 'He was there.' He nodded towards me.

'Anyone else of note?'

'Roger Gretton. Going quite well, too, for once.'

'I thought he was at Windsor,' the Prince said thoughtfully.

'No. He's here, keeping an eye on things,' Lady Val said. 'He likes to do that.'

'You could be right,' Flinty said. 'He came up to me at the end full of friendly chat. Wanted to know what young De Lacey here was doing and how he came to be riding one of your horses, David.'

'The devil he did. Damned impertinence and I'll tell him so the next time I see him. Now, what about that tea?'

Lady Val crossed to the fireplace and rang a bell. Two men-servants brought it in. It was served on silver and was lavish. There were poached eggs and boiled eggs for the two of us who had been hunting, and toast and scones and gentleman's relish, crumpets and fruitcake, all of which HRH ate sparingly while I, who was ravenous, tried to restrain my longings. Lady Val, who guessed as much, typically and thoughtfully pressed me to satisfy them. 'Come on, we'll have a go at this cake,' she said.

Soon the Prince left his chair and began once more, as I had seen him before, to pace restlessly up and down the room.

'Curse this damn break,' he said. 'I'm a prisoner here. I can't even play squash. They say it'll be another week before I'm out again with hounds.'

'There's a point-to-point, the Fernie, on Saturday,' Lady Val said.

'Point-to-points are a dead loss unless one is riding oneself,' the Prince said. He picked up a copy of the *Tatler* and began idly leafing through the pages.

'You're supposed to be presenting the Challenge Cup,' she reminded him.

'Bugger the Challenge Cup,' was the reply. He was staring fixedly at one of the photographs in the magazine as he spoke. 'There's a picture of Roger here chatting to Marston at Belle Helvick's wedding,' he said. 'I didn't know they were all that close.'

'He likes to keep near the seats of power,' Flinty said. 'Let's have a look. Marston got his morning coat out of moth balls for the occasion, has he?'

The Prince gave a short laugh as he handed over the magazine. 'Looks rather like it now you mention it,' he said.

'Roger was out that day you got hurt, you know,' Flinty said. 'I'll bet he was on the telephone to Marston the moment he heard of it.'

They were talking quite uninhibitedly in front of me. Slowly, almost without I or they knowing it, it seemed, I was being drawn into their circle, and Lady Val's next words appeared to confirm this. 'He's devious,' she said. 'If he's interested in you, Danny, look out.' She selected a crumpet, munched it and licked her fingers. Her eyes followed the Prince's every move, and she watched as he took the magazine from Flinty, looked at it again and then threw it down. As their eyes met he smiled and then laughed. 'A pillar of the Jockey Club and mischief-maker in chief,' he said.

They turned then to other topics, and personalities of whom I knew nothing, while I munched away at my tea and looked about the room which I had not had the opportunity of surveying on my first visit so taken was I with the character of its occupant. Over the chimney piece was the Munnings picture of the Prince on Forest Witch – I wonder where that is now – with below it some silver racing trophies, together with the famous or rather infamous photograph of him on Pet Dog hailing a hansom at the Welsh Guards point-to-point which had really started all the rubbish about him being a rotten rider, and another of one of his more spectacular falls, both of which I thought sporting of him to have put there. On the walls were Lionel Edwards pictures, one of the Cottesmore away from Ranksboro Gorse and another of the Quorn at Quenby Hall, and a Snaffles of the Grand National at the Canal Turn. Two deep sofas faced the fire, there was a Chippendale writing desk, the side table with bottles and another with more signed photographs, bibelots and silver cigarette boxes. It was a typical, comfortable bachelor's apartment without any frills.

When the time came for me to leave, Flinty followed me on to the landing outside the door to the Prince's suite. 'I'm off tonight,' he said abruptly. 'You'd better dine with me. Here, at the Lodge. Come to the front. I'll book you in.' He hesitated for a moment as if deciding what to say next and then, half-apologetically, added: 'Black tie, of course.'

I almost said: 'I'll try not to let you down,' but I didn't, and after my bath I tied the black tie with particular care; in fact I wasn't finished with it until the third try. It was a double-ended one, single-ended were in those days regarded as slightly caddish and only to be worn by 'charleys'. As for made-up ones, well . . . Once finished to my satisfaction, the tie went round a wing collar on top of a stiff shirt front held in place by a set of studs from Asprey's which my mother had given me as a sort of going away present. HRH at that time had not made the sensible soft shirt front with dinner jacket acceptable and fashionable.

Flinty met me in the hall of the Lodge and brought me into the bar.

It was a long, well-proportioned room, which I imagine had once been one of the reception rooms of the mansion. A long bar ran down one wall and the whole thing had been tarted up in the glitzy manner of the day with chromium chairs and tables, coloured chromium shelves behind the bar, cocktail shakers and jugs and bottles of all sorts, shapes and sizes. It all looked modern and smart to me then but I suppose we would call it kitsch now.

Flinty led me to a table where a waiter hovered around,

and asked me what I would have to drink. Once again I found myself in a dilemma, but Flinty solved it for me. 'Cocktail?' he said. 'Mario here mixes a rare 'un. Dunno what's in it but it seems to work. Calls it jumping powder. We'll have two of those.'

When these had been brought and we were sipping them, one of the crowd round the bar detached himself from it and came over to us. He was a small man with a round, rather simian face, very broad shoulders and the torso of a prize fighter. Flinty introduced us but in fact I recognised him from his photographs in the illustrated papers, usually being led in on the back of a winner. He was the Honourable Rupert Carleton, one of the leading amateurs of the day, and of whom I remembered my father saying he could stop one as well as he'd win on one – when he wanted to.

'Surprised to see you here, I thought you'd be at Gatwick,' Flinty said.

'Just back from Ireland. I went over to ride one in a bumper that Billy Weldon thought of buying. Told him it was bloody useless. Seen this – no, of course you haven't. It was shown to me when I was there and I kept it.' He reached into an inside pocket, took out a wallet, and from it drew a press cutting which he passed to Flinty. It was a fairly grubby piece of paper which looked as if it had gone through many hands. Flinty glanced at it, frowned, and then handed it to me.

It appeared to be a drawing from an Irish comic paper. Someone had scrawled across the top of it: *Dublin Opinion* and the date. The drawing itself depicted the King and Queen dressed in formal robes and wearing crowns, breakfasting together, if I remember rightly. Beneath was the legend which I do remember exactly, word for word:

The King: *What's the matter, my dear? You look upset.*
The Queen: *It's Eddy. He's sulking. He's on his high horse again.*

The King: *Good heavens! Tell him to get down immediately.*
                  Else he'll fall off!

'Doesn't help the image, does it?' Carleton said as he took the cutting back.

Flinty made some non-committal reply and the other turned to me. 'Staying here long?' he said.

'That depends,' I said. 'On how long Colonel Probert and Captain Terrier are prepared to put up with me. I'm supposed to be learning, you see.'

He gave me a hard look. 'I should have thought you'd have been better in a racing stable,' he said.

'Shovelling shit and sweeping the yard, that's all you'll learn in some racing stables I know,' Flinty said.

'Perhaps. Still, I should have thought with your connections – ' he let that thought hang in the air for a bit and then, as if realising, or pretending to, that he was treading on dangerous ground, he said quickly, 'Though Flinty here will teach you a thing or two I have no doubt.' And with that he got up and drifted away.

Flinty and I finished our drinks and went into dinner, Flinty, it seemed to me, in an unusually thoughtful mood.

Unlike the bar with its modernistic trimmings, the dining room at Braden Lodge had been left much as it was. The walls were panelled and the tables with shaded lights on them were set far enough apart to ensure privacy. Flinty had arranged for one in a corner near a curtained window. 'You see,' he said as we sat down, obviously referring to the cutting Carleton had shown us. 'They don't want him and they'll do all they can to discredit him. That bloody drawing will go round everywhere. Rupert will see to that. If they only knew him as well as I do they'd realise he doesn't want all this Royalty clap-trap either. He's happiest living in the country, hunting and riding races. That's what he'd like his life to be – squire of a couple of thousand acres with a stable full of blood horses.'

'But some day, surely, he'll have to take on all this Royalty clap-trap as you call it,' I said.

'I suppose so,' Flinty said, squeezing lemon over smoked salmon.

'Are you telling me,' I said, 'that there are some who won't have him?'

'They may have to but they won't like it. Your father knew that. As long as they don't take steps to prevent it – '

It seemed, as my mother had said, that by keeping my ears open I was learning more every day. But that was the extent of it just then for he suddenly changed the subject. 'How many winners have you ridden?' he asked. 'He told me to find out.'

'Six,' I said.

'Out of how many rides?'

'I'll have to count.'

'Don't bother. That's not bad for a start. Over banks, I suppose?'

'Yes. Does it matter?'

'Not much. But there is a difference. You've ridden work and schooling?'

'Yes, quite a bit. What is all this?'

'I'm not sure myself. Sometimes he keeps his cards very close to his chest. He was fond of your father and he's furious with the Jockey Club, half of whom he says have never been on a horse and the other half only at some ceremonial parade on an old hack. He likes you and he has a way of taking people up. He likes his own way and by and large he sees he gets it. How could he not – all those tours and that adulation and then everyone here chasing him. But you saw how he went on about presenting the cup at the Fernie on Saturday.'

'Will he do it?'

'Oh, he'll do it all right. Val will see to that. She can handle him. She at least is good for him. As long as it lasts – '

With that he returned to the first part of what he had been saying: 'You know, what he'd like above all to be is a GR. He sort of idolises chaps like Jack Anthony and Harry Brown. He goes to the National Hunt Meeting at Cheltenham semi-officially and those are the people he likes talking to, not the nobs. It'd give him more pleasure to win the National Hunt Chase than three kingdoms.'

We were drinking champagne by this time, and here I was more at home than with those damn cocktails. It was my father's practice to open a bottle at dinner after an especially good hunt, or two, perhaps, if I'd done well in a point-to-point. And if he'd had a decent winner when he was training there was always a case ordered for the cellar at Kilbarry. Even so I was, I think, emboldened a bit by the wine when I asked him: 'But is he good enough? Would he ever make the grade?'

'Why not if he had the stuff under him? It's true he's so hasty he can never ride a waiting race but half of these bumpers can't anyway. You've seen him out hunting. He's unstoppable and, as an old rough-rider said to me once, "It's them what gallops as gets there." But they're trying to stop him riding in point-to-points. They'd never wear him having a go under Rules and he knows it. He's a sweet man, really.'

We went on sipping our wine. I hadn't then nor have I now the faintest idea what brand or year it was, but I knew enough to recognise that it was damn good stuff and went down smooth as silk and not like the acid drops I'd tasted at some hunt balls at home. But then, of course, I also knew enough to realise that it would be. Everything about Braden Lodge reeked of money. The clientele demanded the best and it was seen to it that they got it. I looked about me at the well-fed faces, some of them flushed with wine or gin, the beautifully cut shoulders of the dinner jackets, the jewels and décolletage of the women, and heard the tinsel trickle of laughter as some outlandish exploit, fall or jump out hunting was recounted. I saw, too, the hovering waiters, anxious for their jobs, and eager to obey each gesturing or beckoning finger.

The laughter at a nearby table was louder than the rest and I glanced at it. It was all male and Rupert Carleton was one of them. After a minute or two they pushed back their chairs and began to leave the room. As he passed us Carleton paused and, looking at me more than Flinty, said: 'Poker tonight. Care to sit in?'

'I think not tonight, thanks,' Flinty said.

'Nor your young friend?'

Flinty frowned slightly and looked across the table at me. I took it as a cue and shook my head.

'Perhaps if you change your mind,' Carleton said as he left us. 'We'll be in the card-room. Long sitting, too, I'd say.'

'Do you play cards?' Flinty asked me when they had all gone.

'Not really,' I said. 'Family stuff sometimes, at home.'

'Hardly a preparation for poker at Braden Lodge,' he said. 'Take my advice – don't. Here be dragons as they say. Port? Brandy? No?' He threw his napkin on the table and stood up. We went out for coffee.

I walked back to my rooms that evening, my thoughts in a whirl. I didn't feel like sleep and I knew I should communicate with my mother to tell her how much had happened since I had arrived and what I had learnt, such as it was. There were no cross-channel telephones in those days, indeed Kilbarry was one of the few Irish country houses in which a telephone had been installed at all, and that at the insistence of and chiefly for the use of my father.

So, marshalling my thoughts as best I could, I got them down on paper. I told her about my hunting and meeting with the Prince and Flinty and Lady Val, and I said I thought that on the whole people seemed more interested in me than perhaps was warranted and that I had the impression something was going on, I didn't quite know what, and were there any further riding instructions, as it were, that she would like to give me. That done I did go to bed and, full of good champagne, slept the sleep of the young and healthy.

5

It was two or three days later that things began to happen. A big, rangy horse with quality about him had been picked out by Captain Pat and Pirate from a batch which had been sent over by one of the leading Irish dealers at, if I remember rightly, Buttevant in County Cork. Now horses which have been accustomed to jumping banks often take time to acclimatise themselves to fly fences. Usually they are inclined to stop and pop and have to be rousted up a bit but for some reason or another this fellow, who was called Rockalong, had reversed the process and was proving himself something of a tearaway. The moment he saw a fly fence he made a dash at it, taking it by the roots as often as not, and he had already dumped one of the rough-riders good and proper. He could gallop, though, and I think either Captain Pat or Pirate had his eye on him as a hunter or possible point-to-pointer if they could get him right. I know that one of the instructors from Weedon had come up to throw his eye over things, as they quite frequently did to see if there was anything that would suit the equitation school. He, too, had spotted him but Captain Pat had put him off. 'No,' I heard him say. 'Wouldn't do at all. He's a bit of a hard case.'

Well, that was that; it was none of my business except that I was interested in all that went on in the yard. I was standing that morning I remember, talking to Captain Pat who, as I was to discover, loved a bit of gossip and to learn all that was going on. In a way it was part of his job, for between himself and Pirate they had to sort out the horses, the better ones going of course to the cavalry and the Horse Gunners; but in the cavalry there were racing regiments and polo regiments and to some extent the chargers had to be suited to the requirements of each. Even in the cavalry certain of the more elderly of the COs and seconds-in-command amongst the less fashionable of regiments were not very good or enthusiastic horsemen, so that at times mistakes were made and chargers sent back. Thus it behoved them both to keep their eyes on appointments and changes and to know something of the characters of those to whom they despatched their drafts.

'Mixing in high society already, aren't we?' Captain Pat said to me, giving me that wise old owl look from under his glasses which I came to know so well. 'How is your pal HRH these days? Has he forgiven me yet?'

'He is erecting the scaffold,' I said, and then added hastily and with a grin. 'I think he regards it all as a great joke.'

'He's a sportsman.' How many times during my period at Melton was I to hear that word used about him? 'If we can only keep him here doing what he wants to do. And you? Dining with Flinty at Braden Lodge. In two years I think I've only been in the place twice. How did that go?'

'He was charming,' I said. 'Cocktails and champagne. He's devoted to HRH.'

'So well he might be. HRH has made him. Oh, he can be good company, the best, when he likes. I knew him in India. He's devoted to himself too, still I suppose who isn't, and he's got himself on. And he's done HRH well over his horses. No doubt about that, whatever people say.'

'Lady Val was there at tea,' I said. 'She's a stunner.'

'She's the best thing that ever happened to him. I dunno, though, can she hold his roving eye?'

At that moment the first lot, which I wasn't with that morning, passed us. Rockalong was amongst them and Captain Pat's eyes fell and fastened on him. 'We must get that fellow right,' he said. Then he thought for a moment before blinking again at me under those glasses. 'You'd better take a turn on him,' he said. 'Horses seem to go for you. Do both of you good. Part of your education. School him tomorrow morning. I'll put your name in the book.' He gave me another of his half-mischievous glances and went off.

Next morning I saddled up the big horse and brought him out. He was unfurnished as yet but there was no doubt about his strength. A massive shoulder stretched in front of me and plenty of power came from those great loins. He was, I think, what we thought of then as a 'Grand National type', which has all but vanished now. I could see why my two mentors had fancied him.

A few other ranks, ostensibly on different tasks, had gathered round, to see the fun, no doubt. Actually Rockalong went easily enough as I took him in a quiet canter round the field to settle him down. He came back to my hand as I asked him and I began to wonder if the tales I had heard were not exaggerated. Just to make sure I went round again. Captain Pat had stationed himself beside the second of the schooling fences. 'Come along,' he called when I reached the top of the field again. 'Don't hang about.'

It was as if the big horse had heard him. Once I presented him at it and he saw the fence he took off.

He didn't – quite – take that first fence by the roots, but he did the next best thing. It was only his strength that saved him and, somehow, I remained in the saddle. The schooling fences were well spaced out. I had time to restore myself and catch hold and, for a moment, I thought I had him in my hand. I was wrong. We were off. His head went out and his feet drummed on the ground. Then, suddenly, I saw Captain Pat give a start and peer at the fence. Taking a step back he threw out his arms at the same time shouting at me: 'Pull out! Pull out!'

Nearly knocking him down in the process I just managed it. But the extraordinary thing was that having swerved somehow away from the fence and back on the level, as it were, Rockalong dropped his bit, came back to a canter and trot like, as Flinty would have said, an old sheep.

'Get down, put that damn horse away and come back here,' Captain Pat commanded.

Mystified, I obeyed and returned to find Captain Pat standing at the back of the fence staring at it fixedly. 'Look at that – ' he said, pointing.

Following his finger I saw, stretched between the uprights of the fence about six inches from the top, a piece of wire, tautly strung.

'If you'd hit that at the pace you were going you'd have broken your neck more'n likely,' Captain Pat said. 'And what's more it didn't get there by accident. I've sent for the Colonel. Ah, here he is.'

Pirate came striding along in his masterful way, followed at a respectful distance by the other rank who had been told to get him. 'Well, then, what is all this?' he demanded.

'I think you'd better see this fence, Colonel, or rather what's been done to it,' Captain Pat said, indicating the wire as he spoke.

Pirate took a couple of steps closer, leant down, looked hard at the wire and then ran his finger over it, testing its tension. After standing thinking for a few moments and stroking his chin, he went back a few paces and surveyed the fence. 'I see,' he said thoughtfully, and then, turning to me. 'You were schooling Rockalong, I understand. That's the tearaway Chris Mullen sent over, isn't it?' He looked at Captain Pat.

'Yes, sir,' Captain Pat said. 'I thought – '

Pirate cut him short. 'I'll hear all about that in a moment. You'd both better come to my office. In the meantime you, Wilson – ' he hailed the other rank who was still hovering about ' – Stand by this fence and don't allow anyone, repeat anyone, to approach it without my express authority. Understood?'

'Yes, sir.'

We moved off. It was all beginning to be horribly formal and rather frightening, I thought. Once in Pirate's office it became more so. He took his seat behind his desk. Not knowing quite what to do, and with some sort of memories of the OTC behind me, I tried rather clumsily to stand to attention. Pirate, catching sight of this, snapped at me: 'You're not on defaulters, boy. Sit down if you like. Now, Terrier, tell me about what happened, if you know it.'

I found a chair and listened. When Captain Pat had finished Pirate sat back in his chair, tapping his teeth with a pencil he had picked up. Then he directed his unblinking gaze at me. 'There has obviously been an interference with His Majesty's property with the intention, if I'm not mistaken, of inflicting bodily harm – or worse. This could be a police matter. You're a civilian, De Lacey. Do you want the police called in or are you prepared to allow the military to handle it?'

All sorts of things shot through my mind. The most important was that I definitely did not want any interference from the police which might lead to awkward questions as to my being here, for all I knew bringing up the affair with my father and even dragging HRH into it. I was certain, too, that my mother would agree with me. Actually, as I was a minor, technically, I think, I had no right to make the decision myself, and my mother should have been consulted, but that never occurred to me until long afterwards and I don't think it ever crossed the minds of the two elderly gentlemen (as I then thought of them) in the room with me. I also think, now, with service experience of a world war behind me, that there should have been a formal military court of enquiry, but that did not seem to occur to them either or, if it did, was quickly dismissed. As I've said, and as I was to have further evidence a few days later, Pirate had feudal ideas about running his private army and between them they were a law unto themselves.

'I'll leave it to you, of course, sir,' I said.

'Very well. Have you, yourself, any idea who could have done this?'

'None whatsoever, sir.'

'Who knew you were schooling Rockalong this morning?'

'His name was in the book,' Captain Pat put in. 'The whole place knew it. There was quite an audience,' he added drily.

Pirate frowned and tapped his teeth with his pencil again. 'I'll see Sergeant Major Gleeson first,' he said. 'Get hold of him, Terrier, will you?'

Captain Pat left the office and I heard a shout, followed by an order and the sound of marching. A minute or two later the Sergeant Major appeared. Saluting in fine regimental style and with great stamping of feet he stood to attention before us.

'All right, Gleeson,' Pirate said. 'Stand easy, I just want to ask you a few questions. It's about what happened schooling this morning though I expect it's around the place already.'

'I have heard something, sir. May I say I'm glad the young gentleman wasn't hurt, sir.' He gave a sidelong glance at me.

'So am I,' Pirate said grimly. 'You are aware then, but in any case I'll tell you. Someone strung a wire below the top of the second fence just where it would catch a horse and turn him over. It was either a joke – a joke in very bad taste let me say, or something much worse. These fences are maintained of course. When was the last time any work was done on them?'

'Two days ago, sir. They were built up again after that mad devil – begging your pardon, sir, that Rockalong, made a hash of them.'

'And they haven't been schooled over since?'

'No, sir.'

'I'll want to see the working party that did the job in due course. In the meantime have you any idea who could be stupid enough or, put it at its worst, malevolent enough to do this?'

The Sergeant Major thought for a moment and then shook his head. 'No, sir, I haven't. There are some mad bug – beggars here but I don't see any of 'em doing a thing like that.'

'You were here all yesterday. Were there any strangers about?'

'None, sir, that I saw. There was that Mr Gretton if you remember, sir, but he saw you himself.'

'Yes, of course. I know all about him.'

'Oh, and that Major Westcough, sir.'

'Major Westcough, eh? What did he want?'

'I think he said he wanted to see Mr de Lacey, sir. It was something about a horse if I'm not mistaken.'

'Very likely,' Pirate said. 'Thank you, Gleeson. Just get that working party rounded up, will you? I'll send for them when I'm ready.'

When the Sergeant Major had left, Pirate tapped his teeth again with his pencil and looked at me, appraisingly, I thought. 'Flinty,' he said after a pause. 'He's become rather a pal of yours, hasn't he? Any idea what he wanted?'

'No, sir,' I said. 'He didn't say anything to me about coming round.'

'Something about a horse,' Pirate said reflectively. 'I wonder. But then it would be, I suppose. Very well, you two. I'll be seeing the working party in a few minutes though I don't imagine I'll get much out of them.' We were effectively dismissed.

Once outside I turned to Captain Pat. 'You don't suppose he really thinks Flinty put that wire there, do you?' I said.

'When he goes all broody like that no one knows what he thinks,' Captain Pat said. 'He doesn't like Flinty and that's the truth of it, and when he doesn't like someone – ' He allowed that thought to hang for a bit and then went on: 'But, no, I shouldn't think so. What on earth reason would Flinty have for doing it? He could have seen your name in the book, though.'

'So could Gretton or a hundred others if it comes to that,' I said.

'If you ever see Roger Gretton stooping to menial work, go and have your head examined. He can't even put a saddle on a horse. There are one or two dirty noses in that last batch which that brute Rockalong that nearly killed you came over with. I'm going to isolate them and turn them out. Fresh air and nature are the best cures. Remember that if you ever have to deal with 'em. Come along and give me a hand.'

When I got back to my rooms that evening there was waiting for me a letter from my mother in reply to mine. She had been fascinated, she said, in all I had written, especially about Flinty and HRH. *I remember Flinty well,* she wrote, *Your father was one of the few who liked him and had a good word for him. He said he was amusing and a thruster in everything – especially hunting, racing and, if he was after your girl – look out! Reading between your lines it is, as I first thought but didn't mention until I heard from you, worthwhile now seeing those private detectives again. Your father knew too much about something or someone. We never found out all we should have done about that stable lad who disappeared. It was shortly after that your father got the message and had his stroke.* She went on to give me instructions. I was to phone the firm of detectives for an appointment. They were called Ormsby and Little and operated out of Newmarket, apparently, to some extent anyway specialising in racing matters which was how my father got on to them originally. She gave me their address and telephone number. Major Ormsby, the senior partner, was the man who had dealt with my father. It was he whom I should see and from him obtain details of the lads involved or said to be involved. She had already written him telling him I would be calling and guaranteeing him his fees. *Remember*, she concluded, *don't trust anyone, not even Flinty with whom you seem to be getting on like a house on fire, too far. Your father said that although he liked him and found him good company he was always on the make. I'm not quite sure what he meant by that but perhaps you'll find out!! Your affectionate, Mother.*

The tragedy which had come upon us had, I realised, at least done one thing for us. It had brought my mother and myself closer together. I read her letter again. The peremptory instructions were still there and the toughness with which she was prepared to pursue her objective, but a note of humour and affection had crept in though she could not yet bring herself to use the word 'love' seriously, at any rate towards me; it was still 'your affectionate Mother.'

Next morning I telephoned the detective agency. The senior partner, or 'Major Charles' as his secretary referred to him, was with a client and could not be disturbed. Yes, she knew who I was, they had received my mother's letter, they were very busy and the file had been put away, but she had discussed the matter with the Major and as my mother seemed most anxious and as the Major had known Colonel de Lacey personally he felt he should see me and she thought she could fit me in, let her just look in the book. She didn't seem either enthusiastic or gracious but in the end she made an appointment for two days away.

My mother, of course, had given no thought as to how I was to get to Newmarket. I had no car of my own but Captain Pat had told me that I could use his when he did not want it for himself, and in fact I had run a few errands for him in it already. When I asked for the day off and the loan of it to go to Newmarket he agreed readily, the only comment he made being: 'Newmarket? Not thinking of leaving us for a racing stable are you?'

'No,' I said. 'Not at all. It's a bit of business for my mother.'

When I went to get the car I found him waiting beside it in the garage where the transport was stored. He wanted to see Harry Beeby in Melton, he said; he would drive me there and I could take the car on to Newmarket myself or, he added, anywhere I liked provided I returned it in one piece. He would, he said, find his own way back.

I had spent most of the previous evening thinking how I should approach my interview with Major Ormsby and, as well, wondering how he would treat me. Mostly I thought I should try to find out more about those three temporary lads, in particular about the one who had disappeared to America whose name even, albeit a false one, we did not know. My mother had told me that my father had kept no written records of his or the detective's research, it was almost as if he did not want any account of it to be available to others, however close, to read. Everything had been done by him verbally or in telephone conversations with the agency.

There was one record, however, for all to see, and that was the warning-off notice which had appeared in the *Racing Calendar*. My mother had had a copy of it typed out and had given it to me. I didn't much care for reading it and being reminded of that blackest of all days. I had folded it up, put it in one of those leather writing cases which were fashionable in those days, and tried to forget it. Now, thinking it might give me some sort of line on what to say at the interview and in any event would refresh my memory on what had been said, I took the writing case, opened it, extracted the sheet of paper, and read it. As I did so one name hit me between the eyes. It is sufficient to quote it in full (I have it still) to show whose name it was. Here it is:

The Stewards of The Jockey Club,
Lord Wilberton, The Marquess of
Farnborough and A. R. J. Gretton Esq.
(acting for Lord Benby) were satisfied
that a drug or stimulant had been
administered to a horse under the care
of Lieut-Colonel D.R. de Lacey for the
purpose of affecting his performance
in a race and warned Lieut-Colonel de
Lacey, the trainer of the horse, off
Newmarket Heath.

When I had read the notice first I had paid little attention
to the names of the Stewards, if indeed I thought of them at
all since they meant nothing to me. I did now, though –
A. R. J. Gretton Esq. Could he be, yes he almost certainly
was none other than he who had enquired about me out
hunting and whom Lady Val had branded as devious.
Further, could there possibly be any connection? Could A.
R. J. Gretton Esq., for reasons best known to himself, have
been influential in swinging the verdict against my father?
No, I told myself, that theory, at least, did not hold water
since the disqualification was automatic under the rules,
but, as I read it again, I realised that it merely stated the
bare facts and left the implication open that my father was
concerned with the doping. Could Gretton have had something to do with the drafting of the notice with the intention
of discrediting him, and if so, why? And what had Gretton
been seeing the Pirate about the day before that wire was
stretched? Coincidence? Perhaps, well, probably. My head
began to reel.

All these things were still in my mind when I met Captain
Pat at the garage next morning. His car was one of the early
'square radiator' Morrises, a two-seater with a dickey
behind. Like many of his generation he regarded the motor-
car, literally, as a horseless carriage, knowing nothing and

caring less about what went on under the bonnet. He never changed gear unless he had to and made up for this by putting his left foot on the clutch and spinning the engine. That morning we had gone a mile or so when there was a splutter and cough in front of us. Captain Pat placed his left foot on the clutch, his other on the accelerator, and pumped them both up and down. 'Get on, car,' he commanded.

The coughing continued, Captain Pat swore. There was a final asthmatic snort and the engine died. We freewheeled slowly to a stop. 'Damn thing,' Captain Pat said. 'What in hell is wrong with it now?'

Having a fair idea, I leant across him to look at the fuel gauge. It was registering empty. 'They go better if you put petrol in them,' I said.

'What? Oh, I see. Well, hell what now? We push I suppose?'

'That won't help, I'm afraid. I'd better walk back and get a tin.'

This was going to take some time. It looked as though I would be late for my appointment and I had a feeling that Major Charles Ormsby might not take too kindly to young men knocking his schedule of appointments about. I was opening the door to get out when a car drew up alongside us and a voice called: 'In trouble? Can I help?'

It was a silver-blue Riley runabout, a low-slung, graceful machine, and behind the wheel, setting it off as if it had been designed for her, sat Lady Val.

'We're out of petrol,' I said.

'That's easy. I'll send someone along to fill you up.'

'Could you, please, quickly,' I said. 'I'm in a bit of a fix. I've an appointment in Newmarket and it looks as though I may be late the way things are going.'

'You're in luck then. As it happens I'm going to Newmarket myself. I'll take you there.'

'Bless you, would you – ' I said.

'Pleasure. Glad of the company. But what about you, Pat?'

'I'll be all right,' Captain Pat said equably: nothing ever really fazed him. 'Just send someone out when you pass a garage.'

'Hop in then, Danny,' she said.

There was no offside passenger's door on the Riley and I literally hopped in beside her and settled down in the seat. She let in the clutch and we were off. She drove like the wind with the lightest of touches on the wheel, and the gear changes, which weren't all that easy in the days before synchromesh, went in like butter. We would make up for lost time and I would keep my appointment, I thought, as I watched the hedges fly past. I was quite happy to sit there, silent, in her company.

'The little man and Flinty have gone off horse-coping,' she said. 'He enjoys that, thank goodness, and he's not a bad judge of a horse, either. He's a bit like a caged lion, wanting to get back on to one, grounded as he is since you broke his collarbone.'

'*I* broke it!' I protested indignantly. 'I did nothing of the sort. He did it himself taking on that awful place. I told him he'd break his neck and he took no notice. I didn't know who he was then.'

She laughed. 'The point-to-points are coming along and he'll be mad for them however much they try to stop him,' she said. 'He should have been born a commoner – well a non-regal Duke, perhaps, with vast estates. You're lucky, he likes you and he wants to do what he can to make up for what the Jockey Club, did to your father. He doesn't much care about the Jockey Club and flat racing bores him rigid.' She laughed again. 'He was sitting next to some pompous ass at one of those grand Lord Lieutenant's luncheons that he dislikes so much, and Mr Pomposity, who was some nob in the Jockey Club – actually, now I come to think of it, it was Marston – well, he was going on about the iniquities of steeplechasing. "A bastard sort of sport if it's one at all," he said, and the little man promptly set him back on his hocks saying, "Oh, really, you know the flat always reminds me of dog-racing!"'

'He seems to me one of the most vital and wonderful people I've ever met,' I said.

She sighed. 'If he'll only stay that way,' she said, and then, almost fiercely: 'They say Flinty isn't good for him, but he is, he keeps him human. He makes him laugh. If he was said and led by those stuffed shirts Roger Gretton and Marston he might get pompous himself. Oh, I know he's spoilt, all you bloody men are spoilt, especially elder sons. Are you an elder son?'

'No,' I said. 'I'm an only child.'

'Then you ought to be spoilt, though you don't seem like that to me, though I suppose you were always given the best to ride, that's why you can cross a country. But you had a bit of trouble schooling the other day, didn't you?'

'How did you know that?' I said.

'Everyone knows everything in Melton. Have they found out who did it?'

'No. But it's early days yet.' Privately I doubted if they ever would. If it had been an inside job, the possibility of a fellow splitting on him or him confessing was unlikely in the extreme. If, as I was coming more and more to believe, it came from outside, the likelihood of discovering the culprit became even more remote. So far as I knew, what we now call security was in those days non-existent at the depot. As a civilian I didn't know or for that matter even care or think about whether sentries or a piquet were posted; indeed I scarcely knew what they or their duties were. If the deed had been done the night before, which seemed probable, anyone with the slightest knowledge of the routine, and there were plenty of those about, could have chosen his time and got away with it.

'Whoever did it, it was a damn dirty trick,' she said, and then: 'What brings you to Newmarket?'

Sitting there in that tiny car alone with her, spinning along the empty roads, isolated, almost as if in a time capsule, intimacy enveloped us. I felt an overwhelming desire to confide in her. Also, I can confess it now after all these years, for I still have that trip indelibly engrossed in my memory, I wanted in some way to impress her. Besides, I rationalised it to myself, she had mentioned my father sympathetically and she might be a useful ally.

'I'm going to see a detective,' I said.

'About the schooling affair, is it?' she said.

'No. It's about my father. My mother and I want to clear his name. He didn't dope that horse.'

'But no one who knew him believes that he did.'

'That's not enough. The Jockey Club in their notice didn't make that clear.'

'And you think the detectives can find proof he didn't?'

'They're the people my father employed, Ormsby and Little. We want to find out just how far they got.'

'Well, good luck to you.'

By this time we were in the outskirts of Newmarket. She dropped me at the head of the High Street, saying she had to go out to one of the studs. After agreeing to meet at the Rutland Arms, I made my way along looking for Messrs Ormsby and Little.

A brass plate with their names upon it and nothing else, set into a wall beside a Georgian doorway with a fanlight over it, told me I had found them.

There was a stairway facing me at the end of a narrow hall with a blank doorway on either side. An arrow pointed peremptorily upwards and I followed it. At the top was a landing with a glassed-in box of an office at its back. Inside this sat a sour-looking puss with drawn-back black hair and heavy horn-rimmed spectacles. She slid open a panel and looked at me interrogatively. When I stated my business she said Major Charles would see me shortly, and indicated a door on the left marked WAITING ROOM. I opened this and went in. It was airy and well-furnished with a carpet on the floor, leather chairs and a rent table in the centre, on which were stacked orderly piles of the usual illustrated papers and the current *Sporting Life* and *Sporting Chronicle*. On the walls were Lionel Edwards and Snaffles prints; two tall windows overlooked the High Street. Major Charles didn't seem in any great hurry to interview me and after reading the runners and riders in the dailies I got up and wandered about examining the prints, finally coming to the windows.

As I watched the traffic and the passers-by I saw two whom I recognised on the farther pavement. They were Rupert Carleton and Lady Val, and they were talking animatedly as they walked along. Just at the edge of my vision they stopped and appeared to confront each other. So far as I could make out they were arguing about something, and that in a not very friendly fashion. But then the door opened and sour puss indicated that Major Charles would see me now.

His office was on the other side of the landing. She opened the door for me and ushered me in. He was sitting behind a large reproduction desk in the centre of the room. In front of it were two mock Chippendale chairs. At my entrance he rose, extended a hand, and motioned me to one of them. He had a cropped military moustache and a round, smooth face, entirely unlined, which gave him in some way an air of innocence, which, I supposed, may well have helped him with clients anxious to unburden themselves. But the first thing I noticed about his appearance was that he was wearing a bow tie.

Bow ties in those days in the sort of circles in which I guessed he mixed were frowned upon as being rather raffish and bohemian. This may have been at least partly due to the fact that Winston Churchill always wore one and Winston then was heartily mistrusted by the upper echelons of conservatism as a *flâneur* and an adventurer and the architect of the disastrous Gallipoli expedition. It didn't, however, put me off. I wasn't in love with those upper echelons myself; they had done my father no good and to me it seemed to make him more human and approachable.

'Sit down and tell me your troubles,' he said. 'What can I do for you?'

'It's about my father,' I said. 'You remember him, I'm sure. You acted for him trying to find out who the real doper was in the matter of his warning off.'

'Of course I remember him. I've heard from your mother. How is he, by the way?'

'It's hopeless I'm afraid. We don't know how long it will be but he is not going to recover.'

'How terrible for him and for you both. I liked and admired your father. What a thing it was to happen and ruin an otherwise blameless and successful career. And then the stroke. I'll do anything I can to help.'

'We want as he did to find out who did dope the horse and to clear my father's and my family's name,' I said. 'I believe suspicion fell on three temporary lads in the stable before Ascot. Two of them were cleared but the third disappeared very quickly to America. Has anything been heard of him since?'

'Nothing. Despite all our best efforts and those of our agents on the other side we were unable to trace him.'

'Do we know his name? He must have given one even if it was a false one.'

'The name which he gave when he was in your father's employment was Vincent Rossiter. As you say, it seems probable it was false.'

'I've been thinking about it over and over again. Was any check made about him from my father's stable before they took him on?'

'We looked into that. There was but a very cursory one,

I'm afraid. Things were in a bustle before Ascot but he told your father's secretary that he'd been with Jimmy Connaughton. I don't know if you know, but Jimmy Connaughton's stable has a floating population of lads. He goes over to Ireland, hires them by the boatload for a pittance, and he either fires them or they leave in a few months and he gets another lot in. The head lad told your father's secretary he didn't remember much about Rossiter but he thought he was all right and good with handling horses.'

'And nothing has been heard of him since?'

'Not that we could find out.'

I approached my next question with some caution. 'Did you ever suspect,' I said, 'that someone might have been behind Rossiter, someone with a grudge or other motive?'

'That thought crossed my mind and I mentioned it to your father but he seemed reluctant to discuss it. Reluctant is the word I should use because he didn't dismiss it out of hand. Find Rossiter first was, I think, what he said. It struck me then as a little odd.'

'Did you know that he got a mysterious telephone call to meet someone in the Royal Albion Hotel at Brighton who could tell him who the real culprit was and that it was on the trip to meet him, whoever he was, that he had the stroke? He was found in his car somewhere near Beachy Head.'

He sat up. 'No,' he said. 'I wasn't told that. You see, after the stroke, I could of course get no further instructions from him. Your mother was so upset making the necessary arrangements and everything, and then, if you'll forgive me for saying it, rather hiding herself away, the whole thing more or less petered out. But it was an unsatisfactory enquiry. There was always a bit of an if about it. And what you tell me now leaves even more questions unanswered.'

'Is there any way of identifying Rossiter if, by chance, he turned up again?'

He paused for a moment in thought, then he opened a file which lay on the desk in front of him. 'We do have two photographs,' he said. 'But I'm afraid you won't find them of much assistance.'

'Still, I'd like to have a look at them if I may.'

Wordlessly he took the photographs from the file and passed them across the desk to me.

The first was a group picture of the whole staff at Madagascar House taken, I guessed, just before that fateful Ascot. At the back one head and shoulders was ringed, but, as he said, it didn't tell much. Vincent Rossiter had so positioned himself that most of his features were blurred and hidden by the lad next to him. The second was of two lads larking about. They had their arms about each other's shoulders and this time the features were clear.

'Do you know who took this?' I asked, holding it out to him.

He looked down at the file again and then said: 'One of the other temporary lads, I believe.'

'Can you tell me who they were? I don't think we ever knew their names.'

He shuffled through the file and then read out: 'Norman Graham and Timothy, known as "Ginger" Elton.'

'May I keep these?' I asked.

'You may indeed. Technically they are your mother's property. Do you mind if I ask what you intend to do with them, and in fact what you are going to do now?'

'I thought I'd search for those two lads. They're surely still in racing somewhere, and try to find if they could help in any way.'

'I see.' He drummed his fingers on the desk and then said: 'You may be lucky but we interviewed them and we didn't find them eager to give assistance. In fact they clammed up. I think they thought we were something to do with the police and were frightened of us. Perhaps we didn't handle it very well.'

'Have you any idea where those two lads are now?'

'No. As I say, the file was put on ice when that happened

to your father and the enquiry lapsed. Hold on though – '
He rifled through the file again. 'Yes, here it is. One of my
assistants saw it in a paper and put it on file. Graham was
killed in a motor accident a month or so back, and Elton is
with Rodney Barker and getting a few rides. *Thought this
might be of interest or come in useful*, he has memoed it. And,
as you see, it has.'

I rose to go.

'If I can be of any further help,' he said, extending a hand.
Don't hesitate to call me. Your father and your family have
had a very raw deal.'

I left thinking I had found another friend.

When we got back that afternoon and Lady Val dropped me,
I found Captain Pat waiting for me. 'The Colonel wanted to
know where the hell you were,' he said. 'I am to collect you
as soon as you get back and bring you along to his office.'

'Has he found out something about the wire?'

'Maybe, but I don't think so. I'd have heard something if
he had. Blessed if I know what it is, but it must be something
official, he's got his orderly room expression on.'

We trooped along to Pirate's office and went in. He was
behind the desk with a sheet of paper in front of him.
Without wasting time on preliminaries he picked it up. 'I've
received this amongst other rubbish from the War Office
through the Director of Remounts,' he said, and proceeded
to read:

> The practice of employing unpaid vol-
> untary civilian labour in the Remount
> lines is to be deprecated and if any
> such exists it should cease forthwith.

He stared at me. 'Someone has been telling tales,' he said.
'Someone's arm is being twisted.'

'It looks as though you'll have to go, Danny,' Captain Pat said.

'Go?' Pirate said. 'Go? I'm damned if he does. Bloody cheek, telling me what to do.'

'But what can you do?' Captain Pat said.

'I'll show you.' Pirate took the sheet of paper, tore it into four pieces and dropped them into the wastepaper basket. 'Never got it,' he said. 'Must have got lost on the way. Carry on.'

Once outside Captain Pat was unusually silent. We walked a few paces together and then I said, 'Will this cause any trouble for the Colonel?'

'I shouldn't think so,' Captain Pat said slowly. 'He's seen off other commands and demands before and got away with it. On the other hand, I'm not quite so sure about this one. It's in writing and it seems to come from very high up. If they follow it up with a bigger shot than usual it's just possible, I suppose, that the axe might fall. We don't want to lose him. There's something going on we don't know about. Let me think.' He walked on a few paces and then stopped to peer at me owlishly from under his glasses. 'I'm due a trip to the West Country to look for black horses,' he said.

'Black horses –' I repeated. 'What on earth –'

'For the Life Guards. They're hard to come by. The Irish, where most of our troopers come from, don't like them. They call them "hearse horses". There, that's part of your education. We can often pick up one or two down in the West. You'd better come with me. That's part of your education, too.'

'And it'll get me out of the way,' I said.

'It mightn't be any harm in case they send a major-general down, though even at that I don't think Pirate puts much pass on major-generals. Still, part of your education, as I've said, and I've a leg in a runner at Plumpton. We can look in there on the way back.'

Plumpton, I thought, that would do nicely for what I had in mind. Back in my rooms I found the *Sporting Life*. I had already been through it pretty thoroughly in Major Ormsby's waiting room, and when he mentioned the names of the two temporary lads in my father's stable who had been cleared of involvement, one of them had rung some sort of bell in my mind. Turning over the pages I found it was as I thought and remembered. T. Elton was down to ride at Warwick. It wasn't at all unusual for a lad to progress, or some would say regress, to a jumping stable and, if he was any good, pick up a few rides. It looked pretty well odds on that the T. Elton was one and the same as the Timothy "Ginger" Elton Ormsby had named to me. A glance at the fixture list told me Plumpton was the only meeting on that day next week. If Elton was in the jumping game now, as it seemed he was, he would almost certainly be there, and if so he might well be able to help me with more information about the elusive Vincent Rossiter. It was worth a try and even if he wasn't there someone would know of his whereabouts. If the file on my father was closed, well, I was about to reopen it.

6

I don't intend to dwell on the events of that week we spent
in the West Country which really have nothing to do with
my story, save to say we did find two 'hearse horses' at a
farm outside Wiveliscombe, which I don't really think Captain Pat ever expected to, having, I believe, made up the
expedition on the spur of the moment. Our friendship
flourished and was to last and endure. We talked together
of all sorts of things. He was a fund of stories, many of them
of his time in India and his racing there; he knew everybody
in the horse world – and why not, I thought, for most of
them came through Melton at one time or another. Many of
the soldier riders scoured the Remounts looking for something out of the ordinary, he had a share or a leg in one or
two steeplechasers, and his buying trips in England and
Ireland brought him into contact with those who had horses
to make, break or sell. But it wasn't until the night before
we were due to make our way back to Plumpton and Melton
that we touched on my affairs. We had dined, I remember,
at an inn high up in the Quantocks and, as it was our last
night and since, as he said, he had at least justified our trip
with those two purchases, we treated ourselves to an extra

glass of port. It was I – having learnt from him of all the things and people he knew, and hoping to learn a little more – who brought the matter up.

'What do you know of Rupert Carleton?' I asked him.

'He's an upper-class thug,' was the prompt reply. 'He had to leave India in a hurry. He lives on his wits and his gambling and gets away with it because of his connections and the fact that he's a bloody good rider. Why do you ask?'

'That night I dined with Flinty at Braden Lodge he seemed more than a bit interested in me and how long I was staying and what I was doing, and when I was at Newmarket I saw him deep in conversation with Lady Val. I didn't think they'd be soul-mates, somehow.'

'Why not?'

'It's just that, oh, I don't know – Lady Val is too damn nice for him.'

He looked me straight in the eye. 'Take care,' he said. 'You're moving into deep waters, my lad. That wire didn't get put into the fence by accident, and that letter to Pirate was written by someone with power behind him. The two things add up to rather more than a coincidence.'

'It's all to do with my father,' I said hotly. 'The doping and the warning-off. He was framed. I'm sure of it.'

'I was never happy about that warning-off,' he said. 'And a lot of others weren't either.'

'There was talk of a court action,' I said, 'and the press took it up. My mother said one of the gossip columnists made a meal out of it, had a biggish piece about the possibility of revelations coming out and reputations being tarnished if it came on.'

'Power,' he said. 'It's all about power, and when those in high places feel their power threatened they can be uncommonly ruthless.'

'I don't think HRH could have had anything to do with it.'

'Of course not. He's to be the loser in whatever game

they're playing. You know I was at a dinner party not so long ago, a very grand dinner party. I was only there representing Pirate who couldn't make it. Over the port they started discussing HRH. There's one old boy at Court, Lord Esher, he's a sort of éminence grise, a half pansy who knows all the secrets, and one of the grandees quoted him: "The boy is a Stuart not a Brunswicker," is what Esher said. It stuck in my mind and I've often thought of it since, seeing him around. Esher has hob-nobbed with the great since he was knee-high to a grasshopper and, like most of those fellows with a feline streak in him, he's no fool. Those few words sum HRH up.'

'Another Bonnie Prince Charlie,' I said.

'You've put your finger on it.'

'I saw the detective my father hired to try to find the real culprit in the doping,' I then said. 'That's what I went to Newmarket for.'

'Did he help?'

'Not much, but he gave me the names of the temporary lads whom they thought might be in the ramp. The third, the chief suspect, went to America and disappeared. One of the others is riding now and I thought I might track him down at Plumpton tomorrow.'

'Who was the detective?'

I was anxious to learn more of Major Charles Ormsby in case I had need of him again and, as I've said, Captain Pat knew everyone. In fact it was said of him in the yard that he knew the breeding and background of all the horses and of every officer in the mounted arms, together with that of most of their wives. It scarcely needs saying that this was an exaggeration but still I guessed he would know enough to tell me what I wanted. 'His name is Major Charles Ormsby of Ormsby and Little,' I said. 'I thought I could trust him,' and I added, I hardly knew why, save that it had stuck in my mind: 'He was wearing a bow tie.'

'Charles Ormsby,' he said immediately. 'He was in the

16th. There wasn't enough action for him in the cavalry and he transferred to the tanks, got a DSO and was badly wounded at Cambrai. He went into Intelligence when he recovered, and after he came out set up that enquiry agency. He doesn't take divorce and picks and chooses his clients. Yes, you can trust him.' He chuckled. 'Despite the bow tie. One way or another I think wears it as a sort of brand of a maverick that he isn't bound by his background, that he'll take up a case from anybody if he believes them and damn the consequences. He's mixed it with the authorities once or twice.'

'Maybe he'll have to do it again,' I said.

7

Plumpton racecourse in those bygone days was not noted for its amenities. I forget who it was who said or wrote that the only place you could really see the racing from was standing on the water-butt outside the weighing room. It was an exaggeration but it wasn't far out. Since Captain Pat's parting words to me about his runner as he went off to find his trainer were: 'Not today I think,' this did not bother me much and in any event my main object was to find T. 'Ginger' Elton. With that in mind, having checked with the number board that he hadn't a ride in the first, I made my way to the weighing room. At the door I asked the attendant if a jockey of that name was about and, if so, would he come out to me. In a few minutes he was back, accompanied by a freckle-faced youth whose mop of red hair told me I had guessed right and that this was indeed 'Ginger' Elton, one of the lads I was looking for.

'Got a ride for me, guv'nor?' he said cheerfully.

'No,' I said. 'I'm afraid not. Look, my name is De Lacey. I'm the son of Colonel de Lacey who was warned off. I'm trying to find who did dope that horse. I was wondering if you could help me.'

His face fell. 'Gawd,' he said. 'Not all that again. Hasn't there been enough with those tecs questioning me? I didn't have nothing to do with it. I don't know nothing.' He turned to go.

I put out a hand. 'Hold on for a minute, please,' I implored. 'No one thinks you had anything to do with that doping. All I want is to ask you about Vincent Rossiter.'

'That bastard,' he said succinctly. Then he thought for a moment. 'They did your dad proper, didn't they, the poor guv'nor. I only worked for 'im for a bit, but he was as good a guv'nor as I've ever had. An' because of it all I've had trouble gettin' work, people thinking I was mixed up in it somehow – '

'Then you will help?' I said.

'Mebbe. Things are tough – '

'I'll make it worth your while,' I said.

'You're on, guv'nor. I've a ride in the next. Meet me after the third, round the back of here.'

I watched the next two races, one of which happened to be Captain Pat's, in a fever of anticipation and impatience. To use the word 'watched' is a bit of a misnomer, for in those days there was a mound in the middle of the course and the only stand had been imported from some defunct racecourse which had perished either during the war or before it, so that the remark about the water butt wasn't far wrong. But I did see Captain Pat's horse stuck successfully and unobtrusively 'in the middle' and I saw enough, too, to tell me young Ginger Elton could ride. He had a nice style, rode with a long rein, sat still and finished fourth, which was just about as near as he could have been, I reckoned.

When I got round to the back of the hut which served as a weighing room he was there, waiting for me. At this distance of time I forget just what riding fees for a jumping jockey were in those days, but I think they were in the region of two or three pounds a ride. Anyway, one thing my mother hadn't kept me short of was money, and I had two of those crisp, old-time white fivers ready for him.

'Thanks,' Guv,' he said as he smartly folded them and put them away. 'Now what?'

I took out the two photgraphs I had got from Major Ormsby and showed them to him. 'Is that Rossiter, what you can see of him?' I asked.

He examined them for a little, paying particular attention to the snapshot of the two lads larking about. 'I took that,' he said, holding it out. 'That's 'im.' He pointed to the ringed figure.

'He didn't seem too keen on having his picture taken,' I said, pointing to the group in which he was partially obscured.

'That he wasn't,' he said. 'I remember now. It was after a footer match. 'E saw me snappin' it, said he wished I hadn't, 'e 'ated havin' his picture taken. I didn't put much notion on it at the time 'cos some people don't. But later on when 'e asked me had it been developed and could he have a look at the negative I did think it more 'n a bit strange.'

'Did he get it?'

'Nah. We sort of fell out, like, after that. 'E was always a bit of a show-off and it was about then he started to throw money around. He could never hold his piss, if you know what I mean, always babblin' and lettin' on he knew more'n he did and braggin' about the touches he'd made. We pulled his leg about the money and he didn't like it when we told him it must have bin a mighty touch and why hadn't 'e let us in on it.'

'Did he tell you?'

'Not bloomin' likely. "Touch,"' he said. "What do you think? I'm in with the nobs now", or somethin' like that.'

'You're sure he mentioned the nobs? Did he say who they were?'

'Nah. We thought he was just talkin' big to hide that he hadn't let us in on the touch, but now you're askin' I remember he went up to Lunnon one time and it was when he came back that he was in the money.'

'And was this just before Ascot?'

'That's right. We were only there with your guv'nor for a bit, before the others got well and came back.'

'Did you ever find out anything about him? Where he came from, sort of? It seems likely Rossiter wasn't his name at all.'

'Nah. He clammed up about himself but he liked to play the big fellah just the same. He was a right bastard.'

'Did he dope the horse?'

'If he didn't, who did? Scarpered off to America straight after or so I heard.'

'He might come back. Would you know him if you saw him again.'

'Sure thing. 'E went off with a pair of shoes of mine and a shirt belonging to my mate. That's the sort he was. Couldn't keep his hands off anything. I'd know him all right.'

'One other thing,' I said. 'The doped horse, Bloemfontein. They don't dope test every winner. Everything gets round in racing, did you ever hear of any reason given why they tested him?'

He scratched his head, looked at me and said, 'I dunno. We all talked about it, talked about nothing else for the matter of that, when we heard. I remember, too, there was a bit of a buzz in the weighing room – someone, I dunno who it was, it's only come back to me now, said he heard there was a tip-off.'

'I see. You don't know who gave the tip-off?'

'Nah.'

I didn't think I'd get anything more from 'Ginger' Elton. I'd been lucky to get as much as I had and to find someone as articulate as he. And he rode well too, maybe he'd be champion jockey one day. 'Thanks,' I said, and on impulse extracted another of my mother's fivers, at the same time taking out one of my cards (we all carried cards in those days) from my wallet. Writing my Melton address and the phone number of the Remount depot on the back, I handed it and the fiver to him. 'If you hear anything at all that might be of help, get in touch with me there,' I said. 'I'm usually at that number or thereabouts. There'll be a few more quid in it for you.'

'I hope you find the bastard, guv, and nail him. And if you're ever in the way of gettin' a ride for a claimer, remember me, will ya?' Then he was gone.

A tip-off, I thought. Who, I wondered, would be the recipient of the information? The stewards of the day? All of them or just one of them? And who were they? I resolved to ask Captain Pat if he knew, and if so what he knew about them. At the same time, I told myself, I must not draw him too deeply into this thing. He had his own future in the army to think of and, if those in high places were involved, it could play hell with him were they to suspect he was concerning himself with enquiries into their activities. He loved his work here, and a posting to looking after mules in Belize wouldn't be much fun. All the same it could not do him any harm to ask him that one question. Meeting him shortly afterwards I did.

'If it was a tip-off,' he said. 'It would probably be to the stewards of the day. I'll look 'em up in the Calendar and I might find out who the chairman was; it could have been made to him, though whether, if it was, he'd be likely to give you anything about it is another matter.'

At that moment I heard a voice I had begun to know well hailing me. 'Hey, you!' it called, and I turned to see the tall figure of Flinty striding across the grass towards me. 'I want a word with you,' he commanded as he came nearer. 'Where the devil have you been?'

The 'word' clearly did not include Captain Pat, who made himself scarce when Flinty joined us. As he did so I told myself that it was this approach of Flinty's, in the manner of, 'I am His Highness's dog at Kew, Pray tell me, sir, whose dog are you?', which made him so unpopular in many quarters.

'I've been looking for hearse horses,' I said.

'Hearse horses? What the – ? Oh, I see, you've been off with Terrier on one of his buying sprees. Now listen to me – HRH wants you to ride to work tomorrow morning very early. It's a secret. No one is to know, not even your pal, Terrier. Understand? I'll call for you.' He nodded and walked off.

My alarm clock woke me before first light next morning. Flinty, being Flinty, had not, of course, given me a time, but I was determined to be ready and pulled on jodhpurs and a high-necked yellow polo jersey (yellow being the smart and fashionable riding-out colour at the time) and a hacking jacket. Shortly after I had washed, shaved and dressed, Flinty was at the door in his 4½-litre Bentley. I don't know how many people nowadays – precious few, I imagine – have even heard of those great green battle-cruisers of cars with a distinctive romantic rumble from the exhaust you could hear a mile away – well very nearly. They were all the go just then amongst the rich and sporty, and Flinty was not one to be left out.

We seemed to drive for miles and miles and, as we drove, Flinty, both hands on the string-bound steering wheel, talked. 'Much has happened while you were away,' he said. 'First of all the little man has heard of that drawing Rupert was bandying about, he may have actually seen it, I'm not sure, but he's bloody furious. "I'll show those stiff-necked shits – and the press", was what he said to me. Things weren't improved by that ass Marston coming down and reading the riot act about his riding in races. Some kind friend had showed him the cutting, I think, though I don't know. Then he went on about the broken collarbone and when HRH pointed out that happened hunting, not racing, it didn't have any effect. Anyway I think Marston hardly knows the difference.'

'How is the break?' I asked.

'It's mended, or he says, it has but he had it all done up in an elaborate sling when Marston was here. "How can I ride in a race when I'm like this", he kept saying to Marston, and that was about all the change Marston got out of him. He was hanging about the Remounts too.' Flinty changed gear, double-declutching expertly, making the big engine give out one of its more exciting rumbles as he swung her round a tight corner.

'Who was? Marston?' I said.

'That's right. I don't know what happened between him and Pirate but I rather gather Pirate saw him off whatever it was about – ' Flinty looked sideways at me as if expecting me to say something but I kept my silence. So someone had come down, I thought, as Captain Pat had said might happen. It had been wise of him to take me away.

'Those who meddle with old Pirate do so at their peril,' Flinty said. 'He runs a good show and is known to do so and he has friends where it matters, too. Ah, here we are.' He turned the big car through a narrow gateway and we bumped up a lane that petered out at the edge of a hundred acre field.

When we came to a stop I looked about me. Down one side ran a line of schooling fences which looked as though they had not been used for some time as they were weak, woolly and bedraggled. The rest was good, galloping grass. Above us was a little knoll with a few scattered trees at its crest: beyond and all around was the rolling grassland of the Shires. Nearby a groom held three horses, one of whom I recognised to be my friend Pepperpot; in the centre was another big, blood horse and the third was a lighter, racy-looking chestnut. Drawn up beside them was HRH's Rolls. Its doors opened and HRH and Lady Val emerged. There was no sign of a sling on his bad arm now. As if he sensed me observing this, Flinty said quietly to me: 'Now you see why he wanted this kept quiet.'

We gathered in a little group round Flinty. 'You'll ride Pepperpot,' he said, jabbing a finger at me. 'It's about a mile round. You and HRH will go round threequarter speed. When you come to the last bend, Lady Val will jump in and the three of you come back as fast as you can.'

As I approached the horses I noticed that someone had been shoving some work into Pepperpot. He looked leaner and harder than when I had hunted him. They must have something in mind for him, I thought.

The others moved towards their horses, HRH to the hunter and Lady Val took the blood tit. Flinty legged me up on Pepperpot and we set off. Pepperpot surprised me by jumping into his stride far more quickly than I had expected and, once there, it took me all my time holding him. Round we went, the two big horses held by us stride for stride on the springy turf. I can remember it now and how I thought, God, how wonderful to have the chance of doing this and in this company with the thud of hooves coming up and the wind whipping past my ears, all of it in the pearly light of an early morning in Leicestershire.

When we turned for home Lady Val was waiting for us on the blood tit. She jumped in. With that the three of us set sail. I thought for a moment they were going to lose me, for Pepperpot didn't quicken with them. Then, almost you would say in his own time, he put his old head down and really began to gallop. He drew abreast of the Prince and left him there; with Lady Val leading us a length or so and going like something smart on the flat, we passed Flinty who was standing by the cars.

'Jolly good,' the Prince said as we pulled up, and, looking at Pepperpot, 'the old boy can still go a bit, can't he?' Then he seemed to catch sight of the schooling fences for the first time. A light of pure mischief came into his eyes. 'Come on,' he said. 'Let's have a go.' With that he turned his horse at the first of the fences and set him alight. Willy nilly, I followed.

The horses were steamed up. It was a piece of madness really, it wasn't schooling at all, it was a helter skelter dash. We flew down the line, Pepperpot stretching himself and gaining lengths in the air. They were weak fences and far from suitable for our horses and to this day I don't know how we didn't wreck them both. But that was him all over. When his blood was up he'd take on anything and we were lucky for, as it happened, no damage was done. When we pulled up he turned to me, flushed, happy and laughing. 'What fun!' he said. 'What splendid fun!'

We walked the horses slowly back to where Flinty was standing looking thunderous. 'That wasn't on the agenda,' he greeted us. 'Racing flat out over those rubbishy fences, of all the bloody silly – '

'They enjoyed it as much as we did,' HRH said, slipping to the ground and pulling up his irons.

'Maybe, but that's just luck. One knock and they'd be out for the whole season.'

HRH was not in the least abashed, in fact he was smiling as if re-living those moments of 'fun', though I had the feeling that only Flinty could have got away with thus admonishing the heir to the throne. He then joined Flinty and they went aside, conferring together for a few moments. Lady Val came over to me. 'He's an old darling, isn't he?' she said as she patted Pepperpot. 'He goes for you too, he doesn't for everybody. We wanted to see if he'd quicken. That four-year-old of mine has been placed on the flat.'

I thought to myself that I'd been on trial too and hoped that I'd passed. 'He has the hell of a lep in him,' I said, looking at Pepperpot as a groom took him and led him round.

'All the little man's horses jump,' she said. 'They have to.'

As we spoke a shaft of sunlight broke through the cloud

and fell on the knoll above us. Something blinked in its light and caught my eye, and then I saw a black shape move along below the trees. Realising that the reflection I saw was the sun catching the windscreen of a car, I watched as it gathered speed and disappeared round the shoulder of the hill. Idly I wondered what a car was doing up there at that hour of the morning. When the others had gone and were walking towards the Bentley, I mentioned it to Flinty. Frowning, he said: 'What sort of a car was it, did you see?'

'No,' I said. 'But now you ask it wasn't a farm truck or anything like that. I only got a glimpse but I'd say at a glance it was a sort of expensive job.'

'And what would a sort of expensive job be doing up there while we were working horses below, I wonder,' he said. 'I think we'll take a look-see. He may be still hanging around.'

About a quarter of a mile from where we left the field we found the way up the hill. It was a narrow, rutted lane and Flinty turned the Bentley into it. We climbed upwards round two bends until we came to a short, straight stretch beneath the trees where there was a closed gate at its far end. Here Flinty pulled to a stop and we got out. The gate was locked with a rusty padlock and looked as if it had not been opened for some time.

Flinty glanced around him and than stared at the muddy ground. 'He's gone,' he said. 'And he came up the same way as we did, he didn't come through that gate so he wasn't just passing on his way. Look,' he pointed to tracks in the muddy ground. 'Here is where he turned.' He stared again across the landscape. 'He could see every yard of the gallop from here if that's what he wanted.'

'He was here for a bit,' I said. 'Look, there are cigarette butts.'

Flinty bent down, picked them up and examined them. 'Parkinson of Haymarket,' he said. 'And they are more than just ends. I know of only one man who gets his cigarettes from Parkinson and throws them away half-smoked.'

'Who's that?' I said.

'Never you mind for the moment. The point is he was here watching us. How did he find out where we were? Who told him?'

'One of the grooms,' I suggested.

'Royal servants don't talk. Especially HRH's. Loyalty is their middle name.'

We were back in the car by this time. Flinty's fingers drummed on the steering wheel. 'How fit are you?' he asked.

I'd been off work for that week in the West, and already I was beginning to feel an ache in one or two unused muscles after the gallop. 'Fairly fit,' I said.

'Well, get yourself fully fit. HRH wants you to ride Pepperpot in the Adjacent Hunts at Marleythorpe.'

I gasped. Never in my wildest dreams had I thought of this. 'Is it because of his shoulder?' I said. 'Is it still playing up?'

'Mind your own business,' Flinty snapped. 'Don't ask any questions but be grateful for the ride.'

I had the feeling they were playing some game with me but I didn't care. Here was the chance of a lifetime, or two lifetimes if it came to that. As it happened, the problem of getting myself fully fit solved itself. Captain Pat was preparing Dainty to run in the Veterinary Corps race at Alton in Hampshire which he had won on her the previous year, and Pirate had one put away which he wanted got ready and asked me to ride work on him.

Givenchy was the name Pirate had given his horse after the place in France where he had been wounded and lost his leg. Where he originally came from I never knew, but Pirate liked him so much that he had bought him out. He was quite unlike the usual run of troopers, being a light-framed, thin-skinned sort and, like most of his type, highly strung. Perhaps, I thought, Pirate and Captain Pat had spotted him somewhere and got hold of him for better things. If so their judgment had not belied them; after we had worked them together for a few days it was clear that he could go more than a bit and could leave Dainty, whom we knew was no slouch, standing.

'He seems to suit you or you him,' Captain Pat said as we hacked home one morning. 'I'll have a word with Pirate. He might put you up. Then you'd have two strings to your bow, wouldn't you?' He smiled one of his knowing smiles.

For the news of my riding Pepperpot had got out, as I fancy it was meant to. A para appeared in one of the glossies.

From our correspondent in the Shires and Provinces:

> *I hear that the Prince of Wales who sustained a broken collar bone recently when out with the Quorn has given the ride on his good horse Pepperpot in next week's point-to-point at Marleythorpe to Daniel de Lacey, a young man over from Ireland whom we have seen going so well to hounds in his first season here.*

I wondered what 'the watcher on the hill', as I was mentally dubbing him, thought of that, but my own thoughts were too full of the coming week to allow room for anything much else, though I did find time to ask Captain Pat if he had been able to ascertain the names of the Ascot stewards that day my father had been in before them. Yes, he said, he had, and the chairman on the day had been Major Sir Crispin Merevale, bart. When I asked him if he knew him he replied rather testily that he was a captain in the veterinary corps and did not usually rub shoulders with Ascot luminaries. So that did not get me much further.

8

The days passed in a flash and before I quite realised they were gone I found myself sitting on a bench in the barn that served as a changing room at Marleythorpe, about to pull on my jersey and go out and ride in the Adjacent Hunts race. I could scarcely believe it, there I was preparing to don the Royal colours, 'Red, blue sleeves, black cap'. What a go! to use a phrase current at the time.

In the morning I had walked the course, slowly, carefully and thoughtfully as my father had taught me. In those days point-to-points were still run over a semi-natural country. They were under the jurisdiction and control not of the National Hunt Committee but of the Masters of Foxhounds point-to-point committee, a very different body determined to stress and maintain their independence and to preserve above all their links with fox-hunting and cross-country riding. To that end they laid down in their regulations that, 'the course shall be as natural a character as possible and typical of the country concerned'. They were prepared to send down an inspector if they thought that instruction was not being adhered to, and their letter to secretaries insisted that 'the governing body is very averse to artificial courses'.

The organisers at Marleythorpe had taken these instructions to heart. The fences were cut and trimmed but not much more, and the water, for instance, was just that, an open ditch about fifteen to eighteen feet wide and not, as the poet sang, 'A hollowed out pan with a hurdle to screen it, that cocktail imposture, the steeplechase brook.'

There was one place of which I took particular notice. You came down a fairly steep incline, at the bottom of which you rounded a flag, to be confronted by a fence into a lane with another out of it making it something approaching a modern eventing obstacle. It was a place which needed thinking about and, as I stood by the flag doing just that, I saw that others had anticipated action there. One or two picnic parties were taking their positions and a few press photographers were prowling about, though at the time I did not pay much attention to them.

As I was pulling on my boots, a figure in a long greatcoat with the collar turned up around its ears, darkened the doorway. It looked round and then crossed to where I was sitting. As it approached I saw between the wings of the collar the unmistakable features of HRH, the Prince of Wales. Immediately I began to scramble to my feet.

'Sit down, you bloody fool,' came from his lips, and then, as he joined me on the bench, with that boyish grin which had captivated so many men – and women – of his future subjects: 'I'm riding Flinty's and I hope you're not as frightened as I am!'

I remembered then seeing that Major R. J. Westcough's Bormont II was amongst the entries and thinking that this was probably the thing I had galloped against in that workout. I saw it all now. They had wanted to see how I went and, if I passed, as I had done, in view of Marston's reading of the riot act and the undesirable attentions of the press, they had directed the publicity towards me while he took the ride on Flinty's horse.

Just then Flinty came in. 'All well, David?' he said, and

then, looking across the room: 'What's he doing here? He never rides in point-to-points. Not hot enough for him.'

It was Rupert Carleton sitting quietly in a corner and tying the bow of his cap in a businesslike manner. Flinty, frowning, stared at him for a few more moments before turning back to us and saying: 'Whenever you're ready, David, we'll get weighed out.'

Soon they left the barn together and after a bit I followed them, weighed out and went along to supervise the saddling of Pepperpot. That done I saw him led into the parade ring and walked in myself after him, to stand a lonely figure amongst the groups of families, friends and supporters surrounding the other riders.

Nerves were beginning to get to me and being quite alone made them worse. At that time the thought of falls never bothered me, but the responsibility of carrying the Royal colours was coming home to me and hitting me in the midriff. Up to now I had been buoyed up with the excitement and anticipation of it all but, standing there alone amongst the crowd of presumably crack riders and other swells, most of whom I was sure were directing curious and jealous glances at me, the strangeness of my position came fully home to me and made me feel sick. I wished my father was standing beside me to reassure me with his quiet confidence and presence as he had so often done before. It was borne in on me too that no one had given me instructions and I knew nothing of the other runners. I had been left alone to ride my own race. I dreaded making a fool of myself and the colours I was carrying.

Suddenly I found Lady Val standing beside me. Seeing me alone and forlorn she had come to my rescue. 'Nervous, Danny?' she said.

'I think I'm going to throw up,' I said.

'Don't do that, it would spoil that nice rig you've got on.' Her presence beside me gave my spirits a lift and my anxieties began to dispel. 'Pepperpot has done it all before, you know, and whatever happens the little man won't mind. He knows racing well enough for that. Anyway, nothing will. You've become our mascot, you know. It's the waiting that's the worst. It always is.'

It was then I noticed that she was wearing a habit and looking particularly striking in it. 'Good heavens,' I said. 'You're not going out too?'

'Ladies' race,' she smiled. 'It's the last on the card. 'We're both in it together. So cheer up. You'll be getting up in a minute and then nothing matters. By the way, where is the little man?'

Flinty and the Prince had, probably deliberately, left it very late to enter the parade ring, but as we looked around I saw them coming in, HRH still with the collar of his greatcoat turned up around his ears. They chatted together for a moment and then Flinty, catching sight of me, came over. 'I wonder what that bastard is up to,' he said, looking to where Rupert was the centre of a little group. 'Whatever it is it's no good, I'll be bound. I see pressmen about too. They're not usually here. Something's up. Watch him, Danny. Are you OK?'

'More or less,' I said.

'That old fellow will jump anything and he stays forever. Ride him as you find him. You'll be all right, you'll find.' With that he gave me one of his quick smiles and was gone.

Then we were mounting and going down to the start. There were eight other runners, making a field of nine in all. I had a quick look at them as we milled around waiting for the starter. One or two, I saw, rode 'a good hunting length', didn't look paricularly competitive and, I hoped, were there just for what we called in those days, 'a good bump around'. Three of these were riding in double bridles and sported 'hunting costume' – top hats, believe it or not. Mindful of Flinty's warning I kept an eye on Rupert. For his part he could never look anything other than what he was – a damn competent steeplechase rider. He sat there, shoulders hunched, leathers pulled up, staring out through his horse's ears, taking notice of no one, a man intent and ready for the business on hand if ever I saw one. His mount, I noticed, was lighter-framed than most of ours, and looked more of a racehorse. I wondered where he had qualified, not having bothered to check on the racecard. A line of poetry came into my mind: 'He calls hunted fairly a horse that has rarely been stripped for a trot within sight of the hounds', and its follow up which I thought fitted him too: 'A gentleman rider, well I'm an outsider, but if he's a gent who the mischief's a jock?' I felt very raw, young and inexperienced beside this hard bitten tough. He came past me as we circled, walking slowly, grim and unsmiling. Whatever he had in mind he had a mind to do it. The Prince, on the other hand, was chatting in a friendly fashion to those by him. His seat, too, was a steeplechasing one and his bridle and snaffle. The horse of Flinty's he was riding was, as I had guessed, the one that had gone in the gallop with me a few days back.

We had not long to wait before the starter, a portly ex-Major in the Brigade of Guards, came down on his hack. Puffing and blowing he lined us up and unfurled his flag. Rupert, I saw, had bagged the inside and kept it.

The starter looked around him and kept his eyes on the Prince. 'Are you all right, sir?' he called, and then: 'Well – er – ahem – Go!' He dropped the flag and we were off.

The Prince went to the front straight away as I'd been told he was wont to do. The rest of us jumped the first two fences almost abreast, and after that the race began to sort itself out, the gents in top-hats and double bridles forming a little group at the back who weren't taking the whole thing too seriously. To my surprise the pace was nothing like as strong as I had expected, scarcely more than a good hunting gallop with the Quorn. Pepperpot was into his stride well and truly by this time and it was taking me all I could do to hold him. His jumping was as quick and accurate as I remembered and he was gaining yards in the air. Before I quite knew it he had jumped himself into the head of affairs behind the Prince.

So we came to the top of the slope leading to the place which I have described. Halfway down the descent Rupert came and passed me, his eyes on the Prince just in front, his face set and grim. Then I saw that there was a whole battery of press photographers lined up near the turning flag. One thing race-riding had taught me was that you've got to think quickly and act as quickly as you think. To this day I don't really know what Rupert intended to do, but I believed then and still do that his plot was to bump the unsuspecting Prince off his line, drive him from the course before the sharp turn, into the arms – and lenses – of the photographers. This would make him look a proper Charley on a horse, give the press more fuel for their jibes at him and – though this is hindsight – more material to fulfil the theories of certain people of his unfitness either to ride races or to succeed to the throne. Of course if what was planned came off he might have brought him down, but I don't suppose he cared much one way or the other about that. It might even make a better photograph.

Be all that as it may, I wasn't having it. I drove Pepperpot upsides of Rupert just as he was beginning to make his move towards the Prince. We came together and touched. Pepperpot was by far the bigger, stronger, heavier horse. Rupert's horse was thrown out of his stride and there was a stream of curses from his rider, who had to snatch him up. The Prince rounded the flag safely and sailed serenely on.

I had lost a couple of lengths in all this and the field, what was left of them, began to close up. I never saw the gents in top hats again though I was told afterwards they all finished, delighted with themselves. The bump seemed to have taken little out of Pepperpot. We rounded the flag, jumped the in-and-out without a pause and I set out after the Prince who by this time had increased his lead.

A field of plough faced us after the next but nothing really mattered to Pepperpot; he went through it as if it were slush, and it was as we came out of it that I began to sense that HRH was beginning to come back to me. And here I'd like to state that from where I sat I was in a position to observe his horsemanship. He was riding a race from in front, jumping alone, which is not the easiest thing for a bad horseman to do, yet I could not detect signs of incipient refusals or anything wrong with his presentation at his fences. Not that I thought much about those things at the time. That came afterwards. Then I was intent on one thing – catching him.

So were others. He was never given any quarter in his races and didn't expect any and we were really racing now. A rider in a red cap loomed up on my left and I heard the thud of another's hooves behind me. We seemed to beat off the man behind, whoever he was, and together red cap and I raced for the next, a cut and laid fence. There was a ditch on the landing side of this, I remembered. I asked for a big one and got it. The other chap didn't. I saw the red cap dive towards the ground and then I was alone behind the Prince – but would I get to him?

We were on good firm grass again now and Pepperpot revelled in it. He met two plain fences just right and I knew we were gaining lengths. I didn't look round but there was nothing near me so far as I could tell. It was between me and him. Ahead of me, at the top of a rise, I could see the finish, the roped-off straight and the crowds.

Pepperpot was full of running. Another fence fled behind us. The Prince was still ahead but the gap was narrowing with every stride. I knew it and I think Pepperpot knew it too. We came to the last at the foot of the rise. He threw a tremendous leap, gained lengths in the air and landed running. I sat down to ride and halfway up the straight I caught him.

But he wouldn't give in. The hill was getting to both of us

now. Stride for stride we battled it out. The crowd was roaring on either side. Twenty yards from the post we were still locked level. I was blind to everything except riding that finish. I daren't go for my whip, I hadn't the experience to risk unbalancing a tiring horse. Hands and heels I rode him out. And then Bormont's head appeared by my knee and dropped back. I had him beat. The post came up. We were a length to the good.

Pulling up, the realisation of what I had done came to me. I had beaten the most popular man in the land in a hard fought finsh. He had probably started favourite too. I hadn't looked. I wondered if the crowd would greet me by throwing bottles.

At least there was one who wouldn't. Turning to ride back I found HRH beside me. 'Well done, young feller,' he said. 'I'm always told the best jockeys pick the wrong horse of two!'

Considering he'd just been beaten a length or so by his own horse when he'd looked like winning on another I didn't think that half bad, and, coming back through the lane of spectators, he clapped me on the back. 'Damn good race,' he said loudly so that all could hear. It was the sort of gesture which brought him instantly into the hearts and minds of the country people, and as he spoke a ripple of clapping broke out. I thought then and have never had occasion to alter my view that here indeed was a man among us.

When I had weighed in, after a few more slaps on the back and congratulations in the weighing tent, I changed quickly and went down to the last to watch Lady Val's race. Getting there in time to see the finishing stages I watched her come to it clear of her nearest challenger. She jumped it cleanly to come away and win by what looked an easy four or five lengths.

I had not seen Rupert since our race and had resolved to keep well out of his way if I could, but when I went to fetch my colour bag from the barn I came face to face with him. I rather think he had been watching and waiting for me since there was fire in his eyes and a scowl on his face. As I've said, racing teaches you to think quickly and, seeing these, I resolved to get my say in first. 'I'm very sorry about that bump, sir,' I said. 'I couldn't keep my bloody horse straight.'

'Why, you young cur,' he snarled at me. 'I've a good mind to report you to the stewards for foul riding but seeing whose horse you were on, this weak-kneed lot'd do nothing – '

'But, sir,' I said, pretty feebly I admit, since of all my quick thinking I could only conjure up the first excuse that came into my head. 'It was an accident – '

'Accident be damned. You're going to get a lesson in manners. Come round behind the barn and I'll give you something to remember me by.'

It didn't look too good for me. I could scarcely run away and he was broader, stronger, heavier than I. He could probably have taken me with one hand tied behind his back. The euphoria of my win was rapidly vanishing. But help was at hand.

'I wouldn't do that if I were you, Rupert,' a quiet voice said. 'I'd pick on someone up to your weight or you may have to take on two of us.' It was Flinty who had come up behind us and heard the exchange.

'You keep out of this, Flinty,' Rupert said.

'Oh, I don't think so,' came Flinty's quiet voice again. 'You see I keep wondering who was watching a gallop a while back and smoking cigarettes from Parkinson of Haymarket while he was doing it. It's known as touting, isn't it, not a very attractive occupation, and someone who rode in it, you know who I mean, might wonder why the tout was there. And he might wonder, too, who alerted the press that HRH would be riding today and stationed them at that in-and-out. Who, I wonder, Rupert?'

'Yes, lay off, Rupert,' said another voice beside him, and I saw that Lady Val had joined us. She gave Rupert a cold stare from her cool grey eyes. Whether it was that which finally made up his mind for him, I didn't know, but he backed down.

'You look out. I'll see you in hell before I'm finished,' he snarled at me. Then he turned and walked away into the crowd.

'He had a smashing fall at that in-and-out,' Flinty said. 'It didn't improve his temper.'

'Which is always on a pretty short fuse,' Lady Val said. 'Forget him. Congratulations, Danny, you rode the hell of a race.'

'So did you,' I said. 'How anyone ever takes on racing in a habit and side saddle beats me.'

'Makes it easier,' she said, laughing. 'You can't fall out of one even if you try. Anyway now it's a double event and deserves a celebration. There's a hunt ball tonight. You're coming, Danny. We can't do without our mascot.'

'HRH's quarters at eight for dinner, I was told to tell you,' Flinty said.

'Do you know what *lèse majesté*, means, Danny,' she said, smiling. 'You've committed it and got away with it. He's gone off delighted with himself. He loves old Pepperpot and he thinks the plan he made to keep the press away by switching rides worked a treat.'

'He doesn't know anything about Rupert's little game whatever it was,' Flinty said slowly. 'And it's as well not to tell him for the moment anyway.'

'What was his game?' I said.

'Adverse publicity,' Flinty said. 'It all mounts up. And it all gets home to papa in Buck House. Someone tells him the tittle tattle – and embroiders it.'

'Well they won't this time,' Lady Val said. 'Danny saw to that. There's champagne in the car. We can start the celebrations now.'

After I had fetched my colour bag we adjourned to the car

where we polished off two bottles in no time at all. It was when, back in my rooms, I had bathed and was changing, that I remembered the racecard and that I should look for the name of Rupert's owner. Going to my overcoat I fished it out. The name was there in black and white: A. R. J. Gretton.

9

HRH liked small parties and most of the guests had already assembled when I arrived. Truth to tell I wasn't looking forward either to the dinner or the hunt ball. I was sure I would be by far the youngest at dinner and would know very few at either gathering. The fact that I was the only one wearing black tails amongst the scarlet and hunt facings at dinner didn't help my self-confidence either. The one consolation was that I should see, and with any luck be near, Lady Val again.

She was there, of course, in the room in which we had had tea after hunting, and Flinty, inevitably, but there was also a flashy blonde whose name I didn't catch in the flow of offhand introductions thrown at me, and to whom HRH seemed to be paying plenty of attention. Rather to my surprise Roger Gretton and his wife, a tall, stately, silent creature, were also in the party. To my even greater surprise, seeing me, he came over to speak to me.

'Terrible thing about your father,' he said. 'I'm truly sorry. Is there any hope?'

'None at all, sir, I'm afraid,' I said. 'At least that's what the doctors say.'

He paused and then said: 'It was too bad what we had to do. But there was no option. It's mandatory. That's the rule.'

'Then the rule ought to be changed,' said a voice at my elbow. HRH had come up and had heard the last sentence.

'I'm inclined to agree with you, sir,' Gretton said. 'And so do certain others of us. There have been discussions in that direction. But you know we move slowly – '

'Then you need shaking up like a lot of other things round-about,' was the reply, spoken quite sharply. When he had said this he moved off to pay more attention to the flashy blonde.

'HRH is right you know, Roger,' Flinty, who was standing by, put in. 'Every trainer is at the mercy of his staff, and they're all at it, especially amongst the smaller stables. They're giving gee-up pills and patent remedies all the time they can spare from filling 'em up with slower downers. What's more, everyone knows it. Why did you pick on poor Dick de Lacey, eh?'

'The evidence was there, what could we do?' Gretton said, but he had not answered the question. He was being backed into a corner and was, I was sure, regretting ever having mentioned my father's name. It was on the tip of my tongue to ask him if there had been a tip-off and if so where did it come from, but in that company and at that time I didn't dare. In any event I hadn't a chance. Lady Val joined us. 'We'll be going in any moment now,' she said quietly.

At that moment a footman appeared at the door, HRH made a gesture and we trooped into dinner. The long hunting table in the dining room of the suite glistened and sparkled with silver and napery. Two footmen moved noiselessly about. The flashy blonde, glowing in the attention paid to her, was seated on HRH's right. I found myself at the foot of the table beside Lady Val. Though she kept the conversation going with trivialities more or less, I thought, to cover my strangeness in that company, her eyes were all for the Prince. My other neighbour was Gretton's hitherto silent or monosyllabic wife, whom I suddenly heard speaking to me, asking some question about the day's racing. What she said, which I now forget, fell into one of those spontaneous silences which sometimes afflict a dinner table and HRH took it up.

'Look well at him,' he said laughing. 'Beat me half a length on my own horse this afternoon, what do you make of that? I should have known better than to give him the ride, shouldn't I?'

He was in tremendous form. Gay is a word one is not allowed to use, at least in that context, nowadays, but it is the only one I can think of to describe him there and at that moment. When he was in that mood it was as if a flame ran round the table and touched us all. He had that sort of mesmerism, an electric ability to make people more than they were. We seemed to come alight and move out of ourselves. I am putting this very badly but it is the only way I can express it as it was all those years ago. It certainly wasn't due to drink, since I noticed that with the footman constantly filling our glasses with champagne, his remained virtually untouched. As if suddenly switched on, the party then came alive and the conversation became general, mostly about hunting and racing in which he joined enthusiastically.

'Will you run Pepperpot in the National Hunt Chase at Cheltenham, David?' Flinty asked him.

'By Jove that's not half a bad idea,' came the reply. 'Nothing I'd like better than a crack at the Cheltenham fences, except Aintree perhaps. Trouble is the press would get hold of it, confound 'em, and then they'd, well, certain people, they'd come down on me like a ton of bricks and kibosh the whole thing. Ah, well, we'll see.' The animation died for a moment and his eyes flickered in my direction followed by most of the glances from the others at the table. 'Better to be an ordinary sort of young chap,' he said.

I took a hasty gulp of champagne and didn't know where to look. The flashy blonde seemed visibly put out. She had lost her place, momentarily at least, as the centre of his attention. Lady Val flashed an appreciative look at me. 'You've won the race and now you've stolen the limelight,' she said softly.

We did not linger over the port, that was never his way, and soon we were whisked off to the ball. Here the flashy blonde came back into her own for HRH, who loved dancing as much as he liked pretty women, monopolised her. I, on the other hand, was ignored and forgotten amongst the crowd of socialites who all knew and recognised each other which, in hindsight, was very good for me. This was much as I had anticipated. The only people with whom I could claim any acquaintance were Pirate Probert, of whom I stood in some awe, and Rupert Carleton whom I was determined to keep as far away from as possible though, despite the venomous looks he darted at me from time to time, I doubted if he would dare to start anything in the presence of the Prince. There was a certain amount of cheery rowdiness going on amongst the younger generation but I knew none of them, though again I saw one or two curious looks directed towards me, I suppose because of my winning of the race and my presence in the Prince's party. Of my only real friend, Captain Pat, there was no sign, nor had I expected that there would be. 'Those affairs are not for the likes of me,' I could almost hear him saying.

Feeling rather like a wallflower at a débutante ball, I was on the point of wandering off to hide myself somewhere in a corner with a bottle of champagne when Lady Val came up to me. 'What are you doing sitting there all sad and lonely?' she said. 'You're not dancing. 'We'll soon put that right. Come along.' She reached out a hand.

'I'm a hopeless dancer,' I said. 'I don't know any steps – '

'Nonsense. All jockeys can dance. It's a question of keeping time, that's all. Now then. That's an order.'

She more or less swept me on to the dance floor. She was right, of course. The beat of the band and her presence in my arms with the silken feel of her flesh above the backless gown gave my feet a lightness to match hers.

'"The craze for pleasure,"' she hummed in my ear, '"Steadily grows / Cocktails and laughter / But what comes after? / Nobody knows."'

The ball was held in the great hall of Patworth Castle some miles from Melton. There were antlers, shooting trophies, and armorial racks on the walls from which ancestors stared grimly down on us.

'Roundheads, and cavaliers, every one of them,' she said as we danced. 'They backed both sides in the Civil War and have gone on doing it ever since. That's why they've kept their lands and their money. That's what it's all about in the last issue, isn't it? Get what you want and keep it? "What comes after, nobody knows."' She hummed again.

When the music stopped she laid a hand on my arm while her eyes roved around amongst the revellers. She was, I knew, searching for the Prince and, as I saw, searching in vain. 'We need a drink,' she said abruptly, and led me through an arched doorway and along a short passage which brought us to a terrace. Here there were chairs and tables set out. Leaving her for a moment I went in search of sustenance and, finding a white-coated waiter, told him to bring a bottle of champagne to the table. As I was returning I found myself face to face with Pirate who was chatting to a tall, fair-haired younger man. Catching sight of me, he stopped me. 'Well done, lad,' he said. 'And your head is still off the block, I'm glad to see. By the way, this is Sir Crispin Merevale, your host, he owns the place. You may meet him sometime in his other occupation, too.'

'I'm one of those dire people, a steward,' he said, smiling. Then he suddenly gave me a hard look, as if the name had clicked in his mind. 'I'll add my congratulations,' he said. 'I used to ride a bit myself.'

So this was the steward who had conducted my father's initial enquiry. Covertly I had as good a look at him as I could. He was utterly unlike what I had imagined him to be – far younger, less pompous, and with an amused look in his eye. Altogether he appeared more approachable than I could have hoped if ever I got the chance to make that approach. The time was certainly not just then. I thanked him and passed on.

Back at the table I found the champagne frosting in its ice bucket and filled the glasses.

'Now,' she said, 'you can say you're a man who danced with a girl who danced with the Prince of Wales.'

'And very nice too,' I said.

'Thank you, kind sir. You didn't do too badly yourself. My feet are intact.'

We were both of us laughing now. 'Cigarette me, will you?' she said.

I took out my case. It was a slim gold one which had been my father's and which my mother had told me to take lest it be stolen. Opening it I held it out to her. 'Common fags,' I said. 'Nothing here from Parkinson of Haymarket.'

She drew a deep breath on the cigarette as I lighted it for her.

'Rupert,' she said, 'is a very nasty man. He goes too far always. And everything he's got he gives to the bookies.' Then her eyes fell on the case. 'What a lovely thing,' she said, picking it up from the table where I had placed it between us. 'A present from a rich girl friend – stocks and bonds from faded blondes?'

'It was my father's,' I said. 'One of his owners gave it to him when he won the Eclipse with Sang Froid.'

'You father,' she said. 'I heard Roger asking about him. So there's no hope?'

'None at all,' I said.

Her eyes clouded for a moment. 'What – ' she began to say and then stopped. Suddenly, almost savagely, she stubbed out her cigarette and then got to her feet. 'Let's dance,' she said.

The throb of the music came faintly to us on the terrace. It was one of those balmy nights that sometimes come to the countryside in early spring. Though the terrace was shaded, the formal gardens below were alive with fairy lights. Set on a high bluff as the castle was, the whole effect was magical. We seemed to be floating in some sort of ethereal space. Alone with her I felt I could stay there for ever and I was reluctant to surrender her company to others on the dance floor. But it didn't happen; she showed no desire to abandon me and so I didn't have to share her. Together we danced the night away, and at the very end, as we joined hands to the strains of John Peel and Auld Lang Syne, smiling, she said to me, 'You're coming to Huntercombe for the weekend. No ifs or buts, you're coming. I'll take you.'

'When?'

'Now.'

Together we made our way to the Riley. She had thrown a mink coat over her ball gown and I climbed in beside her. 'I'll have to pack,' I said.

'Don't you have a man to do that for you?' she said as she pulled up outside my rooms.

'Not yet,' I said. 'I'm waiting for the stocks and bonds from faded blondes.'

Dawn had come and gone. The strings were already going out for exercise and the early morning had brought a chill to the air. 'I'm damned if I'm going to sit out here in the cold waiting for you,' she said. 'I'll come in with you.'

I had a sitting room, a bedroom, and a bathroom down the passage. Turning on the gas fire in the sitting room for her, I went into the bedroom to pack.

It occurs to me now, looking back over the years, how heavily encumbered with luggage even the young, as I was then, travelled. There were dinner jackets and tails, at least two suits, flannel or whipcord trousers, a hacking jacket, shirts stiff and soft, collars innumerable, to say nothing of socks and ties and underclothes and, as well, our hunting and racing clothes. No wonder most of us travelled with trunks. Of course if one went by train, as we mostly did over any distance, there were ranks of porters ready and willing to relieve us of the burden of carrying or trolleying the stuff.

But I digress. I changed rapidly out of my tails and threw what I guessed I would want for the weekend into a suitcase. I didn't think she would take kindly to waiting long and I hurried back.

When I entered the sitting room she was standing by the desk in a corner. In one hand was a cigarette and in the other my mother's letter. She was staring fixedly at the two photographs of Vincent Rossiter which, together with the letter, I had left lying on the desk. She smiled at me as I came in. Not a whit abashed, she brandished the letter. 'I always read other people's correspondence if they're careless enough to leave it lying about,' she said. 'How is your mother?'

'Very well, I think,' I said. 'Hunting madly.'

It wasn't until much later that I began to wonder what had drawn her attention so fixedly to the photographs and why, if she was so interested, had she not questioned me about them and had she skilfully turned any possible curiosity of mine about that by directing attention to my mother's letter?

10

A puncture on the way and my changing of the wheel, which wasn't as simple an operation then as now, delayed our arrival at Huntercombe, and HRH's Rolls together with Flinty's Bentley were already parked in the forecourt when we drew up at the front door.

Huntercombe was a Tudor manor house, in size somewhere between a mansion and a country house. She led the way into an inner hall, square and compact, oak beamed with a small minstrel's gallery. There a butler awaited us. 'His Royal Highness, the young lady and Major Westcough are on the golf course, m'lady,' he told us.

'I see. Get William to show Mr de Lacey his room, will you, Jenks,' she said. Then, turning to me, she said: 'I'm going to get out of these duds. You'll want to freshen up, too, I expect. Come down when you like. We usually meet here. Drinks over there – ' She pointed to a standing chest. 'Help yourself to whatever you want.'

I followed the footman upstairs, and along passages until he threw open a door. It was a low-ceilinged room with a canopied bed and mullioned windows. 'You'd care for a bath, sir, I expect,' he said, opening a door in the panelling to reveal a modern, glistening bathroom. 'I'll run it for you.'

When he had gone I stepped gratefully into the steaming water, and let it soak into my bones and muscles. I'd had a hectic twenty-four hours. I'd won a race against the odds from the heir to the throne, had a row with a leading gentleman rider, been to an exclusive dinner party, danced all night with one of the most sought after girls in the Shires and was now a member of the privileged few to be a guest at her home.

Lloyd George's earl, or whoever he had employed to do the work of modernising Huntercombe, had done it well, I thought. The bath was long and deep, there was every conceivable unguent and accoutrement including, unusually for that day and age, a bidet. The only touch of opulence was the yellow gleam of the taps which I assumed to be gold. Apart from that, the bedroom with its deep pile carpet, embossed writing paper on its desk at the window, antique dressing table and Fragonard prints – or were they originals? – on its walls, seemed to typify the whole place which, from what I had seen of it, reeked of taste, comfort and luxury. And it was, apparently, packed with servants. At Kilbarry we lived well, for Ireland, but nothing on this scale.

Idly I wondered how Lady Val did it since she was so often away, and then I remembered my mother telling me that there was a housekeeper who was popularly supposed to have been the mistress of the old man. She had been a sort of nanny and confidante of his only child and had stayed on to run the place with clockwork efficiency and to pander to her every whim. Thinking of these things, twiddling my toes against the taps, I yawned and, in the midst of soaping myself, fell asleep.

It was the water cooling around me that woke me. I had no idea how long I had slept but I knew it was late. My bag had been unpacked. Hurriedly I shaved and pulled on my clothes. Making my way to the hall I found my hostess, dressed in country tweeds, sitting in a big leather chair and reading the *Sporting Life*.

Scarcely had I arrived when a side door opened and Flinty came in.

'A large pink gin, quickly,' he said, crossing to the drink tray on the chest. 'I don't know how he does it. He never seems to tire. It's go, go, go all the time. No sooner were we here than he had us out golfing. Eighteen holes! I'm whacked. Flat out.' He gulped his gin.

'And the lovely Dinah, dear Dinah?' Lady Val asked.

Dinah, I thought, so that was the flashy blonde's name.

Flinty chuckled. 'She rashly said last night, to get into further favour, I suppose, that she loved a game of golf. She little knew what was coming to her, poor creature. After nine holes she showed all the signs of wilting but the little man would have none of it. Eighteen holes or nothing. She's not the greatest golfer either. She's had time to regret those rash words.'

At that moment HRH and the flashy blonde, Dinah, came in. He was wearing the golfing knickerbockers we then called plus fours, a Fairisle jersey, co-respondent brown and white shoes, and looked as fresh as paint. She, poor thing, on the other hand, was suffering. The blonde hair was bedraggled and there were black bags under her eyes which no amount of make-up could conceal. She was wearing, too, I noticed, the sort of country clothes a town person thinks are right and which in the country look all wrong. As they entered I saw an all but imperceptible look pass from the Prince to Flinty, who immediately put down his glass and quickly left the room. In a few moments he was back dispensing drinks after another slight signal had been exchanged between them. The flashy blonde, as I never ceased to think of her, though there was precious little flashiness about her just then, asked with a sort of gasp for a sidecar if there was one going. There was and she probably needed it.

After we had made desultory conversation for a few minutes, Jenks, the butler, came in. 'His Royal Highness is wanted on the telephone,' he said.

'Were you told what it was?' the Prince asked.

'No, sir, but if I may mention it, the person said it was urgent.'

'I'd better see to it if you'll forgive me,' the Prince said.

As soon as he had gone the flashy blonde put down her glass. 'I think I'd like to go upstairs for a bit,' she said. She then gave the ghost of a smile, and added: 'To try to repair the damage.'

'You do that, dear,' Lady Val said and, when the door had closed behind her, she looked at Flinty. 'You arranged that very nicely, didn't you,' she said.

A little later there was the rumble of the Rolls' wheels and, looking out, we saw its back disappearing out of the forecourt and down the drive.

'That's the end of her,' Lady Val said with satisfaction.

'Just so,' Flinty said. 'And I'm left to pick up the pieces.'

'You're good at that, though, aren't you, Flinty,' Lady Val said. 'It's part of the price you pay, isn't it? Time for lunch, I think. If she doesn't come down I suppose I'd better send that bitch up something.' Then she turned to me. 'As Flinty will no doubt tell you, if he hasn't already, I don't like my own sex very much.'

Lunch was plain and unceremonious. As we sat down Lady Val said to the butler, 'Better send Miss, what the devil is her name, Flinty?'

'Carstairs,' Flinty said.

'Have Miss Carstairs brought up something on a tray, Jenks,' Lady Val said.

The butler coughed. 'I understand the young lady is asleep, m'lady,' he said.

'Well if the sleeper awakes and wants something, send her up a tray,' Lady Val commanded.

We had coffee in the hall. Flinty and I refused both port

and liqueurs. Flinty drank sparingly and I felt that I'd done enough drinking over the past day or so to last me some time. When the cups had been cleared away Flinty, who numbered kindness amongst the other virtues the hostile members of that set refused to concede to him, said: 'I really think I should find out what that poor creature wants. She can't be left marooned here for ever.'

'I should think not, and the dungeons have been out of use for years,' Lady Val said. 'All right, I'll get Mrs Beltham to go up to her.'

Soon the housekeeper, having been given her instructions, reappeared with the news that Miss Carstairs had learnt that the Prince of Wales had been urgently called away and felt that she, too, should leave.

'She wants to go 'ome, is that it?' Lady Val said.

'It would seem so, m'lady.'

'Very good, I'll take her anywhere within reason,' Flinty said. 'Where is home?'

'London, I understand, sir.'

'You could put her on a train at Melton,' Lady Val said. 'Good of you, Flinty. Always a shoulder to cry on. You'll be back, won't you? I'll show Danny the horses. You've seen them before.'

The flashy blonde came down looking considerably more spruce but still not quite what she had been on the dance floor. There was a flurry of thanks and goodbyes, rather tearful on her part, I thought, followed by the burble of the Bentley's exhaust as they drove away.

'Cannon fodder. Good riddance,' Lady Val said, drawing on her umpteenth cigarette of the day. 'Come on, Danny, let's look at the horses. They can do all sorts of things but they can't dance and they can't talk.'

The yards at Huntercombe were magnificent. Lady Val had twenty blood horses stabled at Melton but here were young stock coming on and replacements for the all too frequent injuries in the hunting field being schooled and prepared for action if required. Then there were her point-to-pointers, and in a lower yard her store steeplechasers and foals and yearlings for the few she ran on the flat. The whole place was spotless, swept clean and free from any possible wisp of straw or hay. The boxes were painted, polished and burnished, and all of it lay gleaming in the watery sun which had now come out from behind the low clouds.

We walked down the line of boxes. At one we halted. 'This is Prospero, I won on him yesterday, remember?' she said.

We went in. He was a pale chestnut, a colour I didn't and still don't like, thinking them inclined to be ungenuine, and he had certainly had it all his own way in that race, what I saw of it. But there was no denying he looked the part. He was big and upstanding with quarters 'to carry you clean over a town' as one of my poets, I think, had said. And, by My Prince out of a Jackdaw mare he was, as we agreed, bred well enough for anything.

'It's my belief,' I heard her saying as I looked him over, 'that he could go on to better things. They won't allow me to ride against you men, and I'm fed up taking on these fat cows in lady's races. They're mostly out of control and would knock you down by mistake because they don't know enough to do it any other way. A true run race, my foot, there isn't such a thing. Half my time is spent trying to keep out of their way. Will you ride him for me?'

I gasped. Here, indeed, was another such chance as I had never dreamed of, and coming on top of yesterday too. She looked at me quizzically. 'You'll get lots of offers of rides after that win on HRH's horse,' she said. 'They'll be after you. I thought I'd get in first. Well, what do you think?'

'You've taken my breath away,' I said. 'Of course I'll ride him for you. It's just I hardly know how to say it. Are you sure?'

'I wouldn't have asked you if I wasn't, would I?' She

tucked her arm into mine. 'Now let me show you the rest of the place.'

Arm in arm for the rest of that short, enchanted afternoon, we wandered through formal gardens, glasshouses carefully tended, and down through the woods to where a little river ran. Back at the house with the evening drawing in, the curtains closed and a fire blazing in the big stone fireplace in the hall, we found tea and muffins waiting for us. There was no sign of Flinty. He had sent a message to say that he had been detained and would not be returning. Then the dressing bell sounded and we went upstairs to change.

Looking back, now, in the kitchen, with a pizza and a bottle of cheap plonk in front of me, I find it hard to believe that the way we lived then was a reality. Was it I, as a youngster, who found a fire in the bedroom hearth, my bath run, my dinner clothes laid out, my shirt studded and linked? To me it is like a dream, as so many things from that time are now. Bathed and changed, I came down to the hall to see Lady Val standing by the fire, a cigarette in her fingers, looking as lovely as I had imagined in a short silken evening gown which set off her slim shapeliness.

As I joined her she indicated a jade cigarette box and then pressed a bell to summon the butler. 'Jenks creates the best champagne cocktails this side of paradise,' she said. 'It's the touch of the master hand that tells the tale, isn't it, Jenks?'

'Thank you, m'lady. I hope they're to your satisfaction, sir.' He handed me a brimming glass on a salver.

They were. So were those that followed. 'I've always been told that if you open a bottle of champagne you must empty it,' she said. And then, more sombrely: 'Cocktails and laughter, but what comes after. What comes after. There's the rub, isn't it?' And she stared into her drink.

Later we dined together, in candlelight, at a small table set in front of the fire under the beamed ceiling. There were blazing log fires all over that house, and I suppose there was central heating too, yet so carefully was it controlled that it never seemed over-heated like so many houses of today.

With Jenks and a footman hovering about, we spoke mostly of generalities, and it was not until we were back in the hall in deep chairs in front of the fire, our drinks beside us, port for me, brandy for her, that our talk became more intimate. We were both, I think, by that time slightly tight. I know I was.

'And you, Danny,' she said. 'How is your quest going? Did you find out anything from the detectives?'

'Not much,' I said. 'They think one of the temporary lads did it, but we knew that before. They've narrowed it down to the lad who called himself Vincent Rossiter but he's done a bunk. Gone to America and got lost.' Then, suddenly remembering, I said: 'That was his photograph on my desk you were looking at. They don't seem to be able to find out much about him. He was a wanderer, apparently, and never in one place for long. You didn't have him here, by chance, at any time?'

'Good heavens no. I wondered what on earth those photographs were doing there. Gone to America, has he!'

'So they say.'

'It's pretty hopeless, isn't it, Danny? Why don't you chuck it? Concentrate on your riding. You could go places, though I wouldn't count on more Royal rides. That was a one off. He likes to ride his own horses and damn well he does it, whatever they say. Don't take any notice of what's said about his falls – "thrown from his horse" as if he was cutting voluntaries all the time. He sits tight enough. Everyone who rides in front hunting or rides races has falls, it's part of the game, but you know that as well as I do.'

'It's all that stuff in the papers,' I said, thinking of the cartoon that Rupert was passing around.

'The press, damn them. They're beginning to get him down and can you blame him? How would you like it if you were followed everywhere by a bloody barrage of cameras and crowds congregating in the hope of seeing you take a jerk? Look, here's a recent cutting. I kept it.' She crossed to a desk in a corner, rummaged about a bit and then, with the paper in her hands, came back and read out: "The news that the Prince of Wales was a competitor attracted, of course, a gathering that was unusually large for this annual event. Thousands of people splashed and struggled about on the precarious footing offered by the muddy hillside, which, in places, soon became a quagmire . . ." And, do you know, there was a post and rails at one meeting and when they heard he was coming they took out the top rail. He was so furious when he walked the course and found out he withdrew his horses and came home.'

'Good for him,' I said. 'What a bloody insulting thing to do.'

She lit another cigarette and sipped her brandy. '"My falls have become a public topic," he said to me on the way back. "Why can't they leave me alone, let me be a private person? Lots of others have falls. I'm beginning to despair of the jibes at me."'

'If it was me I think I'd pack it in,' I said.

'He'll never do that, not willingly, he has too much guts, more than I ever thought he had. It takes a hell of a lot of guts to go on in the face of what he's had to put up with. But that was one of the reasons he and Flinty rigged the deception yesterday, to keep the press away.'

'It didn't work,' I said. 'Someone split.'

I don't know if she heard me since she went on, unheeding. 'They'll make him give up,' she said fiercely. 'And then what will happen to him? I've talked to several chaps who have given up for one reason or another, and they say the withdrawal symptoms are something horrible, that they can't find anything to put in its place. He'll take up golf, he says. Golf!' She put so much contempt into that word I could almost feel it. 'If he does he'll start to drink. He keeps himself fit for racing, that's why he's off the bottle always now. He only drinks when he's bored, and anyway he's not a golfer, he's no good at ball games, the outdoor sport at least.' Her words were almost falling over each other as she poured them out. 'And when he's bored he'll be easy prey for some floosie to get hold of him.'

'Like the flashy blonde,' I said.

'Her – she's of no account, but there are plenty of married bitches about all too ready to collar him. He doesn't like the Court set now, and if they make him give up, he'll never forgive them.'

I don't know what made me say what I said next. It must have been the cocktails and the wine and the closeness and companionship. 'Do you love him very much?' I said.

'That's my business,' she said sharply and then, so softly I barely heard it, capping the brandy glass in her hands and staring into the fire. 'More than anything,' she said.

Silence fell between us for a little until I broke it by saying: 'You mentioned there were those who would stop him racing and I've heard that there are people at Court who don't want him there. What about Gretton? He's been friendly enough to me but he was one of the stewards who warned my father off.'

'Roger? You never know with Roger but basically he's one of that stiff-necked crew. Make no mistake, Danny, according to that lot Flinty, I and others, you, too, to some extent I expect, we're dross. People may think I don't know the things they say about me – no family background, Lloyd George's earl, new money and the rest. They may need that new money sooner than they think; some of them need it now. Do you know what they said to one chap who applied to come in as joint master? "It's your money not you we're interested in." What bloody cheek! I'd have told them where to put it and gone to take a pack in Ireland or the provinces or somewhere and done it so well it'd show them up. The little man was furious when he heard it.'

'Good for him. Gosh, I'm learning something every day I stay here.'

'It might be better if you didn't stay too long in this jungle of hard men and predatory women. Miss Carstairs – can that be her real name, it sounds like something out of Sapper? – was casting sheep's eyes at you. Oh, yes, she was, I saw it. Are you a virgin, Danny?'

I found myself blushing furiously as I admitted, haltingly, that I was.

'What? A real, male, buck virgin? Did you know that when one of those crosses Trafalgar Square the lions all roar and Nelson comes down from his pillar and takes off his hat. Has that happened to you?'

'Don't mock me,' I said sulkily. 'And I haven't been in Trafalgar Square recently.'

Having rather gracelessly refused a nightcap I was still miserably sulking when I got into bed. Why, I asked myself, did she have to ruin a wonderful evening by reminding me of my inadequacy for, like many young males in that day and age, inadequate was what I felt in not having known a woman. I realise it is all different now, at least from what I see and read in the papers. A male buck virgin she had called me. I squirmed again at the description and all that it implied. Damn her, I thought, picking at the sheets.

At that moment I heard a movement near the bed and, looking up, saw her standing beside it. I had been so preoccupied with my misery and my thoughts that I had not heard the door opening and her coming in. At first I thought that I must be asleep and dreaming.

It was no dream.

She stood there looking down at me. 'My poor Danny,' she said. 'I've hurt you. I shouldn't have mocked you. It was foul of me. I've come to say I'm sorry.

She was wearing a long silk dressing gown, slashed with colour. We looked at each other in silence and our glances held. Her hand went up to the top button of her gown.

Slowly, one by one, she undid the others. It fell open and with a swift, lithe movement, she shrugged it off and stood there, the glow from the flickering firelight casting a sort of nimbus around her. I had never before, believe it or not, seen a naked woman. Speechless I gazed, drinking in the small firm rounded breasts, the nipples proud and hard, the slim waist and tapering thighs. As if to make sure she was there, numbly I stretched out a hand to touch her.

'I'll make it up to you,' she said. With that she lifted the covers and slid between the sheets beside me.

Even now, after all these years, I can still recall the ecstasy (I can think of no other word) of that first initiation, and at times the memory of the silken sheen of her skin under my questing hands comes back to haunt me. She was careful, tender and kind and when, at last, drowsiness was drifting me towards slumber, I heard and can still hear the words she whispered into my ear: 'Nelson is safe now.'

11

When I arrived at the depot next morning I was met by Captain Pat in no very good mood. 'You're late,' he reminded me. He was right, I was. I was still treading air after the most wonderful weekend of my life. 'You were supposed to ride work on the Colonel's horse. That slipped your mind, I suppose.' He was right again. It had done. 'Go to my office, will you. I want to speak to you.'

He came in a few minutes after me while I was looking at a framed photograph of him winning the Indian Grand National some years before. 'Sit down,' he said, taking his own chair behind his desk. 'Your mother asked me to look after you and I'm not sure I'm doing a good job. The Colonel was thinking of offering you the rides on that point-to-pointer of his, but I doubt if he will now. Cutting work is precious near a court-martial offence in his book.'

'I was away – ' I began.

'I know. At Huntercombe. That's another reason. He thinks you may be getting in with the wrong people.'

'I see,' I said. 'Is the Prince of Wales one of them?' This was impertinent and the moment I said it I regretted it. My only excuse was that I was still on what I believe now is called cloud nine. I waited for the wrath to come but Captain Pat wasn't one of those barking officers whose sparks fly off in all directions.

'He isn't, not yet anyway,' he said, mildly. 'But some of those around him are and you must remember that Colonel Probert is one of the old guard.'

'Who is it then?' I asked. 'Flinty, I imagine. Why are they all so down on him?' (I couldn't bring myself to mention Lady Val's name in this context though I had an idea she, too, would be numbered with Flinty.) 'Is it because he doesn't try to stop HRH doing what he enjoys?'

He gave me one of his owlish glances. 'It's not for me to preach,' he said. 'But the heir to the throne can't always do what he likes, nor for the matter of that can you, as you will find out before you are much older.'

I glared at him and he looked mildly back at me through his thick spectacles. At that moment the telephone rang and he lifted the receiver. After listening for a minute he handed it to me. 'It's for you,' he said.

I took it from him, wondering who was making the call and why. It was Ginger Elton, the lad who had told me about Vincent Rossiter.

'I've seen him,' he said breathlessly. ''E's back!'

'Where?' I said. 'Did you speak to him?'

'Nah,' he said. 'He was all toffed up in a trilby 'at an all. Look, I can't talk more. I'm with Mr Barker now and he'd have the hide off me if he catches me usin' the telephone.'

'All right,' I said. 'Where can we meet?'

'I dunno. Leicester races on Thursday maybe. I've a ride in the second.'

'I'll meet you outside the weighing room after the third,' I said.

'Crickey, 'e's comin'. I thought 'e was in the village. I'd better bolt.' The line went dead.

I replaced the receiver, to find Captain Pat looking quizzically at me through those glasses. Although I was boiling inwardly about having been brought down to earth so suddenly and with such a bump, I felt I had to explain the call. 'That was Elton,' I said. 'The temporary lad who knew Rossiter. He said Rossiter is back in the country. He'd seen him.'

'Has he, bedad. Did he say where?'

'No, he's with Rodney Barker and he said his guv'nor would have the hide off him if he found him using the phone. He told me he'd meet me at Leicester on Thursday and fill me in.'

'Leicester on Thursday. You'll be wanting transport. I could do with a day's racing. I'll take you.'

It was a gesture of forgiveness and did, in fact, solve my problems of getting there. While mentally resolving that one way or another I must get myself a car, I thanked him.

'For nothing. I was told to keep an eye on you after all,' he said with one of his smiles. 'Now then, ever seen a bog spavin? No? Well it's part of your education which I'm to instill into you. You'll see one now.'

Together, friends again, we walked towards the line of boxes.

On the Tuesday and Wednesday, I dutifully rode work on the Colonel's horse which was improving all the time, and attended to my veterinary education at the hands of Captain Pat, and I also acquired a secondhand car, an Alvis 12/50 with a sports tourer body. 'She'll do seventy-five,' an enthusiastic salesman assured me, and a friendly bank manager who remembered my father provided the necessary funds. In those days everyone, especially in small communities like Melton and the racing world as it then was, knew everyone else, which certainly oiled the wheels for those in the circuit.

I had not seen Lady Val, Flinty or the Prince since the weekend. They were, I assumed, hunting four days a week at least, and I could not aspire even to one day, as nothing seemed to be ready at the depot just then, so I could not hope to meet them there. I wondered vaguely if I had been dropped, that I had amused them for a day or so and been of some little use and then discarded, though Lady Val had said I was their mascot which could mean anything or nothing.

The morning before we were due to go to Leicester and before I had taken delivery of the car which was, the salesman assured me, being finally checked over, I went into Captain Pat's office to see what he had in store for me that day. I found him frowning over a newspaper.

'Seen this?' he said, looking up as I came in.

'No. What is it?'

'You'll know soon enough.' He chucked the paper, folded and marked at one passage, across the desk to me.

I picked it up. The print stared me in the face: *THESE NAMES ARE NEWS. Son of disgraced trainer rides Royal winner. Daniel de Lacey, whose father was warned off the Turf for doping, rode the Prince of Wales' Pepperpot to victory in a point-to-point race at Marleythorpe last week-end. His Royal Highness, recovering from a broken collarbone when he was thrown from his horse in the hunting-field, was second . . .*

I threw down the paper in disgust. 'They've managed to libel my father and insult the Prince in one paragraph,' I said. 'It's lucky for them my father is laid out and can't sue. And "thrown from his horse". HRH won't like that.'

'If he sees it. I don't suppose he reads the rag. I don't myself. One of the rough-riders brought it in.'

'They'd never have dared to print it, would they, unless someone had been feeding them information about my father?'

'It certainly looks like that,' Captain Pat said. 'But everyone in Melton knows about the stroke and, these journalistic johnnies, they're always hanging about looking for society snippets, the nastier the better; and, remember, the press were there in force at Marleythorpe.'

'I'm not likely to forget it,' I said grimly, wondering if this had scuppered my chances of seeing them all again. I couldn't disguise from myself that mixing in that charmed circle had been heady wine and I wanted more of it. The character or, rather, what we would now call charisma, of the Prince had me in thrall, as of course it did then with countless others. As for Lady Val, subconsciously, I think, even then I realised that she was one of that rare breed of women whose attitude to sex was much as a man's, in that she took what of it that she wanted as and when she wanted, while at the same time remaining basically loyal to one, and that one was not and never could be me. During the night, or what was left of it, that we had spent together, twice I had heard her murmur in our fitful sleep the word 'David', and on the second occasion she had reached out and clasped me to her. It told me that the episode of the flashy blonde must have hurt more than she cared to reveal. All of this, if it did anything, only heightened my wish to see them both again. But no word had come from any of them by the time Captain Pat drove me to Leicester.

When we arrived in the car park at Leicester, Captain Pat went off almost immediately to seek out cronies and his trainer, leaving me on my own to look at the horses and to watch Elton bring his mount home a hard fought third in his race. He was good, I thought, and deserved more rides if he could get them, but it was a tough old life, tougher then than now, and few survived to get near the top. I had liked what little I had seen of him and mentally I wished him well.

Elton was waiting for me as we had agreed outside the weighing-room and I took him off for a drink. 'That's a nice horse you rode in the last,' I said.

"'E's all right; 'e ran a bit green. The Guv'nor said I done too much with him. He's terrible 'ard to please.'

'Do you want to watch the next?' I said as I brought him

a beer. 'This place will clear in a minute or two when they go out. Then we can talk in peace and no chance of being overheard.'

'OK by me. Cheers.'

When someone appeared in the doorway and said, 'They're going out,' there was a general exodus and we were left alone. 'Well,' I said. 'You saw him, you say?'

'Like I said. 'E was got up all posh. What's more 'e's changed 'is appearance.'

'What?'

'S' truth. 'E's dyed 'is 'air fair and grown a moustache.'

'How did you recognise him?'

''E 'ad a way of sort of twiddlin' 'is 'ands when lightin' a fag. That's when I first spotted 'im and 'e 'ad a kinda tee-hee laugh. I was sure it was 'im when I 'eard it.'

'Did you speak to him?'

'Nah. He got away. We was round the ring then an' people came between us, an' when I sorted them out 'e'd gone. I wandered round a bit tryin' to pick 'im up an' then I seen 'im again. 'E was with the books, bettin' on the rails. None of your Tatts layers for 'im. But someone came up to him. He scarpered off pretty quick an' I lost 'im.'

'Would you know him again?'

'You bet.'

I took out another fiver. As he pocketed it he half rose to go, then he hesitated and sat down again. 'Anovver thing,' he said slowly. 'I've just remembered it an' I dunno does it make any differ – '

'Anything at all you can think of may help,' I said.

''E talked a bit like a toff down on 'is luck, if you get me. We thought 'e was puttin' it on an' apein' 'is betters an' we ribbed 'im about it. Now, seein' 'im all dressed up, I'm beginnin' to think it was the other way round an' mebbe 'e was tryin' to 'ide 'is toff way of talkin'. Mebbe I'm wrong. I was just thinkin' things over after you came to me abaht 'im.'

125

Another thought struck me then. 'Did you recognise anyone he was talking to when you first saw him round the ring?' I asked him.

'Nah,' he said and again got up to go. Then he suddenly stopped. 'Now you mention it,' he said. 'He came from Mr Connaughton. Someone there might remember 'im an' help, but they change so quick you never know with them comin' an' goin'.'

Connaughton, I thought, that might well be a lead. Were things beginning to take shape at last?

'Look, guv', I've got to go,' he said then. 'I'm to meet a feller in Tom Matlock's stable. 'E said 'e might get me a ride. What do you want me to do, guv', if I see 'im again?'

Suddenly I realised I didn't know. I was out of my depth. Yet I had to say something, to appear in charge. 'Don't let him know you've rumbled him,' I said. 'But keep an eye on him if you can. See who he's with, who he talks to and if you know them. And keep in touch. Can I ring you?'

'Nah, Mr Barker 'e's terrible strict. I took a chance ringin' you that time. I could try from the village, though, but even then he's awful suspicious like. Thinks we're sellin' stable secrets to the books. 'E's threatenin' to lock us in. But I spect I can manage. You're there most times?'

'Yes, and if I'm not, leave a message with Captain Terrier or his clerk.'

Another fiver changed hands and I watched him leave, whilst a roar of cheering followed by an influx of people through the door of the bar marked the end of another race.

Going back in the car, Captain Pat asked me how I had got on, and I told him of the conversation.

'I wonder,' he said doubtfully, 'if there's any chance he might be stringing you along. Did you give him any money?'

'Yes,' I said. 'A few fivers.'

'A fiver means a lot to these lads and I reckon he thinks there's more to come.'

'Perhaps,' I said. 'But I've a feeling he's genuine.

Anyway, I've got to chance it. He's my only lead at the moment.'

We drove on without speaking for a few minutes, then Captain Pat said quietly: 'Are you determined to go on with this search of yours to clear your father's name?'

'I am,' I said. 'You know yourself what it has done to us. Besides, there's no one else to do it.'

'As long as you realise there may be perils in your path. That wire in the fence – I don't know, it could be you'd be wiser to face the worst, cut your losses and go home.'

'Are you trying to stop me?' I said almost angrily.

'No,' he said, mild as always. 'Merely pointing out the fences your may have to jump.'

'Have they got anywhere trying to find out who put the wire there?'

'They haven't and in my view they won't. I believe it was an outside job and it could have been anyone who wanted you hurt or out of the way or just plain frightened off. And another thing. The Colonel tore up that direction from on high because he won't stand for interference, but neither does he like things happening in his bailiwick he knows nothing about. He knows as well as we do that someone of influence pulled strings to get that instruction issued, but he doesn't know why, nor does he know why you're here or what you're up to.'

'What are you trying to tell me?'

'I'm saying that he is very strict and very strait-laced in certain matters. He's no fool and he's been puzzling over the wire business and the letter of instruction. He's one of the old brigade, as I've said before, and I don't think he's too fond of the Prince. If he thinks, what with your mixing in certain circles and those things happening, you're a disruptive influence then you're out and nothing I can do to stop it.'

'Then I'll go on on my own,' I said.

'You want to stay?'

'Of course.'

'It couldn't be mixed up with your getting too fond of those circles I was speaking of, male and female, could it?' he said, giving me a sly sidelong look. I was reminded again of his penchant for being the all-knowing, wise old owl.

'I can't think what you're talking about,' I said.

He chuckled in the way he had. 'Can't you? I think you can guess. Bear in mind a wise man once said, "Put not your trust in princes." All right, if you must, you must. But you can't do it all yourself, you know. I think you'd better go back to Charles Ormsby. He said he'd help, didn't he? He'll be glad to have a crack at it.'

'That's good advice,' I said. 'I'll ring him when we get in.'

12

The atmosphere from the sour-puss secretary was slightly less frigid this time when I entered the offices of Messrs Ormsby and Little, and the waiting period before I was shown into the inner sanctum considerably less protracted. Major Charles, I saw, was now sporting a different bow tie, crimson with white polka dots on this occasion. 'I gather from what you said on the telephone that you've made some progress,' he said as I sat down. 'You've seen Elton, it seems, and got something from him. Tell me about it.'

When I had finished he sat back and stared at the ceiling for a moment. 'The weakness of all Turf crimes, as you probably know,' he said, switching his gaze back to me, 'is that too many people have to be in the secret, and somehow, somewhere, it leaks out. It's obvious now, isn't it, if Rossiter has changed his appearance and come back and is in the money, he is blackmailing someone.'

'But who?' I said.

'That's what we've got to discover. First thing is to find Rossiter. You warned young Elton not to give himself away if he spotted him. That was wise. Have you got those photographs I gave you?'

'Yes,' I said, and handed them over.

He studied them for a moment and then pressed a bell on his desk. When the sour-puss receptionist came in he brought her round to his side of the desk and pointed to Rossiter's image in the photographs. 'Have Crannitch blow that face up,' he said. 'And then get him to do a drawing of it.' When she had gone he turned to me again. 'If we could get Elton to indicate the alterations, the moustache and the hair, we'd have a sort of artist's impression, enough probably to pick him up and follow him and see where he goes and to whom. What about Elton, is he co-operative?'

'Very, so far. I've made it worth his while.'

'Good. So one way or another we'll find Mr Vincent Rossiter or whatever he's calling himself now.'

'Isn't he taking the hell of a risk going racing?'

'Not really if you think it over. Only a few know suspicion centred on him, and he must believe the hue and cry has now died down. After all, your father, who was the prime mover in the investigation is, sadly, out of the running. He's altered his appearance. I reckon he thinks he's safe.'

'We've no idea who he really is?'

'That's another question, and one I don't think need bother us at this juncture, though what you tell me of his talking like a toff is interesting. The first thing is find him, the second is watch him without his knowing it. I can handle that, I'll put a good man on to it. It would be best if you were to take the drawing to Elton. He might still shy off from one of us. I think we may have rushed him a bit the last time, and since as you say you've made it worth his while, he'll no doubt expect more where that came from. These lads are always short of cash and no wonder with the pittance they're paid.'

'That reminds me of something I nearly forgot,' I said. 'He told me since he came from Connaughton's there might be someone there who could tell us about him.'

'It's true it was from Jimmy Connaughton he came to your

father. It's a gambling stable and up to all sorts of tricks. Jimmy himself is a tough nut. I wonder if we had a look at his list of owners would it tell us anything – ' He crossed to a bookcase and took down the current *Horses In Training* from a shelf. Opening it he leafed through it and handed it to me.

N. J. CONNAUGHTON. *Peterborough*, I read with, underneath, the list of horses and the names of his owners, a whole stack of them. But from the list two names leapt out at me immediately, *R. P. Carleton* and *A. R. J. Gretton*.

'Good God,' I said, staring at them.

'What is it? Found something?'

'Two of his owners are, well, I suppose you could say, interested in me.'

'Well I'm damned. Who are they?'

'Rupert Carleton and Roger Gretton. Do you know them?'

'I know everyone in racing. It's part of my business.'

'Captain Pat told me Rupert Carleton hasn't a bob. How did he get in there, how does he pay his training bills?'

'The answer to the first question is that he has all the right connections, to the second is that he doesn't.'

'How does he get away with that?'

'He gets commission on any new rich owners he introduces to the stable, which is where his connections come in; and as to the bills, he gives Jimmy something when he has a bet, either with the stable money or from information the stable feed him. It's a gambling stable, as I've said.'

'And Gretton?'

'Oh, nothing like that. Roger Gretton is a pillar of respectability. He's an influential member of the Jockey Club and carries weight in Court circles for that matter. I suspect he trains with Jimmy because he likes a bet, but so do certain other members of the Jockey Club, which may or may not surprise you. To me, I'm bound to say, Roger is a bit of an enigma. On the surface he's an affable, easy-going cove, though I've sometimes wondered – '

'Lady Val told me she thought he was devious.'

'Easy-going chaps sometimes get that reputation. He was on the Prince of Wales's staff on one of his foreign trips, I forget which at the moment. They fell out. No one so far as I know, except themselves, knows what about. I rather think it was because Roger wanted to clip his wings.'

'They seem friendly now. He was at dinner with HRH the night I was there.'

'Yes, well, the Prince doesn't bear malice.' He smiled suddenly. 'That's one of the nicest things about him, one of the many reasons we like and admire him so much – apart from the fact that he goes like hell out hunting.'

'Roger Gretton,' I said, 'was one of the Jockey Club stewards who warned my father off.'

'I know. I checked back in the Calendar before you came.'

'That notice,' I said, choosing my words as carefully as I could, 'leaves it very open to the suggestion that my father had a hand in the doping. That's what hurt him so much and which now hurts my mother and me, and that's what's been accepted by the public. That's why we have got to clear his name. There was a gossip column – '

'I've seen it.'

'Do you know who frames these notices or works out the wording?'

'They're drafted by a member of the secretariat who sits in on the hearing. Then the draft goes to the stewards for approval before they sign it and authorise its publication.'

'So they or any of them could alter it and change the wording as they wished?'

'I should imagine so, but my information is that they very rarely do since they're so keen to get at the port. Are you suggesting that Roger may have had a hand in strengthening it or changing it so that it pointed directly at your father?'

'It crossed my mind. My father was convinced and so now are my mother and I that he was framed. And there's another thing I've found out that convinces me of it. You know as well as I do that every winner isn't tested, not by a long chalk. Why pick on him? Elton told me the gossip in the weighing-room was that there was a tip-off.'

'Weighing-room gossip often has a foundation in fact. If we could find out just where the gossip came from, who, if anyone, heard something to give grounds for it, it would help. Who was the chairman on that day, do you know?'

'I do. Sir Crispin Merevale, bart, of Patworth Castle.'

'He's far from being as pompous as he sounds. I know him quite well. He was in the 17th. He's one of the better stewards. We might get something from him. I'll think it over. It all looks more and more as if there was some sort of conspiracy. I wish your father had told me more at the time. Have you any idea why he didn't?'

'My mother believes it was because of a plot against the Prince of Wales that he knew too much about. That's why he kept so quiet, why he refused to take an action or go public in any way. He didn't want the Prince's name drawn into it.'

'And you think Roger may have been one of the plotters?'

'My father never named names and we are only hunting about in the dark, but since I've come here there do seem to be pointers towards him.'

'It's no secret of course that in Court circles there are those who don't care for the Prince or his way of life. But Roger – I wonder. My guess would be that he is too careful, too anxious to run with the hare and hunt with the hounds to get mixed up with anything like that.'

'Perhaps that's just what he's doing, running with the hare and hunting with the hounds and he's in Connaughton's stable and that's where it all began.'

'I'll keep an open mind. Any other names?'

'I've heard Lord Marston mentioned. He's been at Melton recently keeping an eye on the Prince, or so I'm told.'

'Lord Marston of Sevenoaks. He's the éminence grise at Court. It's possible. Though unlikely.'

'He's a pal of Gretton's. They were snapped together at a smart wedding having a confidential chat.'

He got up and crossed to the window. With his hands in his trouser pockets turning over coins, he stood there for a few minutes in silence staring down at the street. In that silence I could hear a clock ticking and located it. It was a grandfather in the far corner of the room. Somehow I had the feeling that a decision was being made which could affect my whole life.

Eventually he turned back into the room. 'If you are right,' he said, 'I think you should know what you are taking on. Accepting for a moment that there was some sort of conspiracy affecting the Prince, those whom you may now be threatening stand to lose everything, as much as your father did. They're in positions of power and influence. Power and influence,' he repeated. 'The instigators of all evil or pretty nearly. They've shown how ruthless they can be and they can do it again.'

'You're the second person to issue me with a storm warning,' I said.

'Who was the first?'

'Captain Pat, but when I told him I was going on he advised me to come back to you.'

'Pat Terrier is all right. He was with us a bit during the war. In fact I think I rode against him in a gymkhana at Amiens. It's just that you should know who you are toughing with and that you may get crushed.'

'I'm in now and I'm staying in,' I said stubbornly. 'I've got to find out the truth however tough it is. But how about you? You'll be in it too.'

He gave one of his brief smiles and then in an involuntary gesture reached up and touched his bow tie as if it were a talisman. 'I've toughed it with tougher,' he said.

13

Driving back I had much to occupy my thoughts but, despite myself, they kept returning to Lady Val. Even the fact that the artist's impression, which had been completed before I left and was in a manila envelope on the seat beside me, could not distract them. Had she, I could not help wondering, cast me aside having, as she might have told herself, completed my education, or did she think that I might have claims upon her and was making sure by her silence and her absence that it was conveyed to me that I hadn't? But I knew that no such claims existed for me. I was only grateful for a wonderful night and was content to bask in her presence and to enjoy her companionship if she would give it to me.

I tried to turn my thoughts back to the present. All of what Charles Ormsby had said made sense and I should be mulling it over, thinking, too, of the Vincent Rossiter likeness and how I could get it to Elton and persuade him to complete it. All of which meant that I wasn't paying much attention to the road. The Alvis was singing smoothly along, the wind whipped past and, as we entered the long straight stretch on the Oakham side of Stamford, the speedometer **needle** was set fair on fifty which was a good cruising speed in those days. Unconsciously I pressed on the accelerator and then watched it as it climbed to sixty which again, then, was quite a speed. 'A mile a minute' was a sort of magic number as was a hundred, 'the ton', a couple of generations later, though even that, I understand, has become commonplace now. I wondered if she would really do seventy-five. It was worth a try. I pressed harder. The telegraph poles began to flash past, another sign of speed we used to say. It was then that I caught sight of a figure standing by the roadside where the straight stretch ended. At first I paid little attention to him, until I realised he was waving me down. If I thought at all I imagined that there must an impediment ahead, cattle across the road or some such thing. Setting my foot on the brake, I slowed. He went on waving and I pulled to a halt.

He came towards me and as he reached me I saw that he had a cap pulled down over his eyes and a scarf muffling the lower part of his face. It was then that I began to come out of my reverie and warning bells sounded, too late, in my brain. He didn't speak but leant against the side of the car, his eyes studying me under the brim of the cap while his hand gave some sort of signal. With that a huge body heaved itself into the seat beside me. A face, or what I could see of it, for he, too, had a scarf hiding his features, was pushed into mine, and a massive hand appeared holding an ugly looking knife which rested against my cheek. The first man stepped on to the running board and spoke. 'Drive in here,' he said, pointing, his tones muffled by the scarf.

There was a sort of recess in the roadway which gave on to an entrance where two rusted iron gates leant askew between battered pillars. Inside was a broken-down gate-lodge where a screen of ash, evergreen and sycamore had sprung up, shielding it from the road.

'Get out,' the man on the running board commanded.

I hesitated, partly because the whole thing had happened

so quickly my wits were scattered, and partly because what there was of them was frightened. That knife point was uncommonly sharp. It had pricked my cheek already and a thin trickle of blood was running down to my collar. Desperately I sought to find a way out of this and failed. I was at their mercy whatever they wanted. Then the gorilla beside me spoke. 'You 'eard 'im. Wake up, sunshine.'

With that a fist like a piledriver slammed into the side of my face. I was flung back against the seat squab and, as I tried to recover, he hit me again. This time my forehead banged against the boss of the steering wheel. Sparks and flashes flew across my eyes and I almost passed out.

Between them they dragged me from the car and into the gate-lodge. My senses had cleared enough for me to see that the room they took me to was all but empty and desolate. The wallpaper hung in strips, the window panes gaped, and there was no furniture save a table on three legs and a rusted, broken, iron bed. The big man threw me, like a sack of coals, into one corner. I hit the wall and it hurt.

'Don't kill him,' the muffled voice said. 'Just half kill him.'

The big man kicked me in the ribs.

'Now,' the voice said. 'How much did he tell you?'

'What is this,' I said between gasps, for most of the breath had been knocked out of me. 'Who do you mean?'

It was the gorilla who spoke next. 'Your fucking father,' he said. 'And if you don't talk you'll get what he got.' Then he kicked me again, picked me up and slammed me against the wall. As I fell another kick came in. I wondered if my ribs were stove in.

'That'll do. For the moment anyway,' the first voice said. 'Now, once more. What did your father tell you?'

'I don't know what you're talking about,' I said.

'I think you do, else why are you hanging around Melton. I'll repeat what I said and I won't do it again. You'll answer unless you want the same of what you're getting and worse.'

Just for good value the big man kicked me once more. I was beginning to lose count. 'He told me nothing,' I said. Despite the pain in my side, my brain was ticking over and I had learnt something. That stroke which knocked out my father had not been a accident from natural causes. Those mysterious marks on his body were now explained. They had beaten him up in an attempt to get information from him and failed. Now they were trying the same medicine on me. And there was, there must be or have been, a plot of which he knew too much. That was clear now. It wasn't any ordinary grudge that had caused him to be framed, or they wouldn't have gone to all that risk and trouble to find out, frame him and cover up. And now it had rubbed off on to me. It must, as my father had thought and hinted, involve someone far bigger than any of us, and that could only mean one man – the Prince of Wales.

What they didn't know, either, was that although those kicks and general beatings up hurt like hell I'd had falls before and could to some extent roll with the punch. The thick motoring coat I wore, too, took up some of the impact. I was hurt but not crippled and I could still think. I groaned and slumped. 'For God's sake leave me alone,' I pleaded. 'I don't know what you're on about. Why are you doing this? I'm in Melton to learn about horses.'

'Liar. You know very well. Why did the Prince of Wales take you up?'

'It was an accident. I pulled him out of a ditch when he broke his collarbone.' So it was to do with the Prince. That confirmed it. 'He befriended me because of it. That's the sort he is.' I groaned again, I hoped realistically, though it was far from all pretence. I was hurt, no doubt of it, and just to emphasise it the big man gave me another sixpenny one.

'You're lying,' the other said. 'And I'm going to hurt you more until you talk. How would you like to have your fingernails pulled out?'

'How can I talk when I don't know,' I said between groans.

'The right hand first, I think,' the voice said. 'Go ahead, Joe.'

The boot came in again and then he grabbed my hand.

But my mind was still working. Their mention of the Prince had given me an idea. They knew of my association with him and I could play on that. It was the only card I had. Main force wouldn't get me away from these two. The gorilla could eat me for breakfast and the other, who was evidently in charge, seemed just as dangerous. 'You do that to me and I won't be able to ride a horse for the Prince tomorrow,' I said. 'He'll see my hands and he'll want to know why. He'll throw the whole works after you.'

'Hold it, Joe,' the one in charge said.

There was silence for a moment or two while I slumped back against the wall as if the effort of speech had been too much for me. The first man strode over and looked down at me. 'Somehow I don't think we're going to get any more out of him,' he said. 'Perhaps he's telling the truth. Can you walk?' he went on, touching me with his foot.

I groaned again and mumbled something unintelligible.

'You've something to remember us by, anyway,' he said. 'And there's always more to come. Pick him up, Joe.'

Between them they brought me out to the car and got me into the driving seat. I hadn't, of course, been booked to ride for the Prince and I wasn't as bad as I'd convinced them. That, in its way, was a small victory. And there was something else running through my mind as I sat behind the wheel, lolling like a dummy, or so I hoped.

The first man leant over, switched on the ignition and pressed the starter button. 'I suppose you can drive,' he said. 'If you run out of road, too bad.' Then he sniggered.

He was beside me, very close. I knew now what had been bothering me about him all along. ''E talked like a toff,'

Elton had said. So did this thug. And that snigger ending in a sort of tee-hee, just as Elton had said, clinched it.

With a quick motion I reached up and pulled the muffler down from his face. The artist's impression stared back at me together with the additions Elton had described, the moustache and the fringes of blonde hair beneath the edges of the cap. I had found Vincent Rossiter.

'I'll know you again,' I said.

He was so taken by surprise he jerked his head back and made a grab at the muffler. Off balance he stumbled, then, recovering himself, he attempted a lunge at me. But I had got the breathing space I wanted. I slammed the gear lever home and let in the clutch. The wheels spun as we took off. Once on the road I rushed her through the gears. I'm not sure if we touched seventy-five on the way back to Melton but I know my foot was on the floorboards for most of it – and the telegraph poles whizzed by.

Back in my rooms I tried to examine the damage. I had a splitting headache from where they had banged my head about but that, I reckoned, would pass. My ribs and round my back where the kicks had gone in, were a different matter. The weals were just beginning to show, but I knew from experience of hunting and racing falls that the real bruising, the haematomas, would come up later. It all hurt like hell when I moved and was tender to touch, and I prayed devoutly that no ribs were broken. I supposed I should go to a doctor but that would mean all sorts of enquiries and explanations which I didn't feel disposed to give. He might well stop me riding, too, which would mean more explanations to Captain Pat and through him to Pirate, putting me in even worse with him than I was already. I also found that my father's gold cigarette case and my wallet with forty pounds in it were missing. Then my eye fell on the buff envelope of a telegram lying on the table. Opening it I read: WILL YOU RIDE PROSPERO NOMINATION RACE HEYTHROP WEDNESDAY. VAL.

That settled it. No doctor.

Taking Rossiter's likeness from the manila envelope which had been lying on the seat and which the thugs had overlooked, I laid it on the table before me. The features which stared back at me were clearly etched in my mind even after that brief glimpse of them, and I did not think I need go back to Elton to complete the picture. Remembering that I had seen Mrs Williams, my landlady, in possession of a box of crayons which she doled out to her grand-children to keep them quiet when they came to visit, I went in search of her.

Whether she thought it a strange request I don't know, but she produced the box in no time at all. 'Are you all right, Mr de Lacey?' she said as she handed it to me. 'You look very pale.'

'Yes, Mrs Williams,' I said. 'I'm fine. Nothing to worry about.'

'It's them horses and all this riding, I expect,' she said.

'It has its ups and downs,' I said, feeling my ribs twinge and giving an involuntary wince.

In my room I found that I had a bottle of whisky and, though at that stage of my life I wasn't much of a whisky drinker, not having yet acquired the taste which seemed to me to be something like tar oil, I opened it and poured a stiff measure. Gulping it down I found it helped kill the pain and sat down to study the artist's impression. Then, when I had tried out the crayons for colour, I selected one and began to shade in the blond moustache. That done I went on to the hair and had a stab at it. The finished article wasn't very artistic but I reckoned Elton was unlikely to do better. Then I wrote Charles Ormsby setting out what had happened in as much detail as I could, slid the letter and likeness into its envelope and walked to the post office. There I sent it off as well as the prepaid answer to Lady Val: YES DELIGHTED DANNY.

As I once more climbed the stairs to my room thinking of

the events of the day, I decided that I ought to try to make sense out of the chain of events that had occurred since I came to Melton, and, most important of all, who was the inspiration behind them. That there was some sort of plot concerning the Prince of Wales was now in no doubt in my mind, but what was it and who was in it? To the first question there was no immediate answer, though it was now clear that his knowledge of it had cost my father his living death. I thought of him lying in a darkened room, unable to speak beyond unintelligible sounds, and my resolve hardened to find those who were guilty and ruin them if I could. It seemed unanswerable that some at least of those whom I now knew and mixed with were implicated in it to a greater or lesser degree. I took a piece of writing paper from my case, sat down pen in hand and began to make a list.

When it was finished it looked like this:

> Vincent Rossiter
> Rupert Carleton
> Roger Gretton
> Lord Marston
> Colonel Pirate Probert
> Flinty Westcough
> Pat Terrier

Of these, Vincent Rossiter, or whoever he might be, was a certain starter, and Rupert Carleton not far off being one. But I had the feeling that there was someone else in it too.

Colonel Probert? Everything shouted at me that he was not the sort to become involved in intrigue, yet he was one of the old guard. Captain Pat had said that he didn't much care about the Prince or his associates and he actively disliked his chief one, Flinty Westcough. Moreover, he had been seen talking to Roger Gretton at the Remounts the day before the wire had been stretched across the fence, and he had not seemed keen on handing the investigation over to the police and, further, his own enquiries so far had been fruitless. It was true he had torn up that instruction to remove me, but might not that have meant that he wanted to keep me under his eye?

That left Flinty and Pat Terrier. I could not bring myself to believe that either was implicated in any way. It was true that Captain Pat was closer to me than anyone, and I had confided in him to some extent so that he knew more of what I was engaged in than the others, but he had saved me from crashing into the wire, he kept himself to himself, far from the circles in which the others mixed. No, he wasn't a starter.

Nor, for that matter, was Flinty. He might be devious (though I had no evidence of it), ambivalent to me and anyone else who could possibly stand in his way, but his whole existence depended on the Prince and remaining in his favour. I drew a line through both of these names, put a tick for certainty against Rossiter and Rupert, one question mark against Roger Gretton, and two against Marston and Pirate Probert.

I still hadn't got much further, I told myself as I stared at the list, and I was going nowhere at all in finding out just what they were up to. Perhaps my mind, dulled by pain, wasn't working as it should. Pouring myself another whisky, I swallowed it with a grimace of distaste. Then I went on staring into the fire. Just what, I wondered, had I got myself into and where would it all end?

14

Forty-eight hours later I stood in the parade ring at the South Oxfordshire point-to-point wearing Lady Val's steeplechase jersey in her colours of black and gold (the racecard strictly enjoined that the Nomination Race would be run ridden in 'Racing colours' so hunting costume was out), and devoutly wishing I was somewhere else. I knew very well that I was in no condition to ride a race. My side was hurting damnably every time I moved and I had done little in the way of sleeping in the intervening nights, most of the first of which had been spent vomiting, assisted no doubt by the unaccustomed half bottle of whisky I had consumed. At least on the second night I had avoided that, but riding out hadn't helped. The bruises were well and truly up by now, and in colour ranged from dark black to deep blue shot with yellow. They extended from my rib cage round to my back. They had, however, with luck, and I thought I needed a bit of luck just then, missed my kidneys.

I should, of course, have cried off and relinquished the ride but there were several strong reasons preventing me. To be honest I must admit that the one which weighed most with me was the longing to see Lady Val and be with them all again. But there were others. If I were to plead illness, Lady Val would certainly want to know just what had brought on this sudden bout after my immediate wire of acceptance. That would entail explanations I was reluctant to give. Beatings up, or muggings as we call them now, weren't commonplace then; there would be questions asked which I would have to answer, followed by possible police action and probing into the motive for the attack which I was determined not to divulge, at least not yet. I had told Charles Ormsby and that was enough.

Walking the course had done little to reassure me. The South Ox point-to-point committee had, like the Marleythorpe people, taken the ukase about natural fences truly to heart, and had included two post-and-rails and a double. I knew something about jumping timber out hunting, though it is an obstacle seldom encountered in Ireland. You took a pull and a steadier and then went pop and over, or hoped you did. But that would be a very different matter from taking it on at racing pace. I supposed and hoped that the horse, Prospero, knew more about it than I did. My general feelings of alarm and depression weren't helped much by the instructions Lady Val gave me. 'Be there or thereabouts at the second last,' she said. 'He has plenty of speed. Keep out of trouble and you've every chance.'

I knew that tying a rider down with voluminous instructions was one of the worst sins an owner could commit, but these seemed to err very much on the side of vagueness. She hadn't told me anything about the damn horse and if he had any quirks or peculiarities. Maybe he hadn't. He'd won that ladies' race easily enough, though this was a different matter. Perhaps it was that she was so used to riding her own horses herself she didn't give a thought to instructions.

She had moved away to talk to someone else, and I was about to get up when I heard a voice at my side. It was the Prince of Wales. 'She thinks a lot of this horse,' he said.

'And she has upped him in class today. But I'm not sure his heart is in the right place. I don't like a horse with small ears. That's a lesson Flinty dinned into me. Don't be too disappointed – '

'Riders up, *please* – ' came the call.

A hand went round my uplifted leg and I was whisked into the saddle.

Down at the start I tried to collect my wits and look about me. The Nomination Race, with its crack riders from far and near, was an altogether more serious affair than the Adjacent Hunts I had ridden in before. There were no cheery top-hatted gentlemen having a jolly, here. Billy Burton-Brown and Mike Annerley, two of the top-sawyers of the point-to-pointing world who rode against each other regularly, were competing today. I tried to pick them out and fix their colours in my mind so that I could see where they were in the race. I didn't know whether it was nerves or pain which was making me feel weak and sick.

Even now, after all these years, I find I cannot recall that race or write about it without a pang of embarrassment and the knowledge that I would rather let it lie buried in the recesses of my memory, but I have to put it down since it has a bearing on all that was to occur in the coming weeks.

The first thing that happened was that they went off far faster than I expected. This was no hunters' half-speed canter, it was a real race. Taken by surprise which I should not have been, I was left in the rear. Clods of earth flew past me. One hit me under the rim of the helmet, nearly blinding me, so that we jumped the first fence all asprawl with me half out of the saddle. The bump as I came down wasn't much help to my ribs. Prospero didn't care for it either. He shook his head as if to say he wasn't accustomed to this and seemed reluctant to get on with things. Somehow I got him balanced again and then he caught hold of his bit and pounded along. We jumped the next fence cleanly but we were still at the back of the mid-division. After that came two more plain fences which he put behind him effortlessly. We managed the double with a quick change and a hop and approached the first of the post and rails. It was then that I started to make a mess of things. Prospero had speed as Lady Val had said and his gallop had taken him to the head of that mid-division. But he was, I thought, going far too fast at that timber. I endeavoured to steady him, not realising quite how much of a passenger I already was. All I did was to make things worse. He missed his take off and hit the top rail a right old belt.

It was his strength and, I thought afterwards, the speed we were going that saved him. He slithered along for a few strides but he remained upright and I remained on top, I don't to this day know quite how. The next fence, the second post and rails, then confronted us. This time I had enough sense to leave it to him. But the bang at the bar had taken something out of him, or else he had lost confidence in himself and his rider. He screwed over it somehow but on landing I saw we had lost our place and dropped back again. By now my side was agony and my muscles one long ache. We were, however, three-quarters of the way round and I tried to take stock. The two cracks were duelling it out up ahead. If I was to put up any sort of a show I had to do something. Giving Prospero a kick, he lengthened his stride and we went after them. The speed was there, he ate up the ground and, entering the field before the second last, we were upsides with them. They heard me coming and in a moment the three of us were racing for the fence, a weak-looking all but purely natural thing set on a small bank.

They had drawn fractionally ahead of me. I kicked as hard as my diminishing strength would let me. There was no response. Christ! I thought. HRH was right. He has no heart for the battle. Setting my teeth I drove him with all that was left in me into the fence. But I was tired and weak and in pain and wasn't sitting as tight as I should. There was a smash of birch beneath us as Propero went through the fence's flimsy top. Down he came on his head – or so I swore afterwards, though I doubt it. He was near the ground but he didn't fall. Unsettled and unseated I slid off his shoulder and hit the ground. It didn't do my ribs any good, but I was more hurt in vanity than in body as I saw the remains of the field gallop by me and watched Prospero's hindquarters disappearing after them.

At least I was spared the long trudge back. Prospero turned aside – I have an idea someone belted him one to get him out of the way – and ended up in a corner of the field. A countryman caught him and brought him to me saying, 'Here's your horse, mister.'

He seemed sound and there were no cuts anywhere that I could see. That was something. I got up and rode slowly back towards the tents and enclosures. Lady Val was waiting for me and one look at her face told me I was in trouble. 'You fell off,' she said. 'Cut a voluntary. And I thought you told me you could ride.'

'Kindergarten stuff,' a voice behind her said. 'Go back to the children's meets. He needs a man on his back.' It was Rupert Carleton.

A groom took Prospero and I got down. 'Jog him up, Thomas,' Lady Val commanded. 'Well at least he's sound. You haven't lamed him,' she commented when that had been done. Then she and Rupert went off together.

Miserably I made my way back to the barn where we changed, and sat on a bench contemplating my sins and their likely outcome. Thinking it very unlikely I would ever ride in it again, I was in the act of pulling my jersey over my head when there was a little hush in the room. Looking up I saw it was the Prince of Wales who had entered and was making his way across to me.

'I've been commanded to tell you that there's a drink for you in the car,' he said.

It may appear strange that the heir to the throne of what was then and is, alas, no more, the most powerful nation in the world should use the word 'commanded' to convey a message. Hurt as I was both in body and spirit it did seem odd to me even then, but it wasn't until years later that I, along with the rest of his subjects, learnt to their cost that HRH was one of those rare men who like to be bossed about by their women. It's a sort of inborn masochism I think. One of the reasons, I believe, that Val did not keep him, although in reality her case was hopeless from the start, was that she was in many ways too nice and did not exert her will enough at all times. 'What about that horse?' he asked. 'Was he dogging it?'

'I'm not sure,' I said. 'I rode a lousy race. He made two bad mistakes which were mostly my fault. They may have knocked the stuffing out of him.'

'Hullo, what's this?' His eyes were fixed on my side and the bruises in all their galaxy of variegated colours. 'That didn't happen today.'

Once more I had to think quickly. 'I had a fall schooling,' I said.

'It doesn't look like a schooling fall to me.'

'I was kicked.'

'He did a damn good job on you then. Have you seen anyone?'

'No, sir.' I was desperate to change the subject. 'Will I lose the ride, sir?'

He frowned, staring at the bruises again. 'We'll have to see about that,' he said. 'And forget about that voluntary. Happens to all of us. Think of the times they say I've done it – and you don't have to worry about the photographers!'

It hadn't been a bad fall as falls go, but even so I thought it had hurt more than it should. I was painfully wrestling with my shirt when a big, ruddy faced man, with the cut of a sporting yeoman farmer all about him, came up to me. 'Me bluidy jockey's gone and broke his leg,' he said. 'Will you ride one for me in the last, young feller?'

'I'm sorry – ' I began.

Before I could continue to say I didn't think I could do him justice he cut me short. 'So that's it, is it,' he said. 'I saw who you was talkin' to. Too bluidy grand, are we? I'm not good enough, that's it, eh?' And he stumped out of the barn. I was not having a good day.

I found them in the car park congregated by Lady Val's chauffeur-driven Rolls. A small group, most of whom I didn't know even by sight, surrounded the Prince and her. They were chattering away and, I guessed, anxious to be seen in their company and hoping for the appearance of a *Tatler* photographer. But Flinty, good old Flinty, was there too, greeting me with his vulpine grin and pressing a silver beaker brimming with Krug into my hand. 'I've put in a word for you,' he said. 'Told her I didn't think that horse was all that genuine. Didn't exactly go down like an oyster. But she'll make her peace: it's started already by her sending the little man along to bid you to a drink.'

In fact she didn't speak to me then, contenting herself with a brief smile and a wave of her hand. She hardly had a chance, I told myself, so besieged was she by the group about her. Already, too, and before I was halfway through the champagne, I could see that HRH, who could spot a sycophant when he saw one, was showing signs of boredom. They piled into the Rolls, I gulped the rest of the Krug, surrendered the beaker to the chauffeur and they drove off.

The champagne had done me a bit of good, since I'd lunched off a dry biscuit and a thimbleful of cherry brandy, but going home a long, wretched, painful and lonely evening stretched before me. I ran a bath and slid into the steaming water. Lying there I felt my bruises and at each touch I winced. I'm not sure how long it was before I heard voices from below.

'Yes, he's in, m'lady. Come in from racin' he did and looking proper poorly. It's them horses – '

'I've got to see him.' It was Lady Val.

'But he's in his bath, m'lady. I heard him runnin' the taps.'

'I don't care where he is. The Prince of Wales asked me – '

'Oh, m'lady – the Prince of Wales!'

'Where is it, the bathroom, upstairs I suppose?'

'Along the passage, m'lady, but he's in the bath, oh!'

There were firm footsteps on the stairs and then the door, which I had left on the latch, was thrown open and Lady Val came in. 'Now then,' she said. 'Just what have you been up to? Let's have a look at you.'

I wasn't accustomed to entertaining ladies in my bath and made a vain attempt to cover up.

'Don't be a fool, Danny,' she said. 'I've seen it all before, remember. Let me see. Good God, what have you been doing to yourself?'

'I had a fall schooling.'

'Tell that to your aunt Fanny. I met Pat Terrier on the way in. He knew of no schooling fall.' She had seated herself on the edge of the bath, her fingers dangling in the water. At least I seemed to have been forgiven and her next words confirmed it. 'I suppose that's why you fell off,' she said. 'You are a damn fool, you know, Danny. Come on. The truth now.'

I gave in and she was silent as I recounted what had happened on the road – or most of it, for I didn't tell her everything. In particular I left out how I had identified Vincent Rossiter and the threat about what they had done to my father. That would mean going deeply into things which for the moment were better left to Charles Ormsby and myself.

'They went to the hell of a lot of trouble to hijack you,' she said. 'Al Capone stuff. Did they get anything?'

'My wallet,' I said. 'There was forty quid in it, and my father's gold cigarette case, the one you admired.'

'Damn swine,' she said. 'But those ribs of yours, they

should be looked at. I'm going to take you to a doctor. Can you get out unaided?' Her fingers, brushing the water, touched my thigh and ran lightly for a second along it. I shifted uneasily in the water, feeling myself responding.

'I see you can,' she said. 'There's life there still. I'll help you dress.'

She took one of the big towels from the clothes horse and I climbed out of the bath. Enveloping me in it she dried me. Her fingers were soft and deft and infinitely aphrodisiac. She was very close to me as she delicately touched the injured area and her breath was sweet on my cheek. I felt an insane impulse to grab her and tear off her clothes and feel once more that splendid body vibrant against mine. She read it in my eyes. 'Not just now,' she said, giving me a gentle pat. 'There's a time and a place for everything. Clothes on, I think. Where are they?'

Dressed and in the sitting room I slumped into a chair. The euphoria of the champagne had long since vanished. I really was feeling rotten and cursed myself for it.

'What you need,' she said, 'is a stiff drink and then the doctor. Is there any brandy?'

'There's whisky, Lady Val,' I said. 'What's left of it. But I hate the stuff. Can't stomach it.'

'We'll lush it up a bit and you'll find it goes down all right.'

'Like an oyster,' I said, feebly, remembering Flinty.

'That's it.' Rummaging in the cupboard she found the bottle and then went to the head of the stairs. 'Mrs Williams,' I heard her call.

There was a brief confabulation and in a few minutes Mrs Williams came bustling in, bearing a tray on which was a jug of hot water, a lemon, a bowl of sugar and a saucer of cloves.

'Hot toddy,' she declared, putting down the tray. 'Just the thing for the young gentleman. Puts life into a man.'

'Not too much life, I think, just at the moment,' Lady Val

said after she had gone and she was expertly mixing the drink. 'And stop calling me Lady Val. We're chums, aren't we?' She handed me the tumbler and our fingers touched.

The doctor proved to be a fatherly old boy, well used to treating riding and hunting injuries as, in Melton, I supposed he had to be. After doing all the usual things with the blood pressure machine, he ran his fingers lightly over my ribs and bruises. 'Any blood in the urine?' he asked as he came to the kidney area.

'No,' I said. 'It's clear.'

'You'll have to be x-rayed for those ribs. I'll arrange it.' Lifting the candlestick telephone on his desk, he asked for a number. 'That's done,' he said when he had finished. 'You can go round right away. Come back when it's over. They'll phone me the result.'

Lady Val, or Val as I began to call her from now on, whisked me off to the cottage hospital and there they stood me in front of their plates, laid me down and turned me over, told me to hold my breath at designated intervals and clicked their cameras. After all that I was returned to where Val was sitting in a grim little waiting-room looking at a worn and tattered copy of *Good Housekeeping*.

'I don't think much of their reading matter,' she said, throwing it to one side. 'Are we off?'

'Just about,' I said. 'Why are you doing this to me, Val? You're too kind.'

'Royal command,' she said, smiling. 'Besides, you're our mascot, aren't you? Can't let the mascot perish alone and in misery, can we?'

In the doctor's surgery there was another wait while he received the x-ray readings and reports. I suppose I'd better explain that in those long ago days of sixty and more years away, everything in Melton, including the medical services, was geared to the horse and its riders, and things moved more quickly then than they do now in the NHS. Anyway here, in contrast to the hospital, there were deep leather chairs, hunting prints and a plethora of illustrated glossies, *Horse and Hound* and suchlike. And, in fact, we weren't kept waiting long.

'You're a very lucky young man,' the doctor greeted me. 'You have two cracked ribs, and some slight bruising of the lung. Going out to ride in a race in that state could easily have damaged them further and even punctured the lung. There's extensive haematoma over the kidney area, but here again no real damage done. You've missed out by a short head, you might say.'

'Thanks, doctor,' I said. 'But what does all this mean? Will I be able to ride?'

'It means I'm going to strap you up. You'll be off all work for a few days until the ribs and the haematomas begin to heal. And no riding whatever.'

'Damn,' I said.

'You're young and very fit, it shouldn't take too long. You're with Captain Terrier as a learner, you tell me. I'll write him a note to keep you right. Nice fellow, Captain Pat. We meet every now and then to compare notes over a drink.'

'Horses and humans, do you ever get them mixed up?' Val asked him with a mischievous look.

'Sometimes, dear lady,' he answered, smiling at her and responding to her in a way, as I found out, most men did. 'And one then wonders which can be the most difficult. Now, I must write this note.'

He crossed to his desk. 'There you are,' he said, signing his name with a flourish, sealing and handing me the envelope. 'That should keep things all in order.'

When Val drew the Riley up outside my rooms, she sat for a moment drumming her hands against the wheel. 'I've been thinking about what you told me of the beating up,' she said. 'The little man will want to know and I think I'll play it all down. He's not in the best of form at the moment.'

'What's wrong?' I said.

'He's been summoned to the Palace. Papa wants to see him and that means trouble. He says he knows he's in for a ticking off, probably about his racing and his friendship with Flinty and he's not going to give either up. He's afraid of his father, that's what's eating him. He's about the only thing or person he is afraid of. But he has all this on his mind. Perhaps it's just as well, otherwise he might take hold of his bit and go into the why and the wherefore of your beating up, and that's not what you want, is it?'

She let in the clutch, the Riley gave a snarl, and she was gone, leaving me wondering what she meant by those final words and how much she had guessed I was holding back.

15

Having sent the doctor's letter round to Captain Pat, I was sitting after breakfast next morning rather disconsolately reading *Sporting Life* when there was a knock on the door and Mrs Williams came in. 'Gentleman to see you, sir,' she said, and a moment later Charles Ormsby entered. That morning he was wearing yet another different bow tie, fashioned in stripes, those of his regiment, I imagined.

He accepted a cup of coffee and, after Mrs Williams had bustled in with it, he said: 'I rang the Remounts and heard you were off duty on sick leave. Those thugs must have knocked you about more than a bit. I see you're up and about. How bad is it?'

'Not much to signify, really,' I said. 'I've been to the doctor. Cracked ribs and bruising. More a damn nuisance than anything else. Can't ride.'

'Can you talk, discuss things?'

'Yes, surely. Fire away. It'll give me something to think about.'

'First, how did the hijackers or whatever you like to call them know that you'd be in Newmarket or how you'd be travelling?'

'That's easy. I've thought about it myself. Anyone or everyone in the Remounts would have known. A call to the office looking for me would have told them. I haven't checked but I'm sure that was it.'

'That doesn't put us much further. I didn't really think it would. But there's another thing. You were taken to a broken down lodge, you said in your letter. Could you identify it on the map?'

'I expect so. I could have a try.'

He had with him a flat leather briefcase. Opening this he took out an ordnance map and spread it on the table before us. Taking a pen from his pocket he traced a road on the map. 'This is where I put it from your description,' he said. 'And the lodge would be there, wouldn't it?' He placed the tip of his pen on a clearly marked entrance.

With a quickening of interest I bent over the map. The drive passed the lodge and curved through marked trees to a large house. It was, apparently, quite an estate.

'Eston Court,' I read aloud. 'That's it. That's the place.'

'I thought as much. Would it interest you to know who that property belonged to?'

'Very much. Who is it? I'll buy it.'

'Rupert Carleton's family.

Rupert! I thought. Here we go again. 'But the lodge was falling down,' I said.

'Exactly. Rupert has gone through all his money and anyone else's he could get his hands on, including his father's. The old boy finally got fed up bailing him out, gathered together the wreck of his fortunes, sold the place and went to live in Cannes. A local farmer bought the land. He had no use for the house and lodge and they fell into decay.'

'So Rupert could have known just the place, made the phone call and could have called or directed Rossiter – '

'It would seem so.'

'And Rupert, then, is mixed up in this plot or whatever it is?'

'Up to the neck, I'd say, and he is also in communication with Mr Vincent Rossiter, whoever he is. I think it might be worth our while to find out. And if Rupert is mixed up in it there's money for him coming from somewhere.' He finished his coffee and put down the cup. 'Are you fit enough to come for a drive?'

'Yes, of course. Anything to get me away from these four walls.'

'I've been on to Jimmy Connaughton to try to find out if he knows anything of Rossiter's antecedents or where he came from. He wasn't very communicative on the phone but then I didn't expect him to be. But he'll see us. If you're ready we'll make a start.'

Once in the car and on our way he said: 'Jimmy Connaughton isn't everyone's cup of tea. He needs careful handling, kid gloves you might say. When we get there don't be surprised at anything and don't take him on or he'll have us out the door in no time, flat. Play it softly, is the motto.'

We drove on through the countryside which was already showing signs of an early spring. Charles Ormsby clearly knew the way and threaded our passage along the narrow cross-country roads. A mile or so outside Peterborough we passed an entrance and then, almost immediately, came upon another where a sign pointed tersely: HORSES. A short drive flanked by elms, through which I had a glimpse of a square Georgian dwellinghouse on our left, led us to a stableyard. In one corner of this was a single-storeyed building with a portico, a miniature lodge of the sort built on some estates for their workers and which had, I guessed, been there long before the stables which looked comparatively modern and which were smartly painted and gleaming in the pale sunlight.

Ormsby parked the car before the portico, we went up the few steps to the open door and entered. There was a short, straight passage in front of us. Clearly Charles Ormsby had been here before; without hesitation he knocked on a door to the right and, in response to a gruff bellow beyond it, we went in.

Jimmy Connaughton, the trainer, was standing by the window and turned to survey us as we entered. He was a man of just above medium height and built like a battleship. A round, bullet head was set deeply into massive shoulders. Thrusting this forward he stared bleakly at us. 'You're five minutes late,' he barked. 'Time's money and I haven't that much of either to spare. What d'ye want, Major?'

As I later learnt, since in years to come I had much to do with him, Jimmy Connaughton was a tough who had come up the hard way, and didn't care who knew it. He had been for twenty years the head lad to one of the leading Newmarket trainers, I forget which. An enormous punt on the Cambridgeshire had enabled him to set up on his own, near Peterborough, with a mixed string, flat and chasers, and some of the owners had followed him and supported him. His habit of speaking his mind and damning the consequences had, oddly enough, not damaged his career. Those of the upper crust who patronised him, laughed at and with him, and dined out on his more outrageous pronouncements and verbal onslaughts. That and the fact that he told his owners the blunt truth about their horses, and produced winners when the money was down, won him patrons and, more importantly, kept them. But I could see from the start that the interview was not going to be an easy one.

'I know that, Jimmy,' Charles Ormsby said. 'And believe me I don't like taking up your time. But it's important to us as I'm sure you'll agree when you've heard me for a moment. This is Dick de Lacey's son. We're trying to find out who shopped him that day at Ascot, because he was shopped.'

'And how the hell do I come into that? I didn't dope the bloody horse.' But as he said it he looked at me and I thought his voice softened a bit. 'I knew your father,' he said. 'A straight man.'

'Well, Jimmy, we don't think you had a hand in any of the business, and there's nothing of that about our call to you, believe me. But we've narrowed down the search to the lad who did it and who disappeared or was shipped off to America pretty quickly after it. Now you know as well as I that these lads never do those things off their own bat. There's always someone behind them, paying them off and paying them well.'

By this time the trainer was behind his desk, his eyes watchful, and listening intently. 'That's true,' he said. 'Why do you think I keep 'em coming and going? Sell stable secrets for sixpence most of them would. An' there's no stoppin' it. It's them bloody bookies. And this doping is a nightmare. We're at the mercy of them. Why don't the Jockey Club alter the rule or bring in a proper system of testing? Why did they pick on De Lacey's horse, eh?'

'We're looking for a lad,' said Charles Ormsby. 'He was called Vincent Rossiter. He was in your yard for a bit before he went to Danny's father. We'd like to know if you found out anything about him before he came, if he had any references or introductions through which we might trace him. Do you remember him?'

'Remember him? How the blazes would I remember one lad from one year, or one month for that matter, from another?'

Thinking about what I had heard of the floating population of lads that went through his yard I almost smiled, but luckily I restrained it.

The trainer sat glowering at us for a minute or two, then he said: 'If you could nail whoever did the doping or whoever was behind it then it might help us all. Rossiter, now, damned if I recall anything about him but my secretary might.' He got to his feet and, moving surprisingly lightly for a big man, went to the door. Opening it and glancing down the passage he bellowed: 'Benson!' Another door opened and another bellow followed. 'Come here you. I want you.'

There were footsteps in the corridor and a tall, thin, nervous-looking man entered. He might well be nervous-looking if he worked for Jimmy Connaughton, I thought.

'Vincent Rossiter,' Connaughton shot at him. 'He was here about, I dunno, a year or so ago. That mean anything to you?'

The secretary frowned in thought.

'Come on, man, it does or it doesn't.'

'This may help to refresh your memory.' Charles Ormsby said quietly. Unfastening the briefcase he took out the two photographs and laid them on the desk before him.

The secretary took them up and studied them. 'That is him all right,' he said after a pause. 'He stuck in my mind. Odd sort of chap, not like the ordinary run of lads.'

'Any idea where he came from? Did he have any identification or was there any recommendation with him?' Ormsby asked.

'There might be something on the personnel file. I'll go and look.'

In a few minutes he was back, a bulky folder under his arm. 'It's hard to keep track of these lads,' he said. 'But after looking at those photographs it all came back to me. He interested me when I interviewed him. He seemed a cut above the usual run somehow, and I asked him what experience he had and if he had any references. He said he'd always lived with horses and he produced a letter. You're lucky. I filed it and he never asked for it back. He left in a bit of a hurry as I recall it now. Here it is.' He opened the file and passed it over to us.

Ormsby took it and I leant over his shoulder. In scrawled handwriting this is what we read: *I know the bearer Vincent Rossiter. He has experience in handling horses, strapping and feeding*. The signature made me catch my breath. It was: *Rupert Carleton*.

'Well, who was it from?' Connaughton barked at us.

'Rupert Carleton,' Ormsby said.

'That bugger,' was Connaughton's comment. 'Why the hell did you take him on?' He glared at Benson.

'We were shorthanded at the time, if you remember,' Benson said.

'I don't.'

'Anyway,' Benson continued, 'he looked to me as if he was down on his luck and I know what that's like. It's happened to me. I was interested. I asked in the yard how he was getting on and they told me he was good at his job.'

'Too bloody good by the sound of things,' the trainer growled. 'It's as well he didn't stay here long. Anything else you gents want? I've work to do.'

'No thanks, Jimmy,' Ormsby said. 'We seem to have got what we came for. We're obliged for your time.'

'I hope you nail that bugger, Carleton,' Connaughton bellowed at us as we were leaving.

'I thought you trained for him,' Ormsby said.

'Not any more. He shopped me once. No one does that to me twice.'

That, together with some belligerent admonition concerning entries, addressed to Benson and ringing in our ears, were the last words we heard from Jimmy Connaughton as we left.

We lunched off bread and cheese and beer in a pub. As we finished Ormsby said to me: 'This afternoon we have another call to make.'

'Oh?' I said. 'Where?'

'Patworth Castle.' He caught my surprised look and smiled. 'I've made it my business to see Crispin Merevale,' he said. 'I ran into him by accident on purpose at Sandown. I sounded him very obliquely about the tip-off in your father's case.'

'How did he take it?'

'He said to let him think it over.'

'Does that mean he'll go back to his other stewards? They'll shut him up, won't they?'

Ormsby gave a short laugh. 'Nobody shuts Crispin up,' he said. 'And he won't go back to his other stewards, at least that's my guess. He's independent and he'll make up his own mind. The only reason he's stewarding is that he smashed himself up so badly in the National in Shaun Spadah's year they told him he'd never ride races again. He wanted to stay inside racing and he was bored rattling around in that bloody great barracks of his. He'd started to run horses on the flat as well as chasing and he'd been elected to the Jockey Club a year or so before. He was young and energetic and he was a godsend to the old stiffs, so he got accelerated promotion. But he takes his own line and sticks to it. He's agreed to see us. By my reading that means he's prepared to talk.'

Patworth Castle, which I had only seen hazily that night of the hunt ball, looked enormous, almost like a small town, I thought, as we drove up. It was set on a cliff and with its crockets, finials, battlements and turrets it towered over the vale below where the best of the hunting country stretched into the misty distance.

We climbed the curving drive to the cliff top and passed under an arched entrance into an outer courtyard. Here another archway led us to a smaller courtyard where Ormsby drew the car up near a vast gothic doorway. 'Half of this is bogus,' he said. 'Victorian Tudor stuff. No wonder Crispin wants to get out of it and go racing. It'd drive me mad.'

We were led through a maze of corridors and finally into a gloomily gothic library, all dark panelling, heavy tracery on the ceiling and ornate, cumbersomely carved bookcases set into its walls. Crispin Merevale was standing by a massive stone fireplace embellished in its centre with a coat of arms, where blazing logs roared their heat up the great chimney. Another man was with him. He rose from his chair as we entered and Crispin introduced us. It was Lord Marston.

'Afternoon, Ormsby,' he said, giving the detective a brief and far from friendly nod and directing his hard stare, it seemed to me, at the bow tie. Then he transferred that stare to me.

Lord Marston had the face of a mournful bloodhound accentuated by two purple veined dewlaps on either side. His eyes were hooded, hard and wary and I could feel them boring into me. He said nothing by way of greeting or otherwise but turned abruptly to the baronet. 'Well, Crispin, I'll be off,' he said. 'Thank you for seeing me at such short notice. No, don't bother about that,' as his host reached for the bell. 'I'll find my own way out. Knew it well enough in your father's time.' He bustled off.

'Sorry about that,' Merevale said as the door closed behind him. 'Had to see me urgently,' he said. 'Bodyguarding business. They're worried about the monarch's health. He's never quite recovered from that accident when he was bucked off reviewing troops in the war, you know. And there's the succession – but we won't go into that. Now then, Charles, it's about that rotten affair of Dick de Lacey's doping, isn't it?'

'That's it, Crispin, we're trying to get at the truth. Someone was behind it. We've heard that the buzz in the weighing-room was that there was a tip-off. That might give us a lead. I hinted about it when we spoke at Sandown. Can you help?'

'I thought as much and I've turned it over very carefully in my mind. It would benefit all of us if whoever was responsible was found. It might even bring about the changing of that rule which I've never liked, but that's another matter.' He turned suddenly to me. 'How is your father?'

'Poorly, I'm afraid. He's just lying there. He can't speak.'

'I'm sorry. Well, as I've said, having given the matter much thought I've come to the conclusion that no harm can be done in telling you what happened, especially if, as you say, it is all round the weighing-room. Someone must have overheard, or else someone talked who shouldn't. It's very hard to keep a secret in racing. Yes, there was a tip-off.'

'Can you elaborate a bit?' Ormsby said. 'Who, for instance, took the tip-off? Was it you?'

'It was a phone call to the weighing-room asking for me by name and saying that it was urgent. I went to the phone and took it. I can't remember the exact words, of course, but it was brief and to the point, that De Lacey's horse in the third was doped.'

'I don't suppose the caller gave his name?'

'Hardly. When I asked who was calling he put down the phone. Because it was an anonymous call I debated whether it might be a hoax and whether I should tell my fellow stewards. Then I decided that – anonymous or not – I must, and when I did they asked my advice. I felt I had to say that we should act on it and if the test proved negative no harm would be done. In the event, of course, it didn't, more's the pity.'

'Can you tell us anything else about the call – the caller's voice for instance?'

'It was disguised, no doubt about that, which was one of the things which made me wonder if it was genuine. I did get the impression, though it was only that, an impression, that what he was disguising was an educated voice.'

'What was the dope? Can you remember?'

'Cocaine, smeared on the tongue it was thought.'

'Cocaine,' I said. 'But surely it's illegal to have it?'

They both looked at me, almost pityingly.

'You can get all the dope you want if you have the money,' Ormsby said.

'And know where to go,' Merevale added. 'There's plenty of it floating around. And arsenic too. A goodly percentage of trainers use it, some of them those at the top. You'd be surprised. They say it brightens their coats and it's harmless used in small doses. That's what they say. I tremble to think what will happen if regular or even random testing is brought in without plenty of prior notice. Goodness knows what heads might roll.'

'How are the ribs and bruises?' Ormsby asked me as we drove back.

'Hurting as of this moment.'

'Six o'clock. Opening time. We'll pull in here. I expect you could do with a drink. I know I could.'

It was a country pub with a creaking sign over the door. Inside was a dark inner parlour to which we made our way. It was early; few drinkers were about in the public bar and where we were was empty and private. 'No champagne here, or cocktails either,' he said. 'What will you have?'

I settled for brandy.

Ormsby brought the drinks. 'What did he mean by body-guarding business?' I then asked him.

'The Sovereign's Bodyguard,' he said. 'It's a sort of social corps d'elite who hold the monarch's hand and those of selected guests at functions. Marston is the great panjan-drum in it. Why do you ask?'

'Bit of a concidence, isn't it, his being there when we were expected? Is he a member of the Jockey Club too?'

'He is. He had a horse once and actually won a race and they elected him. He never goes to meetings, I believe.'

'Still, he might be anxious to find out from Merevale just what we were coming for and what we wanted from him.'

'If he did, and tried to influence Crispin Merevale, he picked the wrong man.' All the same, I thought, I wouldn't strike Lord Marston off my list of suspects just yet. But Ormsby was going on. 'It's true he doesn't like me much,' he said. 'I crossed him once and he never forgets.'

'Do you think Marston may be in it?' I said.

'Possibly, though if he is, he's at the top and we've got to start at the bottom – with Rossiter.'

'And Rupert,' I said.

'He's in it all right, but it's no use us tackling him now. We've nothing on him. We've got to find Rossiter and make him talk.'

'That may not be easy,' I said, remembering my encounter with him.

His mouth set in a firm line. 'First find him,' he said. 'The rest will follow. I'll see to that.' Reaching down to the brief-case he had brought with him and placed by his chair, he opened it and took out the photographs and the artist's impression. These he placed on the table before him and studied them for a long minute. 'It's my belief,' he said, 'that many if not most of the people I mix with don't know their own fathers.' With that cryptic utterance he shuffled the photos and the drawing together, replaced them in the briefcase and we left the inn.

Hardly had he dropped me at my rooms than I had another visitor. It was Captain Pat. 'So,' he said. 'Off work, are we? I came round earlier to enquire but Mrs Williams said you'd gone off with a gentleman in a bow tie. Charles Ormsby, I presumed.'

'That's right. We had some enquiries to make.'

'I see.' He took the doctor's letter from his pocket and glanced at it. 'Haematoma and cracked ribs, the doctor says. I'm supposed to be looking after you, you know. Would it be too much to ask you to tell me how you sustained these injuries? I heard some cock and bull story about a fall out schooling which I didn't for a moment believe.'

'You might as well know since everyone else seems to. I got beaten up.'

Taking a chair he sat down and regarded me through his glasses. 'I see. Well then – ' and he waited for me to continue.

I told him what had happened, ending up by asking: 'Did anyone phone for me during the day and ask where I was, do you know?'

'As it happens I do. I took the call. It was put through to my office. It seemed a very ordinary enquiry. I told whoever it was that you had gone to Newmarket.'

'You didn't ask who the caller was by any chance?'

'I don't believe I did. I was busy at the time. If I thought at all I assumed it must be one of your smart friends: you mix in such high society nowadays. By the way, tell me about that horse, Prospero, of Lady Val's. She stopped me yesterday on her way to see you and we discussed him. She has high hopes and great plans for him, but is he any good?'

'I don't know,' I said. 'I've been thinking about him a lot. I thought I got nothing when I asked him, but then I rode such a rotten race – '

'I know. I was there. I watched him – and you. I asked Billy Burton-Brown about the race when I saw him afterwards. He told me you were going much too well for his liking when you joined them before the second last and he was seldom as glad to see anyone go.'

'HRH did warn me he wondered if Prospero was all that genuine.'

'Did he? He's no fool about a horse and of course he's got a damn good horsemaster in Flinty whatever they say about him. Maybe the horse is a dog, or maybe he's one of those horses who are moody like some humans. On their going days they can be the best, on others they can't live with the worst. I shouldn't be surprised if he's one of them.'

'I'd love to find out. Do you think I'll keep the ride?'

'That's up to Lady Val. She seems to have taken a fancy to you. It's between you and the horse, isn't it?' He gave one of his chuckles and then became serious again. 'But I'm afraid on that subject I've a bit of bad news for you. I fear you've lost the ride on the Colonel's horse.'

'Oh, hell, why?'

'He says if you're off work you can't ride and he wants to run him Saturday.'

'Who has he got?'

'You won't like this – Rupert Carleton.'

'Rupert! For God's sake, why him? I thought he didn't bother about point-to-points.'

'He doesn't usually, but he's been making the racecourse proper a bit too hot to be wholesome for him recently. He ran out at the last on a well-backed favourite at Gatwick the other day. The stewards took no action but that journalist fellow who wrote the bit about you was there and he didn't let it go.'

'What did he say? I missed it.'

'He called the stewards the three brass monkeys – see no evil, hear no evil and speak no evil, if it's one of your chums. It created a bit of a stir appearing in that column of his. And I hear the books are after him, too. So rides under Rules aren't exactly falling over each other. He met Pirate somewhere at a dinner party and asked him for the ride. Pirate said he could tell him more about the horse than you could and he's to have him for the rest of the season – if he wants him. That's it, I'm afraid.'

'Rupert,' I said. 'Everything seems to come back to him.'

'Cheer up, there's plenty more fish in the sea. Rides come and rides go, you'll have to get used to it. I'll drive you to the point-to-point Saturday if you're still under the weather. We'll see how Givenchy goes for Rupert.'

16

Almost the first person I saw when I arrived at the point-to-point meeting that Saturday was Flinty. He came up to me smiling and after asking about my injuries which, in fact, were much better thanks to youth and fitness, he said: 'I have news for you. You've kept the ride on Prospero.'

My heart leaped. 'That's marvellous,' I said. 'And I'm sure I have you to thank for it.'

'It's true I put in a good word for you, but it was the little man who pulled it off. He's ridden enough races to know what it's like to miss out. He told her it was damned unfair even to think of ditching you after that one bad ride, that you were only starting and that it would do you untold harm. His word is law in that quarter as I expect you know. But you only got there by a short head. Someone else was after it.'

'Don't tell me who it was, I can guess: Rupert Carleton.'

'You've hit the spot. Every time a cocoanut or a good seegar. He's been dripping vitriol in her ear ever since that race last week.'

'He doesn't usually condescend to point-to-points you told me. He's got interested in them all of a sudden.'

'He's short of the spondulicks, I believe. Anyway, there it is. She's in love with that horse. Got a fixation on him the way women have. And she has great plans for him. You're to come to the little man's lodgings this eve to discuss them. But it won't be a long session. We're off night-clubbing.'

The Colonel had entered Givenchy in a race confined to members and subscribers (there weren't then any maiden races in the point-to-points where you could give a new-comer a run). It was the second race on the card and to watch it I took up a position on the hill where we had parked the cars. There I was joined by Charles Ormsby. 'I hardly expected to see you here,' I said.

'I get about,' he said. 'I heard Rupert was riding and I thought I'd come along. What about this horse of Pirate's, Givenchy? You've ridden him work. Has he shown you anything?'

'He can go a bit,' I said. 'I don't know about the other runners.'

'Billy Burton-Brown has one in it,' Captain Pat, who had just joined us, said. 'But they're backing the Colonel's horse for pounds shillings and pence. I've just come from the ring. I can't understand it – '

'By God,' Charles Ormsby said. 'I wonder – ' And he hurried off.

He was back in a few minutes with the look on his face of one who has just made a discovery and is pleased about it. 'Come to the car after this,' he said to me. 'I have something to tell you.'

'They're off,' I said, raising my glasses.

Naturally I was interested to follow the fortunes of Givenchy and to see how he went under Rupert's strong handling, so I watched with more than usual interest the Colonel's colours of amber and white. Rupert had him in mid-division most of the way, then when they began really to race he moved him smoothly up. Most of those that were left began to drop back, but two horses came over the last

171

together. They were Givenchy and Billy Burton-Brown's whose name I forget. There followed a desperate set-to up the straight in which Givenchy was subjected to Rupert's full treatment in a finish. He knew how to handle a whip, he was as good as a pro in a tight finish and better than many of them. He got up by a neck. But when a horse was subjected to one of Rupert's roustings in a finish he didn't forget it in a hurry, and this was Givenchy's first time out.

'I hope the Colonel is pleased,' I couldn't resist saying to Captain Pat who hurried off to have, I imagined, a good look at the winner and to see how many stripes of the whip were decorating his coat.

'The money was down,' Charles Ormsby said quietly as we made our way to his car. 'I haven't been idle,' he went on as we settled ourselves in its seats. 'Something about those pictures of Rossiter has bothered me ever since you came in and reopened the case. Take a look at this.' He reached over and took from his briefcase another copy of the drawing from which my embellishments had been removed. 'Remind you of anyone?' he asked as I studied it.

'Gosh,' I said. 'Yes, now you mention it – Rupert!'

'Exactly. He's Rupert's younger brother, or step-brother would be more accurate. I remembered dimly a scandal of sorts in the family. I'd acted once for one of Rupert's ex-wives and remained friendly with her. We had dinner together a night or so back and she refreshed my memory, telling me the whole story. It seems Rupert's father didn't sire this fellow though he had, of course, to give him his name. Gervase Carleton, that's who he is. But the old man knew very well he'd been cheated and he hated this fellow from the start.'

'Who was the father?' I asked.

'No one knows except, I suppose, the mother, and she died without telling. Whether the father's hatred of him had anything to do with the way he turned out I don't know, since there's bad blood in that family anyway, but Gervase or Rossiter or whatever you care to call him proved to be a wrong 'un fairly early. He was expelled from two public schools and did a term in clink for forging someone's signature on a cheque, leaving while he did it a stack of unpaid bills behind him in the West End. Thereupon, fond papa, having picked up the tag, kicked him out bag, baggage, the lot. He drifted into the wrong end of racing having changed his name about three times, and he survived somehow in the way these characters do. He was always good with horses and that helped.'

'But where does Rupert come in?' I asked.

'That's the quirk in the story. The two of them got on well, it seems, birds of a feather, perhaps, but the ex-wife told me Rupert did his best to look after him, rescuing him from the worst of the scrapes he got into and giving him money when he was on the touch which he pretty nearly always was. He helped him when he could and got precious little thanks for it. It was about the only decent thing Rupert ever did in his life, according to the ex-wife, which is the sort of remark you expect from an ex-wife, as I hope you'll never have occasion to find out.' He paused to light a cigarette.

'What then?' I said.

'It's obvious, isn't it? Rupert recruited him for the job of doping your father's horse and he's now either blackmailing Rupert or Rupert has him under his thumb and is paying him off and keeping an eye on him, or a bit of both more likely. One way or another they're in it together. It was Rossiter doing the betting for Rupert today. I thought it likely when I heard they were raiding the ring. I went down and spotted him.'

'Did he see you?'

'I took damn good care he didn't.'

'But we've got them now, haven't we?'

'Not so fast, my young friend. We've still nothing really on Rupert yet. It's no offence to get someone to do the betting for you. And we both know there's more in this than meets the eye. I've put a tag on Mr Rossiter, to find out what name he's masquerading under now and what company he keeps.'

'How will you do that? He may have disappeared by now.'

'I brought one of my chaps with me just in case. I had a feeling something like this might turn up.'

'What if he loses him?'

He looked at me rather bleakly and then appeared to go off at a tangent in the way he had. 'During the war, when I was wounded and recovering,' he said, 'someone gave me a book on Rugby football to read. It's not a game I'm interested in, but when you're lying in bed like that you'll read anything. One phrase in it has always stuck in my mind. Describing a fullback the author said: "When you're tackled by Mowbray," I think that was his name, "you stay tackled." Well, when you're shadowed by one of my chaps you stay shadowed. Keep in touch, I think things may begin to happen.'

When I left him I watched HRH win one of the regimental races which were a feature of point-to-points then. It was some sort of Past and Present race I think, and by the time I reached his rooms at Braden Lodge, corks were popping.

'I gather Flinty has told you,' Val greeted me. 'I want you to ride Prospero for the rest of the season.'

'He has and I don't know how to say thanks,' I said.

'Well, don't then.' But she smiled as she said it. 'Keep it for showing us it on his back. How soon will you be fit enough to ride out?'

'In a few days, I hope. I mend quickly.'

'Flinty is going to help us with the placing and the plans.'

'A couple of nomination races and then possibly a hunter chase. We'll have to see,' Flinty said.

'I'm entering him in the Liverpool Foxhunters',' Val said. 'You'd better be fit.'

'Gosh,' I said. It was all I could say. The Liverpool Foxhunters' was then run over the full National distance. It was every GR's ambition to ride over those fearsome Aintree fences and I was being offered it. This was beyond anything I could have hoped for and it left me speechless. Seeing me, the Prince gave one of those quick smiles of his. 'You deserve all the luck your father didn't have,' he said. 'I hope it goes well for you.'

On that note I left them to their night out in the bright lights. Full of my good fortune, I wanted to share it with someone, and who better than Captain Pat? I found him, as I thought I might, at Givenchy's box. The horse was a sorry sight, listless and drooping with a series of raw, red weals across his quarters. 'He hasn't eaten up,' Captain Pat said. 'And I'm not surprised. It'll be some time before he sees a racecourse again. What the hell did Rupert think he was playing at?'

'He backed him,' I said.

'I thought as much.'

'Does the Colonel know?'

'If he doesn't he'll have guessed. He's been called away or he'd be here. I only had a word with him. He said he didn't think it necessary to give Rupert any detailed instructions. All he said was, "See how he goes, it's his first time out." That should have been enough.'

'What did Rupert say when he came in?'

'He told Pirate he was going so well he had to take Billy on and then there was nothing for it but to battle it out or they'd have been in trouble. He always has an answer.'

'How did he know he was good enough to back him?'

'That's my fault, or mostly. He asked me about him and I told him we thought he might be something special and a cut above inter hunt class. But I warned the bastard he was highly-strung. I have an idea too he had someone watch him work. I'll take damn good care he doesn't ride him again, not that he's likely to. You might be lucky and come in for the ride, whenever it is.'

'I'm lucky twice over then. I've just come from Val Spenlove. I've kept the ride on Prospero.'

'Have you, by Gad. That's a bit of a turn up, isn't it? How did that happen?'

'Flinty and HRH fixed it. She's going to run him in the Liverpool Foxhunters'.'

'I hope he's as good as he looks. Here's the Colonel now. I think it might be wiser if you were to fade gently away. Don't worry, I'll put in a good word for you with him, that is if you're not too taken up with your high falutin' friends.'

Walking back, although I knew that sterner things than riding races should be occupying my thoughts, I could not bring myself to do other than dream of Prospero and Aintree. But the following afternoon I was brought back to reality with a bump. There was a telegram waiting for me in my rooms. It read: *Meet me Buck's Club tomorrow 11 a.m. or nearest. Ormsby.*

17

While I was breakfasting next morning before catching the early London Train from Melton, Mrs Williams bustled in with the post. It consisted of a letter from my mother which I put into my pocket, unopened, to read on the train, and a small, registered package. Breaking the seals on this and untying the string I tore off the wrapping. Inside was a hard object in a covering of tissue paper. When I unfolded this my father's gold cigarette case slid out on to the tablecloth before me. There was no note or letter with it that I could see and after staring at it in astonishment for a moment I picked up the wrapping to examine the address label. But this told me nothing either. It was printed in blue ink and had a London postmark. I was still frowning over it when I heard Mrs Williams' voice from below. 'Mr de Lacey, you'll miss your train.'

Hurriedly pushing the case, wrapping and all, into a drawer, I grabbed my hat and coat and made for the station with a few minutes to spare. The train was in on time and in my first class carriage I took out my mother's letter. It contained little beyond some scraps of hunting gossip and news of her horses until I reached the end. *You seem to be seeing a lot of Val Spenlove*, she wrote. *Beware! Did your father ever read Mr Kipling to you? 'The rag, the bone and the hank of hair', and if you don't know the rest then find out!!!* My mother spattered exclamation marks throughout her correspondence with careless abandon. I need scarcely say I didn't know the rest and I put the letter in my pocket while I tried to figure out where the cigarette case had come from and why. After a bit I gave that up too and picked up *Horse and Hound* which I had bought at the station bookstall.

Buck's Club was the first London Club to install a bar. Its members were rather proud of the fact that they had set a fashion and it was there that Charles Ormsby was waiting for me. 'It has been said and rightly said,' he remarked as he motioned to a half bottle of champagne nestling in an ice bucket on the table before him, 'that some damn teetotaller invented half bottles, but we have work to do.'

'You're giving up an awful lot of time to our affairs,' I said. 'I only hope it's not wasted.'

'I'll tell you why I'm doing it,' he said. 'First, I'm interested in righting an injustice if I can; second it may concern the heir to the throne whom I like and admire and therefore feel it's part of my duty; third, and many people would say most important, your mother has paid me a handsome deposit.'

Mention of my mother reminded me of her letter. 'You know a lot,' I said. 'Do you know a quotation from Kipling – "the rag, the bone and the hank of hair"?'

'Kipling, the soldier's laureate,' he said. 'I do know that thing, or some of it. It goes on, "we called her the woman who did not care but the fool he called her his lady fair."' He paused and looked at me, '"Even as you and I". Why do you ask?'

'I heard it somewhere,' I said, mentally trying to digest it and thinking, too, that my mother could be at times a jealous bitch.

'Hm,' he said, giving me another hard stare and reminding me that here was someone whose probing mind worked all the time. 'Well, I mentioned we have work to do. We've located Mr Vincent Rossiter, or Vernon Radley as he calls himself now. It's odd how these chaps always seem to like to keep their initials. Makes it easier to remember if you're changing them often, perhaps.'

Rossiter – or Radley which I'd better call him from now on – had taken up residence in a block of flats near Marble Arch known, so Ormsby informed me in the taxi, as Co-respondent Court. There was a commissionaire at the door and a receptionist behind a desk in the foyer but neither of them questioned our credentials as Ormsby marched in. He was turned out in the then regulation dress of the soldier or ex-soldier up in town – dark suit, bowler hat, hard collar and the not quite so regulation bow tie. The commissionaire actually saluted him, a tribute no doubt to his military bearing and air of authority. In any event I guessed from its name that the residents of Co-respondent Court would not care to have questions asked about their own or their visitors' comings and goings.

Ormsby led the way to the bank of lifts and we went up to the third floor. There, about halfway along a dark corridor, he paused before a door with a card on it inscribed, Major Vernon Radley. 'Major, indeed,' he said. 'He's come up in the world. He usually goes to the pub round the corner about this time, I'm told. The Bridle and Bit, it's full of the sweepings of the racecourse. That's where he belongs.' As he spoke he took a bunch of what looked like keys from his pocket and bent over the lock. In a few moments there was a click and the door swung open to his touch. 'Kid's stuff,' he said. 'It's a good job we live in a law-abiding society. A child could do it.'

We stepped into a short hallway or vestibule. There were doors on either side, both of which stood open. One gave on to a bedroom whose vast double bed was tousled and unmade, the other to a sitting room and kitchenette. Ormsby went through the rooms quickly, making sure there was no one in occupation.

'I say,' I said, when he came back to me in the hall. 'Isn't this frightfully illegal?'

'I think you said something to that effect before about getting dope,' he said rather crossly. 'Of course it is. That's why I'm doing it.'

Beside us in the hallway was a table with an envelope on it addressed to Major Vernon Radley. Ormsby picked this up and studied it for a moment. Then, taking a pen-knife from his pocket, he slit it open and began to study its contents. 'We've come to the right place,' he said, handing me the letter. There was a cheque pinned to it and it was written on Braden Lodge writing paper. On it was scrawled: *Thanks for your help. We worked it well*, followed by the initials R. C. The cheque was for fifty pounds. It was made out to Vernon Radley and signed Rupert Carleton.

While I was looking at these and pondering their implications, Ormsby was prowling about the living room, finally coming to a stop before a desk in the window. On it stood a half empty bottle of whisky and a used glass. It was littered with circulars and unpaid bills, amongst which was a leather bound book. Picking this up he examined it. 'It's a diary,' he said. 'This might be interesting.'

He took it to a chair and began to leaf through the pages. 'It's a five year diary,' he said. 'It was a year ago your father was warned off, wasn't it? It all began at Ascot, as I remember. Listen to this: *June 3rd*. That was a week before Ascot. *Got the stuff from R.C. Hope it works*. R.C. That's Rupert Carleton, I'll be bound. I think we may just have struck gold. Get that letter from the hall, will you?'

I brought it to him and he looked at it again. 'He signed the letter with his initials,' he said. 'And the cheque, of course, with his full name. That ties him in with the diary entries for R.C. I'll hang on to these.' He replaced the letter and cheque in their envelope and put them in his pocket. 'The cheque would probably bounce anyway,' he said. 'But there's more in the diary.' He turned over the pages. '*June 11*,' he read out, '*It worked! Bf won by three lengths. Enquiry. de L sent on. He must go. Now for the pay-off from R.C.* Even if the rest of it doesn't live up to what we've seen and heard I think Mr R. Carleton is in some trouble. Up a certain creek without a certain paddle, you might say.'

'Why on earth did he write it all down?' I asked.

'So as to have a record and a hold over Rupert, I imagine.'

'And leave it lying about?'

'It wouldn't convey anything to anyone unless they knew what we do. As for leaving it lying about, they're both reckless devils. When did your father have his stroke?'

'Last August.'

He turned back to the diary. 'Good God,' he said and read out: *They seem to have fixed de L!*'

'That must have been when he was in America.'

'It was. Let's see what he says about coming back. Here it is. He's got a bit more expansive: *Fed up with this bloody country. Drinks firewater if you can get it. Champagne like Epsom salts. Returning whatever R. says and he can bloody pay up.*'

At that moment there was the sound of a key in the lock and then steps in the hall.

'Oh, Lord – ' I said.

'Take no notice. Panic not,' Ormsby said coolly, almost as if he had been waiting for it. 'If it's the gallant Major he's in for something of a surprise.'

The door opened and a man came in. It was Rossiter alias Radley and I recognised him at once. Looking at him with what I now knew, despite the dyed hair and the fair moustache, I could see the striking resemblance to Rupert. But there were also differences. It was a far weaker face. Where Rupert looked what he was, a roaring tough and hard nut to crack, this chap's mouth had a curl of indecision under the moustache and the eyes were pale and watery.

'What the hell – ' he exclaimed, coming up all standing as he saw us. 'What are you doing here? Burglars, are you? I'll call the police – '

'You do just that if you wish,' Ormsby said. 'The phone is over there and we haven't tampered with it. But take a look at Mr de Lacey there. You've met him before and he you. There's a small matter of grievous bodily harm outstanding between you, apart from several other things I could mention. Go ahead, what's stopping you?'

He looked at me and recognition together with fear suddenly flared in his eyes. Then he caught sight of the diary in Ormsby's hands. 'What are you doing with that?' he almost shouted, pointing at it. One of those round ebony rulers, fashionable at the time, was lying on the desk. As he pointed he picked it up and made a lunge towards Ormsby and the diary.

It was the quickest thing I ever saw. At one moment Ormsby was sitting there, relaxed, the diary in his hands. The next the diary was laid aside and he was on his feet, clasping the wrist that held the ruler. It went up behind Radley's back and spun him round as you'd spin a top. A single push sent him reeling off balance towards the far wall. He hit it hard and collapsed with a crash on to a spindly sofa that stood there. A picture on the wall above him, dislodged by the impact, came down and splintered on the floor. Radley lay gasping, with shock and surprise, I thought, more than hurt.

'You try that again and I'll break your arm and probably your neck as well,' Ormsby said equably. The bow tie, I noticed, remained impeccably in place.

'What do you want? If it's money I haven't any,' Radley said, his eyes darting about.

'I know that,' Ormsby said. 'It's a little information which I rather think you can give us. How is your brother Rupert, by the way? And what exclusive regiment did you decorate with your presence, Major?'

He lay there looking at us, his eyes darting from one to the other, finally coming to rest on Ormsby. 'Who are you?' he said. 'You're not CID.' Then, recognition dawning: 'I know you. You're Ormsby, the private rozzer, paid for digging up dirt.'

'I wouldn't have far to go to find it here,' Ormsby said.

At that, all at once, having realised we had no official status, he began to bluster. 'What the hell do you think you're doing?' he said. 'You've nothing on me.'

'Is that so,' Ormsby said. 'Try this then.' He began to read the passages from the diary. 'R.C. That's Rupert Carleton, I don't doubt,' he concluded.

But by now Radley was showing signs of recovering his nerve. After all, with his record he must have been in similar situations before. 'That'll never stand up,' he said. 'You stole the diary, you tampered with my letter.'

'Of course I did. What do you think I'd do dealing with crooks like you – and Rupert?'

'You can go to hell.'

'Try pulling his fingernails out,' I said. 'That was what he suggested doing to me. I owe him something, the swine, and for what they did to my father.' Involuntarily I took a step towards him.

'Hold it,' Ormsby commanded as the other threw up a hand as if to ward me off.

'I had no part in that – your father,' Radley said. 'I was in America. It was Rupert and you'll never touch him. He knows too much. He's connected, we're connected, with half the Court and three-quarters of the Jockey Club.'

'Balls,' Ormsby said succinctly. 'We've got you where we want you. That diary will hang you and Rupert too. You'll find out how soon and how quick your precious connections can drop you.'

Suddenly Radley changed his tack again and began to

whine. 'You don't know what it's like being the black sheep,' he said. 'It wasn't my fault the old sweep who called himself my father didn't sire me. I didn't ask to be born, did I? Why take it out on me? It was Rupert who was given everything. All I got were kicks, cold shoulders – and hatred. Do you know what family hatred is?'

'I didn't come here to listen to confessions,' Ormsby said coldly. 'Save that for the dock. Where is Rupert now? He seems to have no fixed abode.'

'He's where you can't touch him. He's in Monte Carlo playing the tables with his winnings. Damn him, he said he'd take me with him. What's in that cheque?'

'Fifty pounds.'

'Fifty quid. Christ! He took twenty times that out of the ring.'

'It wouldn't pay your bookies' or your tailor's bill if you have one.'

Cupidity, fear and venom were all beginning to work on him by this time to take the place of bluster and whine. 'That bloody Rupert,' he said. 'He got me into this.'

'And paid you well for it?'

'Like hell he did. Shipped me off pretty quick to the States when he thought you, you bastard, were closing in on me. A few ponies when I did the job, that's all I got.'

'The job? That's the doping? Why do it then?'

'Rupert said there was money in it, big money.'

'Colonel de Lacey knew nothing of all this?'

'Christ no. He dope one of his runners? He was the Holy Ghost. Not bloody likely.'

I could now guess Ormsby's tactics. He was firing questions at his victim, keeping the pressure up to force more information from him. 'Where was this money coming from?'

'I don't know. You don't pester Rupert for information when he has hold of the bit. All I know is that he said there was money in it. I think he had the arm on someone.'

'And you came home to put the arm on him?'

He sulked at that and muttered something about why should Rupert always be the one who had everything. Then he said: 'He told me the source was drying up. That's why he had to work that bet.'

'And now he's hitting the high spots in Monte. Unfair, isn't it?'

'Damn him. Listen, what's in this for me? You'll have to do something. I'm flat broke. At least give me that cheque.'

'The diary and cheque are staying with me. They'll do as evidence. Would it interest you to know that Rupert has got you mixed up in something that may well concern the Prince of Wales? That's treason. Do you know what the penalty for treason is? It's hanging by the neck until you're dead.'

'Jesus Christ!' He sank back on to the sofa. I've often heard of people turning deadly white but I'd never seen it before. His cheeks really did take on an ashen tinge and he stared helplessly at us. Then he reached for the whisky bottle on the desk, his hand shaking so much that it rattled against the glass as he poured a stiff measure.

Suddenly Ormsby stood up. 'That'll do for now,' he said. 'Just remember we've got you by the short hairs. We can hand on this information at any time to those who can act on it. Come on,' he nodded at me.

It was then I remembered something I had forgotten in the hurly burly of the day. 'You've got the forty quid you pinched off me on the road,' I said. 'That should keep you going for a bit. But why did you send me back the cigarette case? You could have pawned it for a bob or two.'

'Cigarette case?' he said, looking at me open-mouthed. 'Oh, that gold one. I never had that. Rupert took it.'

'What the devil did Rupert want with it?'

'To cash in Monte and add to his winnings, can't you guess,' he said with a semi-snarl. He was gulping another drink and colour was coming back into his cheeks.

Ormsby stood looking down at him. 'That won't last you very long,' he said, indicating the whisky bottle. 'Here – ' He put his hand into his pocket and extracted a crisp white fiver. Laying it on the table, he said: 'Drown your thoughts, you may need to – Major.'

As we reached the door, with a final flash of defiance, engendered no doubt by the whisky, Radley shouted, 'You'll never get Rupert, you know. He *likes* living dangerously.'

Once outside Ormsby turned to me. 'What's all this about a cigarette case?' he said.

'I forgot to tell you before,' I said. 'It came in the post this morning. It was pinched off me when they beat me up.'

'To give some semblance to robbery being the motive no doubt. Did you keep the package?'

'It's in a drawer in my rooms.'

'I'd like to take a look at it. I'll come back to Melton with you.'

But the package told him as little as it did me. He turned it over, fingered it, stared at the address and postmark and finally put it down. 'Beats me,' he said. 'I suppose Rupert had a motive – but what?'

'What will Radley, Rossiter, or whatever you like to call him do now? Will he run to Rupert?' I asked him.

'He won't. He's shit-scared of Rupert – and of us. He'll lie low for a bit with the whisky bottle. I think I'll pay him another visit tomorrow when he's still in shock. I may have to do a deal with him. Your first aim, what you came over for, is to clear your father's name, right.'

'Yes, but I want to nail that bastard Rupert for what he did.'

'Step by step. He can't do much in Monte and I rather think his or their little plot about the Prince may be falling apart.'

'He said Rupert had the arm on someone.'

'And that the source was drying up.'

At that moment there was the sound of a car drawing up outside. Going to the window I looked out. 'It's a Rolls,' I said. Then I saw the door open and a figure step out. 'It's Sir Crispin,' I said. 'What can he want?'

'We'll soon see.'

In a few minutes he was ushered in. 'Afternoon, De Lacey,' he said to me, stripping off his gloves. 'And to you, too, Charles. I thought I might find one or both of you here. I rang your place of business, Charles, and found you were meeting De Lacey in London but didn't expect to be away all day. Riding any more winners, young feller?'

'He has a ride in the Foxhunters' at Aintree,' Ormsby said.

'Lucky chap. Liverpool – there's nothing like it, riding over those fences. Once done – and I hope you do it many more times – never forgotten.'

'If you want advice on riding Aintree you have it right here,' Ormsby said. 'Crispin's ridden it and knows it and won the Foxhunters' a few years back.'

'Take no notice of Charles,' the baronet said smiling. 'You don't want to hear any spiff from an old hasbeen like me, I'm sure.'

'Of course I do, sir,' I said. 'Please tell me – anything.'

'It's not what I came for,' he said. 'But it's nice even talking about it, reliving it in a way, I suppose. Well then, here goes. Listen, mark, learn, and pay no heed at all.' He sat back and crossed his legs. 'I'd let down your leathers at least a hole, perhaps two, for the drops. Depends on whatever makes you feel comfortable. That above all. You've four and a half miles to go, remember, but still I think that's important. Do you really want me to go on?'

'Of course I do. My father always said that you went round the first time and after that you thought about riding your race.'

'True enough. But you want to be in touch. Bear in mind

the old tag that you can give away weight but you can't give away distance.'

'What about the start?' I said. 'Where do you advise to go?'

'It's a matter of preference. Some like the inside because they say it saves ground, but remember this is a hunters' race and some of the riders aren't as good at keeping their horses straight as the pros and there's more of a chance of interference on the inside.'

'Where do you think is the best then?'

'I always liked the middle. Oh, and sit back at Becher's and slip your reins. I know that McRagget, the high priest of the forward seat, criticises us bumpers and says we put too much weight on a horse's loins, but the last chap I knew to try the forward seat at Aintree told me when he got to Becher's the only thing in front of him was fresh air and the next thing he knew he was in it. Here endeth the lesson.'

'Take all that to heart,' Ormsby said to me, and then, looking across at Merevale, 'But you said you had something else on your mind, Crispin.'

'I did and I have. Since you came to see me I've been considering much further the whole matter of Dick de Lacey's warning off. I've always hated that rule as you know. Your object, both of you, I take it, is to clear his name?'

'We were discussing just that when you came in,' Ormsby said.

'Whatever way you look at it,' I said, 'the public think he did dope that horse and for the matter of that the press have more or less said so.'

'Very well. That being so we must try to get the warning-off notice lifted. I've been taking soundings. There is very considerable sympathy but I didn't find it quite as universal as I'd hoped. However, there was a Jockey Club meeting last week and I felt I had enough to mention it in general terms under any other business.'

'How did that go?' Ormsby asked.

'Not quite the way I wanted, to be candid. There was opposition, not much, but some. It was said it might be establishing a precedent. Luckily I was able to cite the case of Bob Sievier who was let back after two years, over a different matter, it's true. If you know your racing history you'll remember it. They mumbled and bumbled a bit but I think on the whole I carried the day far enough anyway for you to make an application on your father's behalf.'

'Who were in opposition?' Ormsby asked.

'Now, Charles, you don't expect me to quote names from a private meeting.'

'No, Crispin, and you don't expect me to plead ignorance on how these things get out. Members tell their wives, there's talk in club armchairs and over the port – '

Merevale laughed. 'Perhaps,' he said. And then, to me: 'I'll draft your letter of application for you and I'll write in in support of it. If they do grant the lifting of the warning-off notice we should try to get them to say that no blame attached to your father in the matter. That will need delicate handling. By the way, have you got any further with finding the real culprit?'

I was about to blurt out a reply when Ormsby quickly forestalled me. 'We're making progress,' he said. 'I'd prefer not to say any more just at the moment.'

'Hmm, well, tell me when you do get anything. In the meantime we should go ahead with the application. I'll take a few more soundings and let you know, De Lacey, when the time is ripe. Good luck with your riding. When is your next outing?'

'The Garth at Arborfield,' I said.

He laughed. 'The famous Arborfield Brook. That'll give you practice for sitting back over Becher's.'

At the door he paused. 'By the way,' he said. 'That Jockey Club meeting, Roger Gretton was there, and Marston who seldom comes.' The door closed behind him, leaving Ormsby and myself looking at each other.

18

Then began what was the most exciting and at the same time most exacting period of my short life so far. I duly won the nomination race at the Garth. Prospero behaved impeccably, the famous brook held no terrors for him, though it floored several of his competitors. I had him in front most of the trip and he came away to win comfortably. My sins were forgiven.

It is a racing truism that lose by a whisker in the best race you have ever ridden and punters, public, and, I regret to say, certain owners and trainers, will metaphorically or sometimes physically throw bottles at you and hold you up to scorn and derision; win on one of your worst races and you are a hero. Never was this more aptly proved than in my case that season. After Arborfield my fall was forgotten and offers of rides came pouring in.

There is no denying of course that my association with the Prince of Wales, greatly exaggerated as such things always are, helped to further my racing career. Those with a horse to sell, and they were many and various, realised that it did them no harm to say, 'that chap, friend of the Prince's, rides for him you know, rode him and liked him,' and many were not above slyly suggesting I slid one into the Prince's stable.

One such, I remember, came to me and brazenly suggested that, 'there's ten-per-cent in it for you if you pull it off.' Fortunately I had enough sense to refuse that ride. Just the same I found that I was being offered rides here, there and everywhere, and sometimes rode through the card except for regimental or confined races. In all this Flinty was of the greatest help to me. He knew everyone and every horse and had them all summed shrewdly up. I told him of the offer of a bribe and then, remembering, recounted how, after winning the race against HRH, the yeoman farmer had approached me. He knew who it was at once. 'That's Tom Satterthwaite,' he said. 'Has a few jumpers near Market Harborough. "Jockey broken his leg" my left foot. Don't believe a word of it. That's a bloody bad brute and he could get no one else to take the ride. He'd probably have broken your neck. Rupert mostly rides those jumpers for him. He may well have put him up to it. Where is that man of four letters by the way? I haven't seen him round lately.'

'He's in Monte.'

'Lying low and playing high, is he?' He gave his throaty chuckle and walked off.

There's no denying I was spoilt. I was young enough to believe that you made your own luck and that I was making it. Recently, in a book of sporting memoirs published the other day, I saw myself described as a pampered brat (I think the author, whom I scarcely knew, thought I was dead) but this is unfair. I had enough sense to keep my feet on the ground and my head out of the clouds. I kept a still tongue in the weighing-room and above all did not try to presume on or make capital out of my patronage by the Prince. Nor did I ever try anything on in a race but, knowing my inexperience, was learning all the time. As a result both Billy Burton-Brown and Mike Annerley accepted me. Once they had done this they did all they could to help, except of course in the actual race when no quarter was asked or given. 'Look after yourself, no one else will': that's what my guv'nor said to me when I started, Billy told me once. He lived up to it and woe betide anyone who tried to come up on his inside. 'You need two stone in hand to get away with that,' he commented to me after one incident which didn't concern me when he had dealt summarily with the offender and put him out of the race. It was a lesson I was not to forget.

What with riding races and work I was absenting myself more and more from the initiation into the mysteries of veterinary science by Captain Pat which was the ostensible reason for my presence at Melton, so I felt I had to make my peace with him. I thought and hoped that I would find him sympathetic and I did. Regarding me owlishly through his thick glasses he said: 'I was young myself once, though you may not realise it, and I only wish I'd had your chances. But I thought I should write to your mother.'

'What did she say?' I asked, a trifle apprehensively.

For answer he took a telegraph form from his pocket and handed it to me. *Give the boy his head. Writing. Marion*, I read. That solved one problem. But it wasn't all plain sailing. As I was to discover later in life, as always, there were clouds in the sky.

The first of these concerned Prospero. I won the next two nomination races on him. That made three wins on the trot and four out of five starts if you count the ladies' race Val had won on him. But despite those I was still not entirely happy about him or his genuineness. Nor were Flinty or HRH. The only person who believed utterly in him and decried our doubts was Val.

'Get him off well, keep him up in the van, let him run his own race and with luck his speed and his jumping will see him through,' had been Flinty's advice to me. This I had done and the luck had lasted. There was no question of his ability to jump, which was invincible, but in the last of those three races I had thought I had detected signs of his sulking, and he hadn't really yet been asked to battle. He had all the class in the world, too much for ordinary point-to-pointing perhaps, and by those standards he hadn't beaten much in the three races (we noticed that a high class horse of Billy's, The Clinker, had been carefully kept away from us) and it was by and large his class and his jumping which had seen him through and pulverised the opposition. But had he the heart for the struggle which would be required at Aintree? That was the question which the four of us discussed endlessly amongst ourselves.

'Carry on the way you're going,' Flinty said. 'After all it's worked so far. What do you think, David?'

'I'm not one to give an opinion on the tactics of race-riding,' the Prince observed with his ready smile. 'I'm far too busy trying to stay in the plate to think of anything else.'

'You're not fair to yourself, as usual,' Val said hotly. 'Anyway, I don't know what the three of you are bothering yourselves about. He has won three on the trot, hasn't he? What more do you want? What is in the Foxhunters' to beat him?'

'There's that thing of Billy's, The Clinker,' Flinty said.

'Is he going in it?' I asked.

'He's in the United Hunts at Cheltenham, or so I'm told,' Flinty said. 'And if he comes out of that all right, he'll go to Liverpool.'

'What about us?' I said. 'Where do we go next?'

'A school at Jimmy Connaughton's on Monday,' Flinty said. 'He lets us do that when the hunter chases start. Then the Hunters' race at Colwall the next week to give him a taste of the racecourse proper. Both of those should sharpen him up after the point-to-points.'

'There you are then, Danny,' Val said smiling. 'And see that you don't smash yourself up in the meantime.'

The second cloud, if that is the way of describing it, concerned my quest for the clearing of my father's name. I freely admit that this should have taken first place and can only plead that I was young, I was entranced by the people I was with, and was consumed with the ambition to ride races and win as many as I could. And when I thought about it I told myself that my father, were he able to have known about it, would have approved.

I did however try to get in touch with Ormsby to find out how he was getting on with Radley or Rossiter or Gervase Carleton or whatever name he was currently going by. It proved surprisingly difficult. The sour-puss secretary kept putting me off with one excuse or another when I rang from Captain Pat's office and when at last I got through to him all he would say was: 'It's going reasonably well but just at the moment the less you know the better.' With that sibylline utterance I assumed he thought that I would be content. But I wasn't. I wondered just what he was up to and if by chance he had been in touch with Crispin Merevale. With some trepidation as to how I would be received I rang Patworth Castle to find out.

The baronet, however, was his usual friendly and approachable self. No, he said, he had heard nothing from Charles Ormsby. 'He likes sometimes to play the man of mystery,' he said. 'But,' he added, 'I have news for you.'

'Good or bad, sir?' I asked.

'A bit of both perhaps. I've had a word in private with Lord Benby who is the senior steward this year. They're going to meet to consider the application. But he stressed its unusual features. Your father, sadly, can't make it himself so, as it's being made by you on his behalf, they want to have a good look at you. That means you'll have to appear before them officially and in person.'

'Oh, Lord!'

'Take heart. It's not unreasonable, you know. It could be that now or in the foreseeable future you might want to take up where your father left off. If you were to apply for a licence to train they'd know about you and have you on record. And, too, there's the question of precedent which is nagging at them. They'll want to be satisfied that they're not laying up trouble for themselves, though Benby doesn't like that rule any more than I do. That's one good thing. The other is that they knew your father and felt for him, so you will at least be in with a chance. I'll brief you about the hearing and go with you to lend support.'

'Gosh, thanks, it's terribly kind of you.'

'Not at all. I'm in it now and might as well go the whole way. You'll get official notice of the date and time. It will probably be in the afternoon when the gentlemen have had an opportunity to digest their port. I asked him not to make it a racing day!'

'I really don't know how to thank you, sir, and I know how grateful my mother will be.'

'Forget it. Go and ride a few more winners and we'll pull this one off, you'll see.'

Two days later we brought Prospero to Jimmy Connaughton's for a school. He was to go over the chasing fences with two older steeplechasers and Jimmy himself came down to watch it. Somewhere in that cold heart of his, Jimmy, as I was later to find out for I had much to do with him in my subsequent career, had a small soft spot for amateur riders, possibly because he had once been one himself, though with little success I had been told. Whatever the reason, unlikely though it was, he always interested himself in their doings and allowed the use of his schooling fences on designated days to point-to-pointers and their riders. Then, as now, point-to-point horses were not permitted to be sent to a licensed trainer, but it was the practice of those moving on to hunter chasing to bring their good horses to a school over training fences, thus to smarten them up for the larger, stiffer obstacles they would encounter on park courses.

There were others besides Jimmy there too, Billy and Mike among them, whether by accident or design the news of

Prospero's coming having been leaked to them, or hearing of it one way or another through the fraternity of the racing game, I never knew. But I noticed that they had finished their schooling when I arrived and they stayed on, their eyes fixed on us to see how we went. Though again, this may have been explained by the presence in the school, which I had not expected, of the Prince of Wales. It must have been one of his wayward, last minute, spur of the moment decisions, I thought, for Flinty had not mentioned it to me, nor did I think he entirely approved of it, for he stood there, frowning, as he watched the horses being brought out. The Prince joined me as we walked towards them.

'I'm coming with you,' he explained as he swung himself up. 'Recognise him?' He nodded to his mount. 'It's your old friend Pepperpot.'

The third member of our party was, I was equally surprised to see, Ginger Elton, riding a big, rakish chaser of Jimmy's.

'Wotcher, guv,' he greeted me. 'I'm back with Mr Connaughton for a bit. Bin ridin' a few winners yourself I see.'

There I was between the Prince of Wales, the highest in the land, and a stable boy, or stable rat as they were sometimes called, one of the lowest, and at that moment a spirit of pure mischief possessed me. 'Your Royal Highness,' I said. 'May I present Ginger Elton, one of Jimmy's work riders.'

The boy goggled and almost immediately I was aghast at my own temerity. In fact, as I realised afterwards, there was no cause for alarm since once HRH was amongst horses and horsemen he was one of ourselves. 'Jolly good,' he said. 'I hope you won't knock me down.'

I later learnt that the introduction did Elton no service as those few words became a sort of parrot cry in the yard, and whenever Elton afterwards appeared, schooling or on the gallops, he was greeted with raucous shouts of 'Jolly good, don't knock me down!'

Jimmy had spared nothing in constructing his schooling ground to prepare his chasers. It was a huge field set amongst the flat acres and bordered by a screen of trees. There were hurdles for the hurdlers, smaller, though stiff, fences for the education of the young, and bigger ones to finalise the youngsters' education and smarten up the abilities of the older and more experienced. These latter were in two lots of three and four respectively, the first containing an open ditch and the second, placed a little way from the others on a curve, contained a replica of a water jump. There was disagreement amongst trainers whether the latter was necessary at all but Jimmy believed it was and had put a chalked out sheet on the far side of a smaller fence to simulate one. Although the horses could be pulled out at the end of the first set of fences, we were to face the lot.

I was placed between the two experienced horses and, with a shout from Jimmy, we were off.

The plan was, so Flinty told me, to take them steady so as to give Prospero a feel of the thing. 'Let him have a look at the ditch, don't worry about the water, he'll jump it as it comes, can't think why Jimmy bothers with that sham of his. Bustle on over the last two if you like.'

That may have been the plan; it wasn't carried out. Straightaway the Prince on Pepperpot jumped into what I can only describe as a headlong gallop. There was nothing for it but to hurtle after him, Elton's old chaser devouring the ground and I, on Prospero, willy-nilly, matching strides with him.

I had never been so fast over first fences in my life. Beside me I heard Elton mutter 'Cripes' as we flew them. For whatever reason the Prince was making this a trial not a school. We had a look at the ditch but not the way Flinty intended. The others stood back and made nothing of it. Prospero put in a short one and fiddled it – talk of letting him have a look at it! But he got away with it and we went on.

In a way, the Prince with the pace he had set had cooked his own goose. Pepperpot was really only a hunter, though a very good one, and these were racehorses, even if Prospero was as yet an embryo. At the bend Pepperpot began to drop back. Elton by now had entered into the spirit of the thing – the wrong spirit to my mind, and I was mentally cursing the Prince – and was setting the other horse alight. It was the next best thing to a race. Together we fled over the mock water, Prospero making nothing of it.

The distance between the last two fences was longer than the others. Here Elton came off the bit and forged past me. Immediately I thought I felt Prospero falter. But the fence loomed up. Whatever else there was about him he loved jumping. He flung it behind him, out-jumped the other and landed running. Then we pulled up.

I slid to the ground to where the Prince, Jimmy and Val were in a little group. 'He's a smasher, isn't he, Jimmy?' I heard Val say to the trainer.

Jimmy stared long and hard at Prospero. Finally he said bluntly: 'He may be a damn good horse, m'lady, but I'll tell you one thing, he's a damn bad colour.'

Beside me I saw those vivid blue eyes of the Prince flash for an instant and I thought we were in for an explosion of the famous family temper. Instead, touching me on the arm, he drew me a little apart and then, with that truly regal ability to make a fact out of an opinion, he said: 'That was all right. Nothing wrong there.'

To my mind there was everything wrong and for the first and only time in our association I could cheerfully have throttled him. Fortunately, having made that statement, he did not wait for an answer and his next words disarmed me. 'She's set her heart on getting a good one to follow up her father's triumphs, and she thinks this may be it,' he said. 'I wanted to find out. I don't want her hurt, especially now, any more than maybe.'

With that he turned back towards the others and I made my way to the cars. Here Flinty, looking glum, joined me. 'I'll come back with you,' he said. 'I came with the horses.'

He spoke very little on our way but when I pulled up outside Braden Lodge and he levered himself out of the Alvis he said brusquely: 'Come in, we'll have breakfast.'

Breakfast proved to be a bottle of Krug, devilled kidneys, kedgeree, scrambled eggs laced with smoked salmon and coffee, a bit different, now I come to think of it, from my present morning meal of tea and toast and marmalade, varied now and then by an occasional free range egg.

'What was that thing the lad of Jimmy's was riding,' I said cautiously since he didn't seem in a communicative mood to say the least.

'Bolivar. He's an old handicapper. The edge has gone off him a bit. I thought he'd be just the thing to schoolmaster you both. What did you make of your fellow?'

'In the school?'

'School?' he scowled. 'Call that a school!'

I thought I'd better tell him the truth as I saw it. 'One thing is sure,' I said. 'He has the hell of a lep in him. As for the rest, I just don't know. I still think he may not battle. He's unpredictable.'

'About as unpredictable as my royal master. He only decided to put himself into the school at the last minute and I had to tell Jimmy to pull his other horse out. What was he playing at?'

'He said he wanted to find out about Prospero for himself.'

'Damn queer time to think of doing it, but that's him all over. I know him better than most and I still don't know what is going on in his mind, but something is eating him and I wish I knew what it is.'

'He said he didn't want her hurt, especially just now.'

'It's to do with those bastards at Court is my guess. They'll want him to drop her.'

He went off then to change for a day's hunting and I drove back to my rooms to bath and dress before resuming my veterinary education with Captain Pat, it not being a racing day.

Apart from Prospero and his problems I, too, had much on my mind. There was the strange silence of Charles Ormsby; there was Rupert, who was presumably still in Monte since I had not recently seen his name amongst the runners and riders, but I had the feeling that he was not finished with me nor I with him. This led to other matters not unconnected with him, for I was beginning to put two and two together about the plot against the Prince which had led to my father's tragedy and to come up with some singularly unpalatable answers.

In my rooms I saw a typewritten envelope lying on my table. Opening it I found a summons from the Jockey Club stewards to appear before them on the coming Friday at the hearing of the application for reinstatement which I had made on behalf of my father.

19

Crispin Merevale was as good as his word. He said on the telephone that he would be with me that morning in good time to give me what he called my 'riding instructions' for the hearing. Before he arrived I received a postcard on which was scrawled *Best of Luck – VAL*. And hardly had I glanced at it than I was handed by special delivery a long, brown, official-looking envelope. Cramming Val's card into my pocket I opened this. Inside was a legal document with a solicitor's letter attached. It was headed, HARDING, HENSLEY AND BARTON with an address in Lincoln's Inn and it was brief:

Dear Sir, it said, *We have been instructed to forward you the enclosed affidavit sworn by Gervase Carleton, otherwise Vincent Rossiter. Kindly acknowledge safe receipt.*

Eagerly I read it, racing down the numbered paragraphs, and then going back to scan them again with care. The original of that document is presumably either locked away in the Jockey Club archives or lost or destroyed. I never thought to keep a copy but I remember the contents well enough to paraphrase them here.

Gervase Carleton, otherwise Vincent Rossiter, gentleman.

(I liked that touch.) Then presently residing at Braxton Towers, Marble Arch, London, made oath and said –

What he said was that under the name of Vincent Rossiter he had been temporarily employed by Colonel Richard de Lacey at Trafalgar House, Newmarket. As such he had been 'solely and only' responsible for the act of doping of the colt Bloemfontein when under the care and supervision of the said Colonel de Lacey and, further, that the said Colonel de Lacey had no knowledge of, or association with, the said act of doping carried out by him which act required the utmost 'secrecy, skill and diligence' (I remembered the exact words) owing to the strict security maintained by the said Colonel de Lacey in all matters concerning the stable and the horses in his care. He went on to say or swear, I suppose I should say, that no other persons in the stable had been concerned in the matter and if he received payment for same it had come from outside sources. After the incident, fearing exposure, he had emigrated to America, but had since returned. He made this affidavit voluntarily and of his own accord from sincere regret for his actions with the object of clearing Colonel de Lacey's name from the obloquy (I remember that word, too) which his action had brought upon it. It was all dressed up in legal language and flummery but that was the gist of it.

When Crispin Merevale arrived the first thing I did was to show him the affidavit and he read it carefully. When he had finished he put it down saying: 'Gervase Carleton, I should have guessed he'd be mixed up in something of this sort. He's a thorough-going bad hat. It's interesting, too, his pointing the finger at someone else with his talk of a reward. That's typical, too. Where'd you get this?'

'It came by special delivery a few minutes ago.'

'I think I see Charles Ormsby's fine Italian hand in it somewhere, but that's for later. You and I don't know it.'

'Will it help?'

'It must. But we'll have to be careful how we use it. The stewards aren't overfond of lawyers or legal documents.'

'Who are the stewards I'll be appearing before?' It may seem strange that I had to ask that question but the fact was that, concerned as I was entirely with my own minor branch of the sport, steeplechasing, and taken up with it and the horses I rode, I had never given thought to the actual names and personalities of those on the flat who would sit in judgment.

'Lord Benby will be in the chair. He's a fair man, he doesn't like that rule and I'm sure he'll be sympathetic. You're lucky it's not Hugh Lonsdale. He knows a hell of a lot about hunting and nothing at all about racing which he tries to cover up by bluster and bullying all and sundry who appear before him. He wouldn't listen to the evidence and he'd fire you out for the fun of it.'

'That's something. What about the others?'

'There's Giles Tevern. Lord Giles Tevern. Some think him a nonentity, but he's not. He has the habit of listening and asking just one or two questions plumb to the point – and Roger Gretton.'

'Roger! Good Lord, how?'

'He was elected this year to fill the annual vacancy. Your guess is as good as mine what Roger will do or how he will go. No one knows which way that cat will jump. Now to more general things. When you go in make sure you're becomingly respectful. Don't put their backs up or you're lost.'

'Will you be able to come in and give me moral support? I'll need it.'

'Not at first, I think. They'll want to see you alone.'

'They'll listen to you more than me.'

'Possibly. We'll just have to see how things run. I've written in as strongly as I can. I'll take care they know I'm on the premises. If they don't ask for me I'll wangle my way in one way or another.'

'Can you tell me a bit more about what it's like?'

'It's sort of formal, informal, if you follow me. They'll tell you the terms of the sitting – that's your application. Then they'll question you. I can't help you there because I don't know how they'll go about that. Each set of stewards has different ideas of conducting an enquiry. It's held in secret, in camera as the lawyers say. Its opponents call it a star chamber but it's not. Often they lean over backwards to be fair. Remember I believe they'll be sympathetic.'

'Here's hoping.'

'Do you want a drink? Jumping powder. I don't recommend it. You want all your wits about you.'

With that we went downstairs to the street. I hadn't slept much the night before, tossing and turning, wondering what questions they would fire at me and, more importantly, how I would answer them. At any rate, I reflected, as I climbed into the Rolls, the tumbril taking me to the place of execution was doing it in style.

It was then long before the Jockey Club moved to Portland Place and their headquarters were still at Newmarket. My heart sank lower and lower as we approached the town, and the fact that we were kept waiting a little while, kicking our heels in an anteroom, didn't do much for my state of nerves. At length I was told I could go up.

'Starter's orders. You're off. Good luck,' Crispin said, giving me his friendly smile.

A steep narrow staircase led to the door of the stewards' room. As I climbed it I could almost hear my knees knocking together. I have since ridden in five Grand Nationals and many times gone out on sketchy jumpers in novice chases, which someone has likened to sitting in a kamikaze with the engine on, but I have never felt so alone and nerve-wracked as I went up those stairs one by one.

At the top across a small landing were the ornate double doors to the stewards' room. As I approached them, wondering whether I was supposed to knock or await a summons, they were thrown open and I was ushered into the star chamber. The whole scene is indelibly implanted in my memory so I had better describe what it was like. Times have changed and I think it is all done by committee now but that was not the way then.

Immediately in front of me was a polished mahogany, horseshoe table. I was positioned to stand at its farther end between the arms of the horseshoe, rather like a felon, I thought afterwards, facing the three stewards who sat at its head. In the centre was the senior steward, Lord Benby, with, on his left, Roger Gretton and, on his right, Lord Giles Tevern. Of Lord Benby I chiefly remember a pair of immense bushy eyebrows and a bald dome; Roger, of course, I knew well by appearance; the third of the trio, Giles Tevern, was slim and erect with a thin pencilled moustache and I remember, ridiculously, thinking of my father's saying that the only incontrovertible rule of betting was never to back a jockey with a moustache. There was also a flunkey in attendance, someone from Weatherby's, I believe, who acted as a sort of secretary. I hadn't long to take in these details for almost immediately the senior steward addressed me. 'We're here today, Mr de Lacey,' he said, 'to consider the application for the lifting of the warning-off notice imposed on Colonel de Lacey as a result of the drug administered to the colt Bloemfontein when in his care and under his supervision. You make this application on his behalf?'

'Yes, sir,' I said. Oddly, rather like riding a race when the flag falls or the gate goes up, I suddenly felt my nerves go away from me and I could concentrate on the job in hand.

The chairman continued. 'Your father, we are informed and accept, is seriously ill at the moment and cannot make the application himself. You will understand that it is a most unusual one. Your mother, I believe, has given her consent and authority for you to act.'

'There's a letter on the file, my lord,' the flunkey said.

'Very well, now I just want to ask you a question about yourself before we proceed. What is your present position?'

'I am at Melton Mowbray, sir, as a learner with the veterinary staff.'

'The horse in health, accident and disease, I take it.' He smiled as he said this. 'Then I assume I am correct in saying you have no personal interest in the matter in that you have no intention or ambition, at the present at all events, of applying for a trainer's licence yourself?'

'No, sir. Not at all. In my spare time I'm trying to become a reasonably competent rider.'

I thought I saw a sympathetic smile flicker for an instant across Giles Tevern's rather saturnine features when I said that, but it was Roger who, to my surprise, spoke next.

'Then surely this application is misconceived,' he said. 'Your father is, to put it plainly, totally and permanently incapacitated. He will never, as I understand it, train again. It gives me no pleasure to say this, but the application appears to me to be quite pointless and indeed without merit. The rule is there.'

So, I thought, Roger, for whatever reason, has for once come firmly off the fence and, if there was to be opposition clear and strong, that was where it would come from. But Lord Benby was speaking again. 'Mr Gretton has a valid point,' he said. 'In the tragic circumstances surrounding your father it cannot benefit him. Briefly then, why is this application made?'

This was the very question I had been dreading. I had racked my brains how to answer it without appearing to criticise or offend them. I wished I had Crispin there to help. But I had to make up my mind what to say. In the few seconds that were left to me to do so I had to decide quickly – like riding a race, I thought wryly. There was a pause while they all stared at me in silence. Suddenly I knew what I had to do. I'd take the plunge and risk it. 'It's to clear his name,' I said.

'Are you suggesting that the notice in the Calendar was misleading,' Roger said, menacingly it seemed to me.

I was into it now and had to go on with it. 'I can only say, my lords and Mr Gretton,' I said, 'that press and public have placed the blame on my father and that is the way it has been widely accepted, and he himself, in the position he is, can do nothing to convince them otherwise.'

'We're not here to cater for press and public,' Roger said contemptuously.

It was Tevern who then intervened. 'Wait a bit,' he said. 'I seem to remember that at the original hearing before us Crispin Merevale, who was chairman of the stewards at Ascot, gave evidence. He very strongly stressed that when De Lacey was before the local stewards he had quizzed him thoroughly as to his stable security and he was satisfied that no blame could attach to him. In fact as I now recall he said that he wanted that recorded. And now I understand that he has written in supporting the application.'

Lord Benby rustled through the papers in front of him and found Crispin's letter. Peering into his half-glasses he took a moment to read it. 'That is true,' he said. 'He repeats it here. I wasn't at that hearing. You stood in for me, Roger. Do you remember it?'

'Vaguely,' Roger said.

'There should be a record of that original decision which was I presume conveyed to Dick de Lacey at the hearing,' Lord Benby said, and then, turning to the flunkey: 'Have you got it, Masters?'

The flunkey produced a massive leatherbound book. Opening it he leafed through the pages, found the appropriate entry and placed it before the chairman. 'It's here all right,' he said when he had read it, 'with the recommendation or whatever ye call it, as Crispin suggested. Let me have another look at that warning-off notice.' Again he rustled through his papers. The flunkey leant over and helped him. 'Here it is, my lord,' he said.

Having read it, Lord Benby frowned. 'It does differ from the record,' he said. 'What De Lacey was told at the hearing, while not actually exonerating him, which it couldn't I suppose, under the rule, does make clear that he was absolved from blame and that it was the rule and the rule only which convicted him. The warning-off notice omits that and it could be interpreted that he was guilty of the offence. There's something therefore in what this young man says. Do you know anything about the omission, Roger?'

'No, I don't, and I cannot see it makes any difference. As I said before, the rule is there.'

'Yes, but what about justice being done, and also being seen to be done. Do you know, I think we should see Crispin. Is he here?' He looked at me.

'Yes, sir,' I said. 'He drove me down.'

'Did he?' He addressed the flunkey. 'Ask Sir Crispin if he'd be good enough to come into us,' he said.

In a few moments Crispin entered. He was immediately asked to sit down and a seat pulled out for him along one arm of the horseshoe. I was left standing in the felon's position, but never was I so glad to see the arrival of anyone.

'Good of you to come, Crispin,' Lord Benby said. 'Now, about this application. You have written a very strong letter in support of it. De Lacey here maintains, as I understand it, that the notice as published could suggest that his father was involved in the doping. I'm told that you went into the matter fully at Ascot and were satisfied he had no part in it – as we would expect, I may say – and again at the hearing: here you wanted it made clear that the warning-off was only by reason of the rule.'

'That is so. I was firmly of the opinion and belief that Colonel de Lacey could in no way be implicated and I hoped, indeed I think I asked, that the notice when published, if it could not say so directly, would indicate that it came about solely by reason of the mandatory provisions of the rule.'

'Well, it didn't. Can either of you throw any further light on this?'

It was Roger again who answered. He had, it seemed, taken on the role of prosecutor. 'How could we?' he said. 'We don't draft the notices, as you know. But I'd like to say that the real culprit, if there is one, has never been found or identified.'

'Oh, but he has,' Crispin put in. 'I think Mr de Lacey has a document which I believe you should see.'

It may sound all but incredible but, what with nerves, trying to concentrate and understand what was going on, and grapple with Roger's all but open hostility, I had forgotten the existence of the affidavit. Now I took it out and unfolded it.

'Hand it in,' Crispin said.

The flunkey came round and, taking the document, brought it to Lord Benby.

'What is this?' he said as he took it. 'A solicitor's letter. Harding, Hensley and Barton, I see. Gervase Carleton, otherwise known as Vincent Rossiter,' he read aloud. 'Gervase Carleton, God bless my soul, what next.' And then, as he read on, 'Good God!' He finished reading in silence and then sat back. 'You'd both better read this,' he said, handing it first to Tevern.

When it came to Roger he looked at the solicitors' letter. 'Who are these people?' he said. 'They may be any East End fly-by-nights –'

'They're a perfectly reputable firm,' Lord Benby said. 'They've been my family's men of business for generations. I think you may take it that it's quite genuine.'

'Gervase Carleton, that's Rupert Carleton's younger brother,' Tevern said.

'Yes, I'm afraid it is,' was Lord Benby's comment. He said then, looking at me: 'You've no information as to who instructed the solicitors?' he asked. 'It was not yourself, I take it.'

'No, sir,' I said. 'I only got it by special delivery this morning.'

'The solicitors won't tell, that's one thing certain,' Tevern said. 'They're hedged about by all sorts of privilege. But there's one other matter. I've heard a rumour that the Prince of Wales is interested in this case.' He looked at Crispin. 'Can you throw any light on that? Has he mentioned it to you or have you discussed it with him?'

'I have, informally,' was Crispin's reply.

'Did he express an opinion? What did he say?' Lord Benby asked.

'Surely this must be pure hearsay,' Roger interjected.

'Are you suggesting I'm lying?' Crispin said dangerously.

Roger went into retreat immediately. 'No, no, not at all, I assure you,' he protested. 'I only meant – '

'Hearsay be damned,' Benby growled. 'This isn't a court of law and the Prince is a member here in any case. What did he say, Crispin?'

'I asked him if he would give it his support and I give you his exact words: "I should think I jolly well will," was what he said.'

'He put nothing in writing,' Roger muttered.

'I believe that is not his practice,' Crispin said, coldly. 'But since you ask I should perhaps add one other thing.' He looked hard at Roger.

'What is that?' asked Lord Benby.

'He said he wondered could there be anyone else behind it as it was all a bit fishy to his mind.'

I thought I saw Roger shrink into himself at that. Certainly there was no further comment from him but there was from another.

'That struck me, too,' Tevern said. 'Especially in view of the tip-off to you which you mentioned at the hearing in your evidence before us, Crispin, and in your recent letter.

And there is in that affidavit a reference to Carleton being rewarded. I made a note of that just now. It all seems a bit fishy to me, too.'

'It's suspicious certainly,' Lord Benby said. 'Perhaps we'll take it into account. Well, then, if there are no more questions – no? Perhaps then, gentlemen, if you would be good enough to wait in the committee room we should be able to let you have a decision shortly.'

Once more we sat and once more we waited. The minutes passed interminably and no summons came to return. 'They're taking the hell of a time,' I said. 'What do you think they'll do?'

'They won't throw us out flat, I'll bet on that. If that was in their minds they'd have us in to tell us it by now. They're arguing about something.'

'With Roger for the prosecution.'

'It looks very like it, and what's more it's not his form. I had a good look at him when I was telling them about the Prince of Wales. Do you know I thought he looked frightened. I don't understand it.'

I thought I was beginning to do just that and could enlighten him, but I held my peace. 'Why can't they hurry up,' I said. 'I thought going in was bad but this hanging about is worse. Like going out for a race magnified ten times.'

'Wait till you get to Aintree,' he said with a smile. 'Ah, here we are.'

The door opened and we were summoned once more to the stewards' room. This time I wasn't in the felon's position but was told I could sit. The flunkey actually pulled out a chair for me. I hoped it was a good omen.

Lord Benby peered at us over his half-glasses. He had a sheet of paper in his hand, notes of the verdict, I assumed, as I waited on the edge of my seat for what it was to be. Then he addressed us.

'We have discussed this case, application, perhaps I

should say, gentlemen,' he said. 'And have come to a certain conclusion. Because, however, of the unusual nature of the matter and – ' here he glanced down at his notes ' – because of the apparent confusion which arose between what was recorded at the hearing before the stewards previously and the subsequent notice in the Calendar we have decided it would be prudent to obtain legal advice as to the published wording of our decision. This is solely to avoid any further confusion or misapprehension concerning what we have decided and what we intend to convey. As soon as we receive such advice, and we shall seek expedition, the notice will appear in the Calendar.'

'But – ' Crispin said.

Lord Benby held up an admonitory hand. 'I'm sorry, Crispin,' he said. 'That's all I can say at the moment.'

'So we still have to wait,' Crispin said to me as we drove back.

'Days and weeks perhaps.'

'I think not. There's been a lot of talk about your father's warning off and news of your application has already filtered out in the way these things do. They'll want it in quickly to clear the air and put the matter at rest once and for all. If Benby puts the pressure on his men of business and says he wants a quick answer he'll get it.'

And with that, I had, for the moment, to be content.

Crispin dropped me at my rooms. On my table were two letters delivered by the afternoon post offering me point-to-point rides and a belated – typically – telegram from my mother wishing me luck. I ought to write to her, I thought, telling her in detail of the events of the day. That telegram and its message reminded me of Val's card which I had hurriedly stuffed into my pocket when the affidavit came. Now I took it out along with my father's gold cigarette case which occupied the same pocket. Lighting a cigarette I looked at Val's card and read its brief message. How kind and thoughtful it was of her to send it, I said to myself, and perhaps, who knew, it had brought me luck. Then, turning it over, I glanced at the address. As I did so my eyes fell on the cigarette case lying beside it and then went back to the card. Something clicked in my mind as I read the lettered words. There could be no mistake. A cold hand closed round my heart.

20

It had been a strange week of waiting I thought as I crossed the paddock at Aintree on my way to change for the Foxhunters', and the ultimate test of Prospero – and myself. First and foremost in all our minds was the progress or lack of it of Prospero and what was going on inside his head. 'We'll know more after Colwall,' Flinty had said earlier. But the trouble was, we didn't. It was a disaster. Colwall Park has long since disappeared from the fixture list. In a rural and picturesque setting near the Malvern Hills it was far from being one of the lesser gaff courses and was well appointed for its time. The fences were stiff but fair and the three miles of the hunter chase made it for our purpose an ideal of what is now called a prep race for the sterner task to come. Its date, too, soon after Cheltenham, meant that there would not be many runners: in fact there were eight, none of them of much account since the cracks had mostly been at Prestbury Park. As a result Prospero, by reason of his point-to-point form I imagine, was made favourite, if an uneasy one.

Flinty couldn't travel so I had to see to the saddling and the declarations. I hadn't therefore had much time to assess the other runners but down at the start I surveyed them. They were a fairly motley lot but the one which drew my attention was a big, slab-sided brute named, as I learnt from its rider – and aptly enough, as I was to find out – Blunderbus II. He was in a highly excitable state, sweating and squealing and generally dancing about. His rider, a youth of about my age, was in much the same case. He was green about the gills as we used to say, talking very fast and excitedly to anyone near him. 'I can't hold this big bastard,' I heard him say. 'It's my father, he makes me ride him. He was as near as a toucher away with me coming down, only I pointed him up someone's bottom. I can't hold one side of him. Oh, my God, we're off!'

We were and at first all went well. I had Prospero in front, lobbing along and jumping perfectly. So far as I could tell his rider had succeeded in anchoring Blunderbus but coming events were to prove me wrong. It was at the first of the ditches it happened. I was letting Prospero 'have a look at it' or thought I was, when he came up behind me at a rush, totally and entirely out of control. I don't think the horse even saw the fence. He hit it about halfway up with an almighty smash and turned over straight in my path. There was nothing we could do about it even if Prospero had been clever enough to try, which at that stage of his career he wasn't. We went into a tangle of legs and fallen horse and down we came.

For me it was the softest of falls. After the field had gone by I got to my feet cursing in fury. The other chap didn't get up. He was lying a few yards away, groaning, and shortly afterwards was carted off in the ambulance. I never saw him again and don't know what happened to him. Perhaps his father directed his energies elsewhere.

Prospero was none the worse and ate up that evening, but that did little to salve our disappointment, nor did Flinty's laconic comment, 'That's racing,' when told of the day's events. He had seemed preoccupied and, to me, from what I had seen of them, there had appeared to be an air of tension or premonition, perhaps, about the little coterie of friends. Not that I had much time to spare for thinking about anything except myself: the growing certainty hovering in my mind that I had found the key to all that had happened; the anxiety about the ride on Prospero ('You won't sleep for a week,' Billy Burton-Brown had cheerfully assured me when discussing Aintree after one point-to-point); and hanging over me the result, whatever it might be, of the enquiry. On the Wednesday I had rides in a point-to-point and the following day, Thursday, saw the opening of the National Meeting.

I didn't expect to be asked in the Royal party, nor was I, but Captain Pat, kindly and loyal as ever, took me under his wing.

Pirate, I remember, was laid up. I can't recall just why; I think his war wound was troubling him. There was much to do at the Remounts so we decided to give the first day a miss and reserve ourselves for Grand National day, then a Friday, and, of course, the Saturday, when the Foxhunters' was run.

On the Thursday morning I went early to Captain Pat's office to see if I could lend a hand and also to find out if by chance there was anything in the Calendar about our enquiry since Thursday was publication day.

'Are you feeling all right?' Captain Pat greeted me. 'I've thought you were looking a bit under the weather recently. You're not doing anything silly like wasting, are you?'

'No,' I said. 'I'm not doing that.'

'Well then, here's something to give you that Kruschen feeling – ' (I'd better explain: 'Kruschen' was the name of a popular brand of liver salts much advertised by drawings of a man, alive with health, jumping a five-barred gate and carrying the slogan, 'Gives that Kruschen feeling'.) He had an opened copy of the Calendar in front of him. Passing it across to me he indicated an entry with his finger. Lord Benby's request for expedition had been effective. I read:

> The Stewards of the Jockey Club, in view of further evidence now made available to them and for the purpose of clarification only, desire to state that no personal involvement was ascribed to Colonel D. de Lacey in the warning-off notice required by Rule 176 regarding the administration of a drug to the horse Bloemfontein when under his care. The said warning-off notice is withdrawn.

I read it twice, taking it in. When I put it down I felt that one of the weights had been lifted from my mind.

'That's what you came for, isn't it?' Captain Pat said. 'Now go and win your race and you won't call the King your uncle.'

'I must send a telegram to my mother,' I said.

He pushed a pad of telegram forms towards me. 'When you've done that,' he said, 'we'll start our rounds. I've got our vouchers, by the way.'

Those were the days when vouchers signed by two accredited persons (I forget exactly who) were required for entry into the members' enclosure and access to the County Stand where a standard of male dress was expected.

I suppose few save some old stiffs like me now remember the supremacy of the Grand National Meeting as it was held in those far-off days, the glamour and excitement of it all. It was the acme of the steeplechasing scene and, indeed, of the winter social scene, too. Special trains were run from London and other centres and people made up parties to travel on them to the course. There were then none of the 'semi-classic' chases in the fixture list, run on park courses throughout the season to attract the top horses, as there are now. The Cheltenham Gold Cup was in its infancy. The National was the be-all and the end-all, the culmination of ambition and achievement, the crown every owner, rider and trainer strove to gain.

All the best and indeed some of the worst horses were aimed at it. Endless were the discussions as to what was 'a National type' and deep were the pockets out of which money was poured in trying to find one. No other race came near it in either prestige or prize money. It inspired myth and legend and had an atmosphere all of its own which largely disappeared after World War Two and the rise of the Gold Cup. Its winner, wherever he came from in the handicap, was the hero not only of the day and hour but of the year. The celebrations on the Friday night in the Adelphi Hotel were something out of the ordinary even in that free-spending era.

And the Foxhunters' Chase then run over the full National distance of four miles 386 yards was its amateur equivalent as a test of hardihood in horse and man. The fences then were great green straight-up barriers with none of your present day sloped off aprons and softened tops to facilitate some damn cast-offs from the flat and pacify the do-gooders. Horses in those days were, many of them, built like battle-ships to stand and survive if they could the shock of impact with those unforgiving obstacles, but whatever they were they had to gallop and jump if they were to win or be placed at Aintree.

Captain Pat had engaged a room for me near the course. 'You're not going to join those celebrations in the Adelphi on Friday night, my lad,' he said. 'Not if I have to chain you to the bed. You may not sleep a whole lot but you'll be fit and well the morning of the race if I have anything to do with it.'

I don't think I have ever felt so lonely in my life as I dined alone in those rooms. There were battles yet to come, and a confrontation I dreaded above all things to be made. I had no one to talk to or confide in. Even if there had been a confidant, I could not share what I knew or thought I knew until I had made certain. I had to solve this one alone, even as I had to ride Prospero alone and find the answer to his problems by myself. There was never anyone behind you in the saddle and I remembered and repeated to myself Billy Burton-Brown's words of wisdom: 'Look after yourself, no one else will.'

To distract my mind I turned once more to the form book and the entries for the Foxhunters'. There were eighteen probables, Billy's The Clinker and Mike Annerley's Raison d'Etre amongst them. I saw, too, that Mr T. Satterthwaite had a runner, Kindly Note. I didn't need a form book to tell me what I already knew, that Billy had duly won the United Hunts at Cheltenham and Raison d'Etre had been unplaced in the National Hunt Chase, but I thought I'd check on Kindly Note. Doing so I found that he had run in an amateur's steeplechase back in February. Its rider then was Mr R. Carleton, and as I looked at the entry I began to wonder. When, next morning, I opened the *Sporting Life* and saw the confirmation of Mr R. Carleton as the rider of Kindly Note in the Foxhunters', it didn't do anything for me at all.

But Prospero moved smoothly and well in the early morning warm-up, showing no signs of temperament, and the feeling of strength combined with unleashed power beneath me helped to build my confidence. It was while I was walking back from this that I heard a voice hailing me. 'Goin' ter win today, guv?' it asked.

Turning, I found myself face to face with the cheerful countenance of Ginger Elton. 'I'll tell you that in a few hours' time,' I said. 'What are you doing here? Mr Connaughton hasn't a runner, has he?'

'Mr Connaughton, nah. I'm not there any more. A new

batch of lads was comin' from Ireland. He told me since I'd bin hob nobbin' with royalty I was too high an' mighty altogether to ride 'is 'orses an' he chucked me out.'

'Who are you with now?'

'No one, guv, I've gone free lance.'

'Good lord, that's taking a bit of a chance, isn't it?'

'Things are tough OK, but there's allus room at the top, isn't there? You wouldn't have a quid or two about you to spare, would you, guv?'

It was he who had found Rossiter for us, and had it not been for him we would still be back where we had started. Besides, I liked his cheeriness and I wished him well. I felt in my pockets and dug out a fiver.

'Thanks, guv,' he said. 'Best o' luck this afternoon.' He moved away and then stopped. 'That school we 'ad,' he said. 'I was talkin' to one of Mr Burton-Brown's lads that came with the 'orses. He told me they stayed on to see 'ow you went. That one of theirs, The Clinker, isn't it, he said he's the 'ell of a 'orse. But 'e needs to be held up. He's only got one run and it's 'ard to get it right. There's a long run in here, guv. He'll be comin' after you if yer in front. Thought that might help.'

I was digesting this piece of information when I was joined by Crispin Merevale.

'Who was that you were talking to?' he asked curiously.

'A lad called Ginger Elton. He was with my father when the crash came,' I said. 'It was he who put us on to Rossiter. He's gone free lance now to try to make his way. He's had a few rides and I've seen him. He looks good. Perhaps you'd give him a chance sometime,' I added, remembering that he had the name of being kind and encouraging to the young.

'I'll bear it in mind,' he said. (He did, too, and gave him his start. A few seasons later when Elton was amongst the top ten in the jockey's list we would sometimes laugh together about how we had met and he had made his way.)

'I've been away in Scotland or I would have been in touch before,' he added. 'You've seen the Calendar?'

'Yes,' I said. 'It's a marvellous result – thanks to you.'

'Thanks to Benby I should think. We were lucky. He has always disliked that rule and he is trying to bring about a change. The trouble is he's only in the chair for a year and then someone else comes in who has other ideas.'

'I can imagine,' I said, thinking of Roger Gretton.

'It may take time,' he went on. 'You know, that mysterious affidavit didn't do us any harm at all. Ah, here's someone who perhaps can throw some light on that.'

Charles Ormsby was strolling towards us, a copy of the Calendar under his arm. 'You've seen this,' he said to me holding it up. 'Satisfied, I hope?'

'More than that,' I said. 'And as I've just been saying, it's all due to you both. Otherwise I couldn't have done anything.'

'That was a very interesting document which arrived in De Lacey's rooms the morning of the hearing,' Crispin said. 'A sort of strange coincidence, you might say, or very accurate timing, maybe. You wouldn't know anything about that or how it was obtained, would you, Charles?'

Ormsby's smile, like that of the Heathen Chinee in the poem, was childlike and bland. 'I can't imagine what you're referring to,' he said.

'I rather thought you wouldn't,' Crispin said. 'But perhaps you can help us on another matter. Gervase Carleton – just where is he now and what has happened to him?'

'As a matter of fact, I can. By one of those coincidences you mentioned I was just about to tell you. Unregrettably, I suppose you might say, and unregretted certainly, he has left the country for the country's good – and he won't be coming back.'

'But – ' Crispin said, and then stopped.

'Quite so,' Ormsby said, and I noticed that the grim look I had first observed in Gervase's flat had returned to his features. 'Do you know, I don't think I would pursue the matter any further if I were you – either of you.' He gave a brief nod and then wandered off.

Crispin's eyes followed him as he went. 'That's the way it goes,' he said. 'Some go up, some go down, and some just go away. But for you it's over, isn't it, and it couldn't have turned out better.'

But of course he was wrong. For me it was far from over. There was the unfinished business in which I had become entangled to be cleared up, the how and the why of what had brought my father to the state in which he was now; and there was Prospero's race to come.

Somehow I got through the intervening hours before I entered the weighing room to change and weigh out. It was a mixed card in those days and the only other jumping race on the Saturday was the Liverpool Hurdle. The atmosphere in the jockeys' room before a race over the big fences was then, and I imagine still is, despite all the changes, like nowhere else in the racing world. The tension is almost palpable: people talk to each other hurriedly or in jerks or fall glumly silent. There are frequent visits to the loo and on that day I remember someone in one corner was being quietly sick into his handkerchief.

Nothing, however, could quell Billy Burton-Brown's spirits or ebullience. He had been up all night or most of it, he confided in me, at the Adelphi celebrations. 'I've a head like an over-ripe melon and a mouth like the bottom of a parrot's cage,' he said. 'Oh, my God, why do I do these things?'

It was then that Rupert Carleton came in. He stood in the doorway, surveying the room and all that was in it as if he owned them, which was the way he had. His eyes fell on me and he strode over to where I was trying to master my shaking fingers into securing my scarf round my neck. He didn't take long to come to the point. 'What have you done with Gervase, you little rat?' he said.

I stared at him in amazement.

'Don't play the idiot boy with me,' he snarled. 'He's disappeared and you're behind it somehow. I should have done you before. You look out. I'll get you for this, if not today, later. You wait, you little swine.'

He moved off but not before I had time to recall that Charles Ormsby had said that the toughest of us all have our weak spots and the affection he felt for Gervase was his. I noticed, too, that he had put on weight during his absence from racing. His face was fleshier and didn't have that tight, hard look which comes from the constant riding of work and races. But his presence and his warning were not the best of preparations for the next half hour, and a few minutes later we were called out.

They were in the ring, waiting, Val, Flinty and HRH, together in a little group. I walked up to them, touched the brim of my cap with my whip and gave the 'half nod, half bow' described by Pirate and which protocol demanded, to the Prince. I was rewarded by a brief smile but immediately I was struck by how quiet they were, not chatting or joking amongst themselves as I would have expected; even Flinty's accustomed cheery grin was absent. 'What can I tell you,' he said to me after a moment. 'You know him better than any of us. Keep him there or thereabouts. Let him run his own race. That's how you've won on him before.'

'You will win this race for me, won't you, Danny,' Val said.

The saddling bell rang then. HRH walked with me to the horse. This in itself was a sort of accolade. He could and perhaps should have remained aloof and on his dignity, but that was not his way.

'Good luck,' he said when Flinty put me up. There was a wistful air about him as he added quietly, looking up at me: 'I only wish I was coming with you.'

A Mersey mist was hanging over the course as I rode out on to it past the packed stands, and it occurred to me that those on them would see little of the race that day save what happened in front of their eyes. For myself I was in a tangle of emotions. Nerves had gone as they mostly did once I was on the back of a horse but something must have happened to cast a cloud over my friends and there was Rupert and his threats to be borne in mind. If I had time to spare in the race for anything other than looking after myself, I had better watch out for him. I had memorised his colours, green with a white sash, and to my dismay when I lined up in the middle I found them beside me. We formed a ragged line and the starter mounted his rostrum. His hand was on the lever. Out of the corner of my eye I saw Rupert edging forward.

'C'mon, jockeys.' The starter's hand went down, the gate flew up – and Rupert pulled straight across me. I can hear his hoarse laugh yet. He was a far better rider than I. His horse was perfectly balanced and he was off and away. As for me it was enough to make me snatch Prospero up and to throw him out of his stride. By the time we got going most of the field was streaming along ahead. There was no hope now of lying well up from the start. Placed somewhere at the back of the mid-division before we had got to the Melling road, I knew that my worst fears had been realised. Out of the place where he wanted to be, Prospero was sulking. Plodding away he showed none of his accustomed freedom and fire, and as we approached the first I wondered apprehensively if he would bury me. My fears were unjustified; jumping was what he liked and enjoyed; he stood back and threw it behind him as fluently as ever.

So it went on. At Becher's he never touched a twig and the drop meant nothing to him. But we were toiling. 'Let him run his own race,' were my instructions. I knew they were right and knew instinctively too that were I to get at him in any way it would only make him sulk the more. On this of all days he was having one of his moods, just because he was not up there in the firing line. Rupert's manoeuvre had worked better than he can have thought. There was nothing for it but to sit and suffer – and hope.

We floated effortlessly over the Chair which I have always thought the most difficult fence on the course whatever they say about Becher's. And then, as we galloped on, and to this day I cannot explain it, suddenly, nearing the stands, Prospero appeared to wake up. Whether it was the rumble of noise from the enclosures or the sight of the crowds packed and expectant, I don't know, but all at once it was as if he changed gear. His stride lengthened and he landed yards over the water before going out into the country again. There was a feeling of unleashed power and I knew that once more I had a racehorse under me.

Gradually we began to pick up our field. His jumping, as always, helped, since we gained lengths in the air. Unwittingly – and unwillingly – I had done what the experts said should be done at Aintree over the full course – ride it like a hunt first time and then go after your race. Prospero, too, had conserved both of our energies, and some of the others were tiring. He made nothing of the second Becher's and at the Canal Turn, to my astonishment, I found myself in the thick of it, amongst the select few. The leaders, though, one of whom was Mike Annerley, were well ahead. Where Rupert and Billy were I had no idea.

Coming to the third from home I was clear of the pack but with little hope of catching the two in front who, if anything, had increased their lead. It's a formidable obstacle to meet towards the end of a long race, for it is five feet high and has a five foot six inch ditch on the landing side. Prospero, however, had all his running still in him and I went into it full of confidence. As I did so I heard a shout behind me and on my left. 'Pull out! Pull out, you little bastard.' It was Rupert.

He was coming on my inside. That he meant having me in some way, foot beneath the stirrup, perhaps, as he bowled me over, I had no doubt. But he hadn't two stone in hand. At that stage of the race he had precious little if I was any judge, and he wasn't as fit as he might have been. Thoughts of my father lying there like a vegetable, and what he had done to make him so, flashed through my mind as I heard that hated voice. He thought he could do what he liked with me. It was either him or me and I had learnt to look after myself. I slammed the door in his face.

There was another shout and an almighty crash as he went out through the wing. I hadn't then nor have I now any remorse for what I did and its consequences. He had taken his chance and paid for it.

Prospero's strength and his jumping, bless his heart, kept us both upright. We survived the far side ditch with only a nod.

But the race seemed long gone from me. The two in front appeared even farther away. Races, however, can change in the instant. At the second last both of them came down and I was left in front. There was the pack, what was left of them, behind me, and Billy, too, to be reckoned with, if he was still standing. Remembering Elton's warning of that one devastating run of his and Prospero's doubtful courage, I kicked for home to put as much daylight between us as possible. I had to get over the final two fences safely, and with Prospero still full of running and where, through no skill of mine, he wanted to be, I did. We landed over the last and then that long, interminable straight stretched in front of me.

At the elbow I was still in front, apparently unchallenged. But Prospero's stride was beginning to shorten. Where were the others? More important, where was Billy? Then I felt rather than heard that there was someone behind me, someone who was coming at me. It could only be Billy. I sneaked a look under my arm (which I shouldn't have) and there he was bearing down on me, unleashing his run.

He was gaining with every stride. Would Prospero hold on? He heard those hooves, too. Would he pack it in? He seemed to be falling apart beneath me. Oh, Christ, where was the post?

I prayed Billy might be feeling the effects of the night before. He was driving for all he was worth, but perhaps he'd timed it wrong, perhaps he'd tire before the horse. Would Prospero pack it in?

I have a theory that some horses who are not genuine battlers won't actually compound until they are collared. The threat behind them keeps them going. It is cowardice not courage that urges them on. So it was, I'll always believe, with Prospero that day. He rallied, gave a last desperate surge. Billy could get no further. In the little that was left, Prospero held on. We passed the post a diminishing length to the good.

The first thing I remember was Billy reaching across to take my hand. He was puce in the face, speechless, and blowing more than his horse. 'I thought I had you caught,' he got out between gasps. 'Why the hell didn't you stay at home?'

Minutes later I was getting down in the hallowed winners' enclosure under the canopy and Val was throwing her arms round me and kissing me. Then, as I sat on a bench in the changing room and someone was opening champagne, Flinty came in to tell me that I was wanted in the royal box. Perhaps I should describe it as the box where royalty was, since so far as I can remember there was then no royal box as such. The royal party for the Grand National at Windsor stayed with Lord Derby at Knowsley and were entertained in his private box. They, however, with the other grandees, left after the National. They were not present on the Saturday when, on this occasion at any rate, the box was turned over to the Prince of Wales and his party, and his standard flew.

There weren't many people about when I got there. As I've said before, HRH, who I think was in many ways a shy man, did not like large gatherings; he had enough of them, he said, on royal tours and official functions and, of course, anyone who had the remotest connections with the press on account of the way they pestered and persecuted him, was anathema.

Flinty was there as ever, dispensing drinks and hospitality, and Val, and, amongst the throng, Roger Gretton. He came up to me immediately, smiling his ingratiating smile. 'You'll have seen the Calendar,' he said. 'I was very glad we were able to do that for your father and the family. You may have been surprised at some of the questions I asked but, you know, someone has to play the *advocatus diaboli* at these enquiries, as I'm sure you'll understand.'

I wasn't at all sure what an *advocatus diaboli* was and I felt like kicking his teeth in; fortunately I was spared having to reply by Flinty coming up to me. 'He wants to see you,' he said. 'He's outside.' He nodded to the front of the box.

I found him there, alone, staring out at the course. 'Well done, Danny,' he said, and, looking back, I think it was the first time he had addressed me directly by my Christian name which weren't, in any event, bandied about so freely in those days. 'You've pulled it off. Lucky chap. Everything is in front of you now. Make the most of it while you can.'

There was about him an air of indefinable sadness, as if something was coming to an end. He stared out over the abandoned, empty racecourse, its huge fences, great green bulwarks in the gathering dusk. 'A battleground for bravery,' he said, almost to himself, quoting – and I'm sure it was unbeknownst to him since he never to my knowledge opened a book – Will Ogilvie's lines about Leicestershire. He was silent again then; the moments passed and I was wondering if I was dismissed when he spoke, still looking out over the course, his hands on the rail in front of him: 'They're going to make me give it all up,' he said.

I hesitated and then, greatly daring, and I can only think it was the euphoria of winning the race that impelled me to it, I said: 'Is it your father, sir?'

'No,' he said. 'It is my mother. I can refuse my mother nothing.'

This is hindsight but even then I think I saw dimly that deep in him he longed for matriarchy. It was his and his mother's tragedy and, I think, the nation's, and certainly that of all who loved him, that he found it in someone who I truly believe never really cared for him. She added to the domination he longed for the spice of sex and so captured him and held him in thrall all the rest of his days.

We stood together in silence for a moment while, still motionless, he stared out over the battlefield. Then there was a stir in the box behind us and he turned to go. As I stood back to allow him to pass he paused to give me that brief, intimate smile of his which somehow captured all his charm and which once received was never forgotten. 'There's nothing like it, is there,' he said. 'Don't let anyone ever tell you otherwise.' Then he was gone.

Following him I came face to face with Val. 'Thanks, Danny,' she said quietly. 'You've been avoiding me. Why?'

'You should have kissed the horse,' I said. 'He won it. I didn't.' Our eyes met, and I knew then that she knew what I had guessed and that my guess was right and I knew she was going to be hurt and that I would hurt her more and that there was nothing I could do about it. Without waiting for a reply I went on: 'I want to see you urgently and alone,' I said.

'Very well,' she said. 'We're going somewhere, I'm not sure where but I'll be back. Come to Huntercombe.'

'Tomorrow?'

'Yes, before noon.' Then she, too, was gone.

Captain Pat and I dined together that night at the Bell in Melton. Champagne flowed and we discussed the race endlessly as one always will.

'What about the horse, Prospero, now,' he said.

'I wouldn't be surprised if he never won another race,' I said. 'Except, perhaps, on his own terms. Billy should have won it. He might if he hadn't been up all the night before.'

Captain Pat smiled. 'Bacchus, or so I've heard it said, always renders his bill. And it's as true in racing as in other matters. Rupert Carleton is badly smashed up.' He looked hard at me. 'Did you know that?'

'No,' I said. 'I didn't.' In all the flush and flash of victory I had not thought to ask and no one had told me. 'How bad is he?'

'Pretty bad. He's unconscious and will be for some time. There is a fractured skull and multiple injuries to his back. I don't know the details.'

'Will he live?'

'They think so. If he wants to when he comes round and they tell him what the future holds. You didn't give him much room.'

'My father didn't get any room at all,' I said. 'Anyway, how did you know what I did?'

'I was down at the last fence and could see it. You were lucky there was that mist and no view from the stewards' box, and that there aren't stipendiary stewards here as there are in India, where I did most of my racing.'

'He was going where he had no business to be,' I said.

'And you are growing up,' he said.

It was brandy time by now. The waiter had placed a bottle marked 'Extra' on the table before us beside our coffee. 'With the compliments of the management,' he had said. I poured myself a stiff measure while Captain Pat surveyed me closely.

'You've won all along the line,' he said. 'You've cleared your father's and your family's name; you've won the race of your life; they're calling you the find of the season amongst GR's; you're something of a Royal favourite and you don't seem very happy about it. Is it Rupert?'

'No,' I said. 'It's not Rupert. He got what was coming to him.'

It was true all he said. Everything had gone my way these past weeks. I'd won the enquiry and the race and the whole thing was dust and ashes in my mouth.

21

Next morning I drove to Huntercombe. Jenks told me her ladyship was in the library. He showed me in and closed the door behind me.

I remember every minute of that interview as if it was yesterday. The library was a compact room panelled in warm oak between its bookcases with their gilded wire fronts. None of the rooms in that house were grandiose or overlarge which was what, I believe, gave it its air of serene comfort. There was a blazing fire in the hearth, two deep sofas flanked it, between them was a low table on which were a small stack of current glossies and the daily papers freshly ironed. She stood by the fire, one hand on the chimney piece, the other with the inevitable cigarette between her fingers.

She was wearing, I remember, one of those tweed costumes of mannish cut, fashionable at the time and made by a male tailor. On her feet were handmade brown brogues.

Above the chimneypiece was the Orpen portrait of her father. He was a handsome man with a snowy moustache like that of Lloyd George from whom he had bought his title. I came to know that portrait well, and whatever

232

motives urged him to that commission I was sure they were not those of pretension. Perhaps, I thought, he wished to secure something besides his fortune for the daughter he loved. Orpen had painted him, as I believe was his wish, not as a racehorse owner surrounded by his winners and his trophies, but in the sombre clothes he had worn as a plain ironmaster, a wing collar and a dark tie. The only hint of his racing successes was a framed painting of a horse in the background. Now he gazed into the room with the same level glance from his grey eyes as his daughter was directing at me, and I knew from the expression in hers that she knew why I had come, just as I recognised that she would never avoid the issue or a hard question as she would never turn away from a difficult fence out hunting.

I took the cigarette case from my pocket and laid it on the table. 'Thank you for returning this,' I said, and then placed beside it the wrapping in which it had come and the card she had sent me wishing me luck. 'They match very neatly,' I said. 'The writing on the card and the print on the wrapping. You're not a very good forger, are you, and you didn't even think to change your ink. I see it now. You were behind it all. You betrayed him. Why did you do it?'

'I wanted him for myself,' she said simply. 'I was in love with him. You ought to understand that. You're half in love with him yourself.'

'There are two of us then,' I said. 'I fell for it and for you. My mother warned me. "The rag, the bone and the hank of hair", she said.'

'That was kind of her. She never liked me nor I her.'

'You used me,' I said. 'You kept me on a string, under surveillance. That was why you took me up, gave me the rides, why you put me up on Prospero. There were others. Why didn't you put up your pal, Rupert? I wondered at the time but I was blinded. It seemed such a marvellous opportunity. I know better now.'

'It wasn't quite like that,' she said. 'It's all been torturing me. But how did you find out?'

'I first began to wonder,' I said, 'when I saw from Charles Ormsby's window you and Rupert together in Newmarket, just after the business of the wire in the fence. Then there was the leaking of that private gallop to Rupert. No one but you could have done it though I tried to persuade myself otherwise.'

She made a small gesture as if to interrupt me, but I had rehearsed what I wanted to say through a sleepless night and again coming down in the car. 'Let me go on,' I said. 'Then, later, when you came to see me after I had been beaten up: I don't believe HRH sent you, that's not his way, you came because you wanted to find out just what had happened and perhaps, I don't know, to discover if I'd talked, told them something they didn't know. I remembered how you had seen Gervase Carleton's photo on my desk after the hunt ball. I guessed then that you had recognised him from the likeness to Rupert and realised I was on to something. And you told me to keep the beating up from the Prince, didn't you? I still don't know why you sent the cigarette case back. To keep me quiet perhaps. "The fool he was and he made his prayer/We called her the woman who did not care." I've memorised those lines – '

'You have a right to be bitter,' she said. 'But you don't know it all. Since you have guessed so much I'll tell it to you.'

We were sitting now, facing each other across the low table, one on each of the deep sofas. She lighted yet another cigarette from a silver box beside the magazines and pushed it towards me. As I took one I looked at her and all my bitterness seemed to have been drained from me by my speech. I found I couldn't be bitter in her presence, a presence which had captured me from the first time I had seen her in HRH's rooms, a moment which seemed aeons away now.

'It all began with Marston,' she said. 'My association with HRH was common knowledge, let's face it, in the Shires and the drawing rooms, and the Court didn't like it. They felt it had gone too far and was getting too deep. Marston sent a message he was coming to see me. He came and it was to warn me off. "If you think he'll marry you, you are out of your mind," he said. I remember those exact words. "Apart from the fact that he is an inconstant man, fickle in his devotions" – they wanted to blacken him in any way they could, you see – "it is out of the question that he should marry a commoner, above all, and I shall put it quite bluntly, one of no family at all."'

'He was playing it pretty tough,' I said.

'They are tough, these people, when they've decided that the stakes are high. "So you want me to give him up," I said. "That," he said, "is our present intention." He didn't mince his words.'

'I met him once with Crispin Merevale. Horrible old snake, I thought.'

'Wait till you hear the rest of it. We were silent for a while, as he pondered something and I thought about asking Jenks to throw him out of the house. Then, finally, he said: "Of course, there is another alternative." I asked him what he meant and here, again, I remember his exact words, they're engraved on my memory. "There is," he said, "a strong feeling at Court and amongst certain of those close to him that he does not want to be King. It is felt, too, and I will say no more than that, that he may not be temperamentally suited to kingship. If he were to be per-suaded upon to renounce, it would solve many problems. Perhaps you could be the means of doing this, and I may say you would be doing Crown, state and yourself a signal service were you to succeed. Think it over, my dear." He actually called me his dear. Then he took his leave.'

'What did you do?' I asked.

'I thought on it.' She looked up at her father's portrait.

'And the more I thought, the more it seemed to give me hope. He'd often said to me how he wished he'd been born without the trappings of royalty, as he called them. I wanted him so desperately, you see.' She drew on her cigarette and continued to stare into the fire. 'I knew him so well I was certain such a suggestion could not come directly from me. Because he's been badgered by the Court and its minions and that old father of his all his life he is deeply suspicious of anyone close to him giving him advice or trying to influence him. That's half of Flinty's secret. He goes with him, gives him his head, never interferes or advises except over horses and racing and he'll take that, though even then Flinty plays it pretty cagey.'

'But where does Rupert come in?' I said.

'I'll tell you in a minute. It really was mad, it seems far madder now than anything Marston thought about marriage, but I was, as I've said, desperate, and love makes us all mad at times, I think. I was sure if I didn't do something Marston and his lackeys would get him away from me and somehow crush me. Rupert was riding for me then. We were fairly close. I didn't know what I know now, that if there are two ways of winning a race, the straight and the crooked, Rupert will always choose the crooked. And that goes for everything in life too. I had no one to turn to. I couldn't mention it to Flinty. I talked to Rupert.'

'So it was Rupert's plan, whatever it was.'

'He said if we could orchestrate the press to step up their campaign about his reckless riding and how it was endangering the throne, it would help to persuade him he wanted his sport more than the throne and he'd chuck the succession away. If he did the press would leave him alone and he could then live like a private person and break his neck without second thoughts if he wanted to. It's all been artificial, you know, that press campaign. Rupert was behind a lot of it. He has always courted the press to see that he got good notices for his good races and to keep quiet when he shopped one or stopped one. That's why he hates this new chap who has come into journalism and who wrote that article about the three brass monkeys. He says he was at Eton with him and he's letting the side down – imagine!'

'I can. But what happened next?'

'He said he wanted money to set it all up and like a fool I gave it to him. I persuaded myself it was harmless but what I didn't realise then was that with Rupert he can never stop. He has to push all he does to its limit and then go beyond it – like his riding. And he was always short of cash from his gambling. He wanted more and more and then he had to bring Roger into it.'

'I thought as much by the way Roger has been carrying on. But how did he do it?'

'Well, they're cousins, you know.'

'No, I didn't know. Good God, is everyone in this set related?'

'Pretty well, you could say, save for me and a few others. Roger, anyway, was easy prey. There's a vindictive streak in Roger. He's never forgotten that row HRH had with him a year or so back on tour. I never knew the details and David never speaks of it, I'll bet it went out of his mind ages ago. Besides, Roger loves intrigue, and I think he sees himself as Marston's successor as the éminence grise.'

'I shouldn't wonder. He's tricky enough for anything.'

'Rupert got him to step up the whispering campaign at Court against David, so that it would be borne to him on the grapevine that none of the present crowd wanted him and would be happy to see him go.'

'And all the time Rupert was bleeding you of money.'

'Yes, and worse. David would enter his horses in point-to-points all over the place to try and put the press hounds off the scent. Several times Rupert tricked me into letting the cat out of the bag and telling him just where he was running. Then, as I discovered too late, he alerted the press to the correct meeting. David was furious and couldn't understand how the press were always there in force when he was riding. It gave Rupert another hold over me. He threatened to tell David it was I who had spilt the beans.'

'He blackmailed you?'

'That's it, damn him. Oh, Danny, why am I telling you all this? I must, I suppose. I owe it to you. I'm coming out of it awfully badly, aren't I? The things we do. Let's have a drink. Maybe that'll help – ' She went to the bell and rang it.

When Jenks came in she told him to bring a bottle of champagne and open it. While this was going on I sat thinking over what she had told me, and when he had gone and the glasses were filled, I said, 'I can understand this, or I think I can. But I have to know – how did my father come into it?'

'That's where it all began to go hideously wrong. The plan Rupert came up with was for Roger to persuade HRH that it would be better for Crown and state, those were the words Marston used to me, and he would be far happier himself if he were to renounce. He'd often said and made little secret of it and they'd heard him say it, that he'd be better off as a "plain lousy aristocrat". They thought they could play on that.'

'It would never have worked, though, would it?'

'It might well have done. At that time he was disgusted with everything except his life here. The press campaign of denigration and ridicule, stoked up by Rupert, was at its height. The stuffier members of the Court whom he disliked and distrusted were pressing him to mend his ways. They wanted to make him their servant, not their master. He can be swayed but not driven. He might have fallen for it if the right approach had been made.'

'And it wasn't, I gather.'

'No. Roger, being Roger, and as devious as he is, reneged at the last moment. He said it wasn't his place to go to the Prince, using as his excuse that there was some personal feeling between them. They'd have to get someone else. They picked the wrong man.'

'My father – '

'He was close to HRH at the time. Roger suggested him, and they went to him. They dressed it up, of course – been taking soundings, disquiet at Court at the prospect, the Monarch worried, Roger at his smoothest, blah blah, blah – '

'And then?'

'Your father saw through it all. I don't think he thought much of either of them anyway. As I said, they picked the wrong man. He exploded. Said he'd see them damned first, and then he threatened to go to HRH and tell him the whole thing and expose them. They were terrified. So was I.'

'So they framed him.'

'Rupert did. Rupert was behind it all. Your father was in the Royal party that Ascot, which made the disgrace all the more spectacular. The press, as you know, made a meal of it.'

'I begin to see it clearly now,' I said, putting the bits and pieces together in my mind. 'When they thought they had him securely disgraced and muzzled they heard he might be taking a libel action where everything could well come out. They lured him to Brighton.'

'Rupert again. It was he who did that. I verily believe he meant to kill your father and dump him and the car over Beachy Head. I once heard him say he wouldn't hesitate to commit murder if it was worth his while and he thought he could get away with it. They had an encounter. Rupert tried to beat him up. He had the stroke and Rupert left him there. He boasted of it to me, thinking if I knew of it, it would increase his hold over me.'

'Don't forget Roger. He was up to the neck in it. He managed to get on to the stewards' panel who sat in judgment on my father. How did he do that?'

'It would be easy enough. They're all chaps together. He

could say to one of the sitting stewards, "You won't want to take this, old boy. Very embarrassing. I'll do it for you."'

'And that would give him access to the draft notice for the Calendar and he could fiddle it. They weren't leaving much to chance.'

'They thought it had worked a charm. But as I told you, Rupert could never lay off and he wanted to go on bleeding me. He continued to gee-up the press and do what he could to stir opinion against HRH. Then you came along. They had never heard or thought of you and when you appeared they started to panic again. Rupert put that wire in the fence. That's what you saw me arguing about with him in Newmarket. He told me I'd started something I couldn't stop, shrugged his shoulders and took himself off.'

She paused and sipped her drink. 'But I tried to,' she said. 'Giving away that gallop was the last thing I did. By that time I knew I was about to wreck your life as well as my own. I told Rupert he could go to hell, do what he liked, he'd get no more blood money from me.'

'He told Gervase, that's his brother, I remember, that the money was drying up. It must have been about then that you got the cigarette case back and sent it to me. Why?'

'The swine, I thought, when you told me of it. They wouldn't even leave you with that memory of your father. I went to him and demanded it. He laughed at me. "Take it to your fancy boy," he said when he threw it to me. "That's what you're down to now."'

She looked at me while I fiddled with the stem of my glass. 'I know what you're thinking,' she said. 'But you're not right, you know. It wasn't the way you're seeing it – my taking you up, using you, you say, giving you the ride on Prospero. I wanted to help and I hated him for what he had done to your father – and to me – and was trying to do to you. And, Danny, I was, I am, fond of you: do believe that.'

I hoped I could believe her. But I was not finished yet. There were more explanations which had to come. 'Rupert is out of it now,' I said. 'He's had his comeuppance. But what about Marston and Roger?'

'Marston knew nothing of the plot against your father. All he was concerned with was pulling strings.'

'But Roger did. He was in it up to the neck.'

'Not quite as deep as that. He'd never have condoned what Rupert did to your father. I believe he was horrified when he learnt of it. He was frightened then and he is terrified now.'

'I still don't think he should be allowed to get away with it,' I said.

She looked at me steadily. 'Do you know your Bible, Danny?' she said.

'I've heard it often enough at school and in church,' I said, surprised. 'I was brought up in protestant Ireland, and in Ireland all protestants go to church.'

'Do they? I didn't know that. We were originally chapel folk. It's another thing they laugh at me for. The good book says there is a time to love and a time to hate. You've had your share of hating, Danny. Don't go on, it'll eat your guts out. And you can't win them all. Roger was only a catspaw, a go-between. Let Roger be. He's got to live with himself.'

'Are you asking me to do nothing about him?'

'Yes.'

We stared at each other for a long minute. Suddenly I saw that she was right. I made up my mind. 'Very well,' I said slowly. 'I was thinking of going to Crispin Merevale and asking him to bring what Roger has done to the attention of the Jockey Club, but I won't now.' As I spoke it was as if a poisonous cloud which was putting a canker in all I did had been blown away.

'Well done,' she said quietly. 'And it all may have been for nothing in the end,' she went on. 'It looks as if pressures the other way have won. Did he say anything to you?'

'HRH? He told me his mother has asked him to give all this up. To change his way of life, I suppose.'

'None of them understands him. He's not really one of them. He's some sort of throwback, Danny.'

At that moment Jenks came in. 'His Royal Highness is on the telephone, m'lady,' he said.

She was away some time while I sat on sipping the champagne and looking at the portrait of her father. I could have liked him, I thought, a no-nonsense ironmaster who had fought his way up through the thickets of influence, social prejudice and snobbery. I thought of what Marston had said to her of her being of no family at all, and I wondered if HRH went away what would happen to her, and indeed to Flinty, about whose heels the jackals would surely snap.

There were portraits of Spenlove's two Grand National winners on the walls. I wandered over to inspect them with their little plates on the frames setting out their victories and achievements. In his quiet way he had shown them, I thought, that a plain man could conquer their world even if he could not be one of them.

At last she returned. She wore that same sad look that had haunted them all during the past week, only now it was stronger and sadder. She sat down twisting a handkerchief between her fingers and it was a little while before she spoke. Then: 'It's all over,' she said. 'He's going back.'

'What did he say?' I asked.

'They've won,' she said. 'We've known something like this was coming. It's been in the offing all this past week. It's his family this time. If it was only the Court, Marston and that lot, I think he'd go against them just for the hell of it. But this – ' She drew a deep breath, fought back tears and lighted yet another cigarette. 'He's giving up Braden Lodge. That's the start. He says he'll come up regularly for the hunting. They're allowing him that, but I know he won't. They'll play on him and fiddle his engagements to keep him away. It will be out of sight out of mind for us here.'

'But his racing?' I said. 'That's surely where his heart is?'

'It's in abeyance until next year. He says he may persuade them to give him one more season, but I know and I think he knows that it's all over.'

'And Flinty?' I said.

'They'll get him too, you'll see. He'll be despatched pretty smartly back to his regiment in India. The War Office will see to that. It's finished, Danny, finished.'

She was right, I knew. I, who knew him so little compared with her and Flinty, could feel it. It was like a light going out of our lives. If I could feel that, how much more must she be shattered?

'Do you still hate me, Danny?' she said then, breaking the silence.

'You know I don't,' I said. 'Not in a thousand, ten thousand years.'

'What will you do now that what you came for is over?'

It was true. I, too, was alone now, aimless, rudderless, lost, after all that had happened. I would never go back to the University, nor did I feel ready to return to Kilbarry and my mother, where I would be even more alone with only my memories, and I was too young to live on them. 'I don't know,' I said. 'It's happened all at once. I haven't had time to think – '

She stood up and came towards me. I rose to meet her. 'You'd better stay here, Danny,' she said.

'Why?'

'Someone has to look after the horses – '

'Is that the only reason?' I asked.

'No,' she said, and now she was very close to me. 'It's not. There must be something left still. For you, anyway. And you were once our mascot, weren't you?'

HUMPHREY CULLENDER'S
Second Statement

I had not finished reading the typescript when it was time to leave De Lacey. With his permission I took it with me, and it was late and in bed before I turned the last page. Next morning at breakfast Max Melville was silent and abstracted. Looking at him fiddling with his toast, I guessed that the printer's ink, or whatever it is that authors have in their veins, was flowing again, and that he was anxious to take up his pen. Certainly when I told him that I wanted to see De Lacey to clear up some unanswered questions before driving to the airport, he readily agreed, and disappeared into his study.

'I shall have to see my partner,' I told De Lacey, whom I found once more in his father's living-room surrounded by books, papers and memorabilia, the detritus of a life. 'But nevertheless I think I can assure you now we shall take the book on if you agree.'

'Of course,' he said. 'It was a strange beginning to a long life, wasn't it? I don't think anything was ever the same to him again.'

'Then he stayed?'

'He did.'

'And her? I feel I must ask you that. It's obvious – '

'That I'm not her son?' He smiled. 'You are quite right. She was killed in a point-to-point the following year. She was never really in love with Father, you know; she couldn't love him as he was in love with her, but she was fond of him and he filled a gap in her life. All her love was squandered on the Prince, and he knew that, I think. When the Prince went out of her life she was filled, I believe – from what little he let fall: sometimes towards the end he did talk rather more than before – with a sort of death wish.'

'What happened to him then?'

'The two people whom he loved and admired so much had gone out of his life and it nearly broke him up. But she left him all the horses and a stack of money to go with them. He threw himself into his racing, taking rides on any old thing that was offered and I've been told it was as if he, too, wanted to break his neck. But he didn't, though he broke nearly every other bone in his body, some of them twice. He was successful; he rode all those winners I told you about.'

'Did he ever see the Prince again?'

'Sometimes. He always said HRH was never a fair-weather friend. On the rare occasions he came up to Melton after that season, and Lady Val was right, they were rare, the mandarins saw to that, he sought father out; and when in the end they made him sell his string he gave him Pepperpot, saying he wanted him to have a good home. It was the sort of quixotic thing he would do, I gather. Father never for a moment deviated from his hero-worship and admiration for him.'

'The abdication didn't change him as it did so many?'

'Never. The text he used to quote – that there was one throne he could not abdicate, and that was in the hearts and minds of Leicestershire folk who had known him there – was true, too, of father and the few who stood by him. He blamed all that followed on "that creature" as he called her. He said she meant having him from the first. As you can imagine, he read everything he could lay his hands on about them, and he found two passages in particular which he showed me on one of my visits here when he was writing the book. I've kept them for you if you are interested.' He went to the table and picked up two books opened at passages he had flagged. One was the Duchess's correspondence. *I've had my mind made up to meet him ever since I've been here*, I read in a letter to her Aunt Bessie. The other was from one of the better of those 'Royalty' books fashionable today: *Few of those who served Edward VIII had in their hearts accepted him as King*. Both passages were heavily scored and underlined.

'He wanted, he said,' De Lacey remarked as I closed the books and handed them back to him, 'to try, in however small a way, to tell something of the other side of the story. So much of denigration had been written about him and he had nothing but contempt for those who either abandoned him or turned on him. Didn't someone call it "rat week"?'

'I think so,' I said. 'I'm a bit hazy about it myself. He lived to a great age. What happened afterwards?'

'He tried to get into the RAF in the last war but he was too old to fly. They made him an intelligence officer and he was badly smashed up in a bombing raid on an airfield. My mother was his nurse and he married her. It wasn't a great success, I'm afraid. They had little in common and they drifted apart. After the war there was talk of putting him up for the National Hunt Committee, but the Establishment have long memories, and anyone who had close associations with Edward VIII was carrying weight, to use his own expression, and nothing came of it. He took a pack of hounds in Ireland while my mother stayed in England and brought us up. Like a lot of those who have lived that sort of life, and more than most with him, I think, it was downhill all the way. Memories of those months at Melton were always with him.'

He picked up one of the marked books, glanced at it and put it down. 'You know,' he said, 'I think he was right. She ruined him. She played on his worst instincts and she bled him white financially. And she was determined to alienate his old friends, Flinty among them. They said Flinty was hurt he received no appointment at Court when he came to the throne. That was her doing. No one was allowed even faintly to come between him and her. Since talking to Father and reading what he wrote there in his book I've been boning up on the period. In a recent life of Edward VIII I found the author saying that he was loved by many till the day he died. Father was one of those many, and what he has written is a sort of testament to it.'

I took the typescript, put it in my case, and caught my plane. As we soared out across the lush green fields of Cork and over the Irish Sea, I told myself the visit, which had started out so uncompromisingly, had not been in vain. Max Melville was writing again, I had been afforded a glimpse into a society as remote to me and my generation as the sands of Ozymandias, and into the character of a man who might have been.

IAIN JOHNSTONE

Wimbledon 2000

It is the year 2000 and Peter Winston has become the first Briton to reach the men's singles finals at Wimbledon since Fred Perry in 1936. Only the Japanese player, Shimizu, going for a hat trick of Wimbledon triumphs, stands between the Englishman and glory. But who is Peter Winston? And who is, or was, his identical twin brother, James, who died disgraced?

'Sex and suspense, a carefully developed construction . . . Johnstone has a flair for ending chapters with oomph, saving the most dramatic moment until the last, like rallies finished off with startling smashes'
Sunday Times

'Here is a novel packed with historical anecdotes on the sport, details of today's circuit and descriptions of matches lively enough to rival any television commentator'
Sunday Telegraph

'Lands with the force of a Boris Becker serve . . . *Wimbledon 2000* contains enough sex and skul-duggery to turn the All England Club's old green ivy a whiter shade of pale'
Birmingham Post

SIMON WILLIAMS

Kill the Lights

Dominic Gallagher is an unpretentious film star, a reformed alcoholic recently separated from a wife he can't stop loving. Worried by a message from his paralysed father, spelt out in Scrabble titles, he agrees to take on the role of Professor Higgins in a West End revival of *My Fair Lady*. But in so doing he becomes enmeshed in a nightmare of blackmail and betrayal. As rehearsals progress, he finds himself at the centre of an intrigue of fraud, treachery and murder, racing against time in frenzied pursuit of a psychotic serial killer . . .

'Deaths and disasters accumulate . . . Simon Williams spins a devilish yarn, with an electrifying finale'
Sunday Times

'A truly gripping murder mystery full of unexpected twists'
Woman & Home

A Selected List of Fiction Available from Mandarin

While every effort is made to keep prices low, it is sometimes necessary to increase prices at short notice. Mandarin Paperbacks reserves the right to show new retail prices on covers which may differ from those previously advertised in the text or elsewhere.

The prices shown below were correct at the time of going to press.

☐	7493 1352 8	**The Queen and I**	Sue Townsend	£4.99
☐	7493 0540 1	**The Liar**	Stephen Fry	£4.99
☐	7493 1132 0	**Arrivals and Departures**	Lesley Thomas	£4.99
☐	7493 0381 6	**Loves and Journeys of Revolving Jones**	Leslie Thomas	£4.99
☐	7493 0942 3	**Silence of the Lambs**	Thomas Harris	£4.99
☐	7493 0946 6	**The Godfather**	Mario Puzo	£4.99
☐	7493 1561 X	**Fear of Flying**	Erica Jong	£4.99
☐	7493 1221 1	**The Power of One**	Bryce Courtney	£4.99
☐	7493 0576 2	**Tandia**	Bryce Courtney	£5.99
☐	7493 0563 0	**Kill the Lights**	Simon Williams	£4.99
☐	7493 1319 6	**Air and Angels**	Susan Hill	£4.99
☐	7493 1477 X	**The Name of the Rose**	Umberto Eco	£4.99
☐	7493 0896 6	**The Stand-in**	Deborah Moggach	£4.99
☐	7493 0581 9	**Daddy's Girls**	Zoe Fairbairns	£4.99

All these books are available at your bookshop or newsagent, or can be ordered direct from the address below. Just tick the titles you want and fill in the form below.

Cash Sales Department, PO Box 5, Rushden, Northants NN10 6YX.
Fax: 0933 410321 : Phone 0933 410511.

Please send cheque, payable to 'Reed Book Services Ltd.', or postal order for purchase price quoted and allow the following for postage and packing:

£1.00 for the first book, 50p for the second; **FREE POSTAGE AND PACKING FOR THREE BOOKS OR MORE PER ORDER.**

NAME (Block letters) ....

ADDRESS ....

....

☐ I enclose my remittance for ....

☐ I wish to pay by Access/Visa Card Number ☐☐☐☐☐☐☐☐☐☐☐☐☐☐☐☐

Expiry Date ☐☐☐☐

Signature ....

Please quote our reference: MAND